Seventeen & Crazy

Seventeen & Crazy

Bridgit Elizabeth

2018

First Printing: 2018

ISBN 978-1-7751980-0-0

This book is a work of fiction. If you find uncanny likeness in here to people, places, or events occurring in your lifetime, also be aware that the author had no conscious foreknowledge of these correspondences.

Content Warning: Oh, boy! Where to begin? Uh, discussion of sexual themes, sexual violence, D/s, blasphemy, heresy, rape apologism, drug use, ableism, homophobia, misogyny. Just—this book is not for the faint of heart. Okay?

Dedication

This book is dedicated to my loving wife, Sonja, whose unending patience with my artistic process is a truly humbling inspiration.

Acknowledgements

I would like to thank all the people who previewed this novel and gave excellent feedback: Mark and Alison, for their honest appraisal of Amymone; Ron, for his constant support; Matthew Trafford, for providing extremely professional oversight at a critical moment; Josie, who reminded me that I had better watch my unquestioned racism; Jeannie, who thought the Hallowe'en party was written before anything else; Sonja, for her loving support; Ana, for always believing in me; C.L. Lynch, for her care and attention to detail; Brewster, for her honesty in disagreeing with the message here; Natasha, who thought Mirella was unknowable; Rhea, who thought she was in Mirella's head (or vice versa); and Reana Deng, for her late-game excitement about the project and for the cover art. And thanks to Sarah, for her formatting work on the e-book. Anyone I've missed in these acknowledgements, please know that this book would be less without you, and that if I've neglected your name, it's just because of my human failing.

Entry #1: Tuesday, September 7

  As was my people's custom in ancient times, I begin this work, this diary of my senior year of high school, with an invocation:

Oh, owl-oueille, l'hibou-eye
Goddess of Wisdom
Goddess of War
Mother of Athens
Home to my ancient tribe
Mother of spiders
Lady Weaver
You who comfortest Daphne in autumn
You who piercest Zeus upon the throne
You: oh great brilliant Goddess
You: oh Lover of Knowledge
Athene

Keeper of Mysteries
Teller of Lore
All-seeing, All-knowing, All-wise
Always
Athene

It is to your Illustrious Grace
I do dedicate this
Journal of the end times

AΘHNE

I, your humble servant, Amymone Lerner
Do vow to know myself.
Grant me prudence
Grant me skilled words
Grant me a sharpened tongue.

Blessèd Be.

Teachers are idiots. This is plain and true. When I left junior high, I remember being excited for the chance to learn philosophy and to finally play in a full orchestra. But mostly, I was excited to be among the learned. Not students, of course. Those are idiots too. I thought for sure, angelic learned lions would be breaking down the door to pronounce my name correctly.

Stupid, naïve child!

It's not that I hate being called Amy, it's just – well, that's not really my name, is it? Everyone else gets to hear their name in full at role call. What do I get?

Amy—Aemaimoh—Ahm-ee-moan. Am-I-moan? Am-I-moan-ee?

You would think that with all the meetings teachers have had about me they might have had one about the way to pronounce my name. It's Lerner, not Learner, too.

Amymone Lerner. (ah-MY-mohn-ee. LEHRN-er.)

Amy Learner.

Which would you prefer?

You'd prefer your name.

See, because apparently if you have a name like the freakish new girl – Mirella Lantigua – your name is easy to pronounce.

Mirella Lantigua, the new girl with the violin solo. She of the greasy caramel locks. She of the baggy, non-descript clothes. She of the bobble-headed, glass-eyed countenance that marvelled at you in slack-jawed wonder without saying a word, looking not so much at you as outside you. That Mirella Lantigua. Like I don't already suffer enough slings and arrows, titters and glances? If anyone found out she bowed to me – because she totally bowed to me.

It was private. We were in a storage room in the basement. Not exactly a college practice room, but surprising acoustics. We were alone together because I'm tutoring her this year. That's how I know that at least Ms. Baccarat can pronounce her name not just correctly, but with a Spanish accent.

"Amy Learner – Mirella Lantigua."

"You're kidding, right?"

"Problem, Amy?"

"Mirella, can you spell your name?"

"Yes-s!"

"I mean, would you spell your name for me now?"

She did.

You see my problem? How come *she* gets perfect pronunciation, and I don't? Since when is double-l pronounced like a 'y'? "Come on, Mirella. Let's jam."

I told her my name on the way to the basement, and she repeated it back to me. It was slow and soft. Like a kiss. She nodded, then said it again, full of recognition.

I watched her resin up. There's something about this girl, with her sweeping fluidity. She talked to her bow, too. Then she remembered that I was in the room and gave me a nervous glance, eyes downcast. But she wasn't able to hide the whispered cooing she gave her instrument once she'd tucked it under her chin.

Then, she stopped. Stalk still. And suddenly I was catching her violin. She dropped everything, and stared at the ceiling, eyes closed, teeth clenched and bared. And I had her violin in my hands. Caught it by the neck, just centimetres from the floor. Miraculous.

It took the girl a good twenty minutes to snap-to, during which time I practiced my inversions. I didn't want to leave her, you see, not knowing what the hell was going on. How conscious was she? Would she know what was going on if I just left her there? Would she panic if she came to and me not there to calm her? I feel slightly out of the loop on this one, and slightly extremely set up to fail.

But the music? Beautiful. She played the "Canzonetta" from Tchaikovsky's "Concerto in D" and it stunned me. Sheer, lucid musicality. I welled up with tears. The consternation on her face. I don't want to be pissed at her because she's got the solo this concert. She kind of deserves it.

On the other hand, what can I teach this girl? I'm a second-row violinist and sometime harpist. She, as far as I can tell, is ready for a solo career, reaching for that most extreme B-flat like that, and nailing it spot on.

And when she's done, she bows. Not, like, for applause – that would have been weird enough. No. She bows to me. Down on her knees, *forehead on the floor*! So, I laughed. What else could I do? And she gets up and bolts from the room. Awkward? Not remotely.

By the time I got to AP English, the school was rife with rumours about the new kid. She's an idiot savant lesbian Persian-slavegirl psychotic retard who sold her soul to the devil for violin lessons. Or something. But whatever she is, she was sitting in Jeremy's seat. Right in the back corner of the class, where we goths have been known to sit since time the-past-two-years-memorial. Jeremy and I were about to give her hell, but Felicity chimed in first: "Another innocent mind, ripe for the taking!"

Thanks, Felicity. Always playing the benevolent corruption angle, and never to *your* inconvenience, oh no!

When she said that, Mirella – who'd been gritting her teeth at the ceiling again – came to and stared at me in awe. Again. Of course, being a goth, I'm used to being stared at, what with the cobra coiled up my silver-plated ankh, and the dark fashions, and unconventional lipstick shades. Adults glare us the once-over and cluck their tongues or mutter something under their breaths about Satanism. Teens sneer and state outright things about Satanism. Kids – kids are the best. They gawk like they've never seen vampires in the sun before – ancient and powerful for all the blood they've drunk living and undead. None of this sparkly powder-puff, teeny-bopper sparkle-shit!

But with Mirella, there were two things wrong with her stare. First, she wasn't looking directly at me, but outside of me again. Second, she looked at me – not all of us, just me.

So, Mickey says, "Looks like Amy's got a secret admirer. This bird really is a lesbian slavegirl!"

And of course, because that's offensive to all the rest of us, including Jeremy because, you know – gay – we all made noises for him to shut up. To which, of course, he rolled his eyes and shook his head as though we have no sense of humour. Like slavegirls are funny, right? Mickey and his lez-crazy bullshit! He's got a new laptop desktop of two girls kissing. Who are they? We don't know, but they're kissing.

Fortunately, Mr. Myer chose that moment to start the class and Mickey had no choice. He had to shut up. But get this. This is a bright point in the day. When Mr. Myer took role call, he pronounced both our names correctly. Mirella Lantigua. Amymone Lerner. Finally! I have a feeling I'm going to want to do very well in this course. I almost called him Sir.

Entry #2: Wednesday, September 8

I don't believe it! Yesterday she was brilliant, and today she sucked! Where was the passion? Where was the love? Where was the tuning, the precision, the bowing technique? Where was the – what did I call it yesterday? Sheer lucid musicality?

We're playing *Danse Macabre*. She (for some reason) has the solo. I know what I heard yesterday, but no one else does. Everyone thinks Ms. Baccarat is playing favourites and everyone's baffled how Mirella got to be her favourite.

Ms. Baccarat told me after rehearsal that she was hoping I'd bring Mirella out of her shell. Both of us have heard what she's capable of. Ms. Baccarat told me if anyone could, it's me. So, that's something.

We're also playing "Un bal" from *Symphonie Fantastique*, for which I'm backing up that insufferable Mariette Dupont.

Mariette's another virgin, with a heart shaped face and strawberry blonde ringlets that she keeps close to her ears. She's kind of a pissy satellite to the core posse, being too uncool to fit right in (e.g. She knows I'm going to hell, but she's still sometimes nice to me.)

That being said, today she was on me about how dark clothes and dark eye makeup attract the "wrong kind of boy".

"You don't want a boy who's going to want to use you up and leave you to raise a child up on your own, Amy," she said. (This is her being nice.) She said: "If you dressed more modestly, and, like, brighter, then guys wouldn't think of you that way."

"Really."

"Yes. But not too bright. If you wear too much colour, then boys will think you're a hippie girl, and you know how loose those girls are."

"So, what? Like, beige?"

"Yeah! Beige."

(Because that goes right with my skin tone.)

"Thanks anyway, Mariette."

"Look," she said, "do you want guys to think you're loose? Do you want to go through life having abortion after abortion and ruining the womb that God gave you? Are you really that depraved?"

"Well, to be honest, it all seems so complicated, attracting the right kind of boy. I'm wondering, these days, if it's even worth it. You know? Like, maybe I should switch to girls. Wanna kiss, Mariette?"

I said it to shock her, to disgust her – shut her up – but at that point, Ms. Baccarat tapped the podium, and mostly everyone shut up instead. Which means, everyone overheard. A trumpet called: "Dyke!" and everyone laughed. Mariette wrinkled her nose and said, "You're disgusting."

Tactical failure: as ill-conceived a plan as Mariette's unsolicited advice.

Evening:

Last month, I was so grateful to be entering my senior year. *Sigh.* Will I ever be wise? How could I still have the same hopes that I did when I was fifteen? *Oh! People will pronounce my name correctly; people will smarten up and mature by the time I graduate. Someday, my prince will come.*

So, Mickey finally finished his car over summer break, and it looks really good and doesn't even have that sterile new car smell. It smells like him. So when he offered me a ride home, of course I said yes.

So, we're walking and joking down the hall toward the back door, and we open the door and I almost trip on my violin student. She was sitting on the stairs reading an old paperback, waiting for me. I didn't see her till it was almost too late – horrible visions of shattered violin wood and Amymone brains on the concrete.

"Jesus Christ, Mirella! Hide in plain sight much?"

Pause. "Yeah."

"Okay. Whatever. See you tomorrow."

"Wait!"

"What?"

"You – I –"

"You – are in my way. I – am not in the mood."

"But you need my hands."

"I don't, actually. Got my own. But thanks. Go home."

She backed up a stair, biting her lips, looking down.

"But Cecilia told me—"

"What? Who's Cecilia?"

She just stood there, stunned.

"Go home, Mirella. I don't need your help. Despite what your imaginary friends say."

"She's not my—" Her voice caught in her throat. Then she ran away.

"She's fuckin' nuts!" said Mickey.

"I don't know what I'm gonna do with her."

"Sucks to be you."

"You have no idea."

He took me home, and he parked in my driveway, and he turned off the car. And he looked at me.

"Nice ride," I said.

"Thanks. I like it."

"You should be proud."

"I am."

"Good. Thanks."

I picked up my bookbag, music folder, violin, but he grabbed my arm.

"Yeah?"

"Listen, Amy – Amymone."

"Uh-huh?"

"You and me. We're good together."

"I – suppose."

"We should be together."

"You mean, like, together together?"

"Yeah. Don't you think?"

"Um. No. No, I don't think?"

"Why not?"

"It's just not a good time for me right now."

"What are you, on your period?"

"Mickey!"

"Look, I'm sorry. That was stupid. But I'm serious, Amy. There's never been a better time for you. Everyone at school thinks you're a slut, so if you get a boyfriend—"

"I don't need a man to save me. And the last thing I need it a pity date."

"How can someone so smart be so stupid? Did you know they're saying you had an abortion over the summer? The pissy posse's stepped up their game. They're gonna try to make your last year of school a living hell. I can help you. In fact, the way I see it, I'm the only choice you've got."

Dumbfounded. Speechless.

"Well, hey," he said, "you wanna be alone and miserable? So be it. Maybe that freak new girl? I hear you're switching to chicks."

"Mickey!"

"No, Amy. You give the cold shoulder to every guy in school who gives you a warm glance, but some stable boy comes onto you one summer and you can give him a tumble? Someone takes you seriously, and it's no – no way – but if someone from out of town wants a quick lay, you're all over him? Fuck you, you cow. I hope you get herpes. Get out of my car."

"Mickey!"

"Get. The fuck. Out."

There it is. Put out or get out. I was so stunned. Now, it's not that Mickey's a bad guy or ugly, or hard to get along with. We brood together, laugh together, smoke hash together. He's a great guy, really, but... his sense of style? It lacks lustre; it lacks confidence. There's something that's inauthentic about the way he dresses. Like he only dresses that way so he can hang out with outcasts. Which is weird because we're outcasts.

I mean, just because you put a pair of fishnets on your arms and a Bad Religion t-shirt over it does *not* make you a badass. It just makes vanillas *think* you're a badass. And plus, he's a straight guy and he knows I'm bi. How long would it be before he'd want me to kiss some other random girl for his amusement?

But even more than that. It really is *not* a good time for me right now. I can't explain it. It's not like I want to focus on school more, or that I'm heartbroken, or, like, anything like that. I just feel something – I don't know – shifting in me. Changing me. Now is not a good time to have a boyfriend. That's all there is to it.

So, I've got all this going on in my head in one instant, and Mickey's pissed like I've never seen him, I didn't have my bag clear and I shut the door on it. Mickey was already in gear and the tires chirped as he pulled out of my driveway, toppling me as he went. My violin case went flying into the street and bounced open producing my bow. The bow snapped, along with the bridge, and the body got chipped. Mickey stopped, opened the car door to drop my bag, and raced off.

Me, I scrambled to my feet and into the street before anyone could turn the corner and run over my violin. That violin was made in 1910. It was my grandfather's. He gave it to me before I was born. It got him through two world wars. And it nearly got destroyed because Mickey Filloon can't handle rejection.

Sure wish I hadn't been alone in that car. Sure wish I'd taken Mirella along. Man, that imaginary friend of hers – Cecilia? – really knows her shit.

Entry #3: Thursday, September 9

Guys are such shits! Do you know how long it's going to be until my violin is repaired? A month! A fucking month! And do you know how much it's going to cost? $500. That idiot Mickey! Absolute bastard! Way to get me between a rock and a hard place. I didn't realise if I said no he was going to treat me like shit, though I guess I should have. Fucking asshole! I trusted him!

Entry #4: Friday, September 10

The weather is perfect for a picnic, so I've come out to my secret sacred spot. You cross the track field, duck into the woods, walk along the clear footpath for about thirty paces. Then, noting the elm tree on your left, carefully, carefully pick your way right, through the brush. You come out of the brush and meet a briar patch, but in between there's a footpath. By now, you're completely hidden from view of the main path, so you walk (quietly as you can) toward a pretty oak tree, having turned left on that bramble lane. The whole thing's pretty fairy tale. I'm surprised I've never been here when someone else is around, but I never have. No one's ever followed me here, either. I love this tree.

Strike that, dammit! Here comes someone right now.

It's Mirella.

Evening:

Mirella's actually pretty sweet. She heard I lost my violin – not quite true, thankfully, but close enough – and she went to the spot to be with me. I told her what happened. She looked at me with these doe-y eyes, all innocent.

"You needed my hands?"

"Fine. I needed your hands."

God, I hope no one followed her. I doubt it, though. You can't just follow a body with your eyes to that place. You have to be pretty close. And nobody was. If anyone followed us, they heard our conversation, and I didn't hear anything about that in the afternoon. Thank whatsisname for small mercies.

I'd made myself some CLT sandwiches and a Greek salad. Mirella had a tomato she ate like an apple.

"So, how did you end up here?" I asked.

"Walked."

"N-no. I mean – how did you end up at this school?"

She shrugged. "How did *you* end up at this school?"

"I – live in the – catchment? Zone? I think that's what it's called."

"Catchment? Did they have to hunt you?"

"No. I was herded."

"Then I was too."

"So, how'd you get the solo this semester?"

She shrugged again. "Cecilia told me if I played for the casino lady, she'd let me stand alone."

"Did you play the 'Canzonetta' for her?"

"No. Mozart."

"I see. So – that Saint-Saëns yesterday. What happened?"

"I need – time – before I play."

"Why?"

No answer.

"What are you doing when you're talking to your violin?"

"You won't understand." She said it with a weird certainty. Most people who have deep secrets (myself, for instance) when they're pushed to tell them to people who "won't understand", they get defensive. She just said it. In fact, she was pretty even through the entire intense conversation, now that I think about it.

I said: "If it helps you play beautiful music, I have to try. I think music is more important than what you do to play it. As long as you're not, like, bathing in pig's blood or something. 'Cause that can get dangerous."

"You don't know. You can't know. You won't like it and you'll call me crazy. Everyone does."

"Please, Mirella." I put my hand on her knee. She looked at me. "If you give no one else a chance this year—"

"I want to tell you things, but—"

"Okay. Okay. So, Cecilia's not your violin, but you talk to her before you play, yes?"

"Yes."

"And you need time to do that?"

"Yes. But Cecilia's not her name, but she won't tell me what her name is because she says that I won't understand, and even though I tell that I will, she still won't. So, maybe I won't. And if I won't understand *her*, how would you understand *me*? Not even the doctors believe me."

A tear rolled down her cheek. Her face was blank, but a tear rolled down her cheek. My hand went to my mouth. Her hand went to wipe the tear away and she got tomato on her face.

"Fuck."

"So, is that what you were doing, facing the ceiling for half-an-hour before you played?"

"No. She can't hear me when I'm like that. I can't even think when I'm like that. It's a bunch of noise."

"What is it?"

"What do you mean?"

"Why do you do it?"

"I don't mean to. The pills make me do it. They put up a wall, too. She can sometimes hear me and sometimes not."

"Okay. Okay. Well, we have some time until the concert. This is just the start of the semester. Okay?"

"Okay."

Her tummy gurgled.

"You want some salad?"

She shook her head.

"Oh, come on. Yummy feta." I popped a bit in my mouth, but she shook her head again.

"Look. You're clearly hungry so have something."

She picked up a chunk of tomato.

"Tomato, eh?"

She nodded.

"Is that all you eat or something?"

She looked at me out of the corner of her eye, bit her lips, nodded.

"Hm. Good to know. Go ahead. Eat your fill."

You know that deeply good feeling you get when you watch pets eat food you've given them? That. But, you know, with a girl.

There's something about this girl who eats only nightshade and talks to an imaginary friend named Cecilia. Something profound. Something – familiar? Well, whatever it is, thinking about it just gives me chills.

Mirella swallowed and looked at me.

"What?"

She paused.

"What?"

"Your aura's inside out."

"What?"

"You don't believe me."

"I don't even know what it means. My aura's inside out?"

"It's – kinda hard to describe. I've never seen it before, really. Maybe once. Most people project their aura – it shines from them. But yours – is – oh, words! – how can I say this? It's like is this thing – this, like – magick—"

She gasped when she said magick, and looked at me with that fear. Like I might hit her for saying it.

"Magick what?"

"Magick – bend – time – aura – plastered on a canvass of green." I watched her move her hands around her head as she struggled to put words to me, like she was pulling thoughts from her temples. This chick is no retard. I'm guessing she'd never heard words to describe what she was talking about, and if it's that rare I might not have either. Except I have.

"Anomaly?

"Yes-s-s! Green time anomaly – space? Oh! But thanks. I've been trying to find my word mind ever since we moved."

"The computer geeks have been calling me Anomaly since I was twelve. You can use my word mind if you need it."

"Okay. Just for a little bit, though."

Then I asked her what was so inside out about my aura. She sighed and said: "It's like it's putting you together."

"So, instead, of pro-jecting me, it's, like, in-jecting me?"

"Like – it's the being and you're the result."

"Yeah!" Like I recognised it, right? Like I knew exactly what she was talking about? But for like, an instant I did. I felt like I was comprised of stuff. But then I remembered that everything is comprised of stuff and I lost the feeling.

But you should have seen the smile on her face – just lighting up the grove. It was like I was the first person she'd seen in ten years. Then she tried to kiss me and I pushed her away.

Well, what was I supposed to do, really? But she bolted, and I didn't see her for the rest of the day.

Entry #5: Monday, September 13

Mickey managed to get a letter to me today via Felicity. It's posted here.

> *Dear Amymone,*
>
> *I'm sorry your violin broke. And I'm sorry my pissy attitude was partly to blame.*
>
> *You're so unapproachable sometimes. I hope you let me pay for some of the damage.*
>
> *Mick.*

Some?

Some of the damage?

Try *all* of the damage. I mean, look at what he did to me!

Of course, if I'd been nicer to Mirella, this would never have happened, but there's no reason in the world he should understand that. Chances are he'd wouldn't believe it anyway, but he'd probably definitely take the opportunity to absolve himself of all blame.

Okay. Here's the thing and the thing is this: I wish I could fall in love. I do. And maybe that tryst three years ago with my cousin's fiancé was a bigger mistake than I thought. Obviously, this isn't the first time I've had this thought. People have always called me precocious. No one's ever called me sexually precocious, but I am. Sexually precocious. I like that. Early adventures in light eroticism. Mostly with guys a couple years older. But they were still just boys, right? And when they went around doing it to other girls, that was cool with me. (I know that's weird, but it's the truth.)

But when a man – not a boy, a man – showed his interest in me – *in* me – for the first time. I guess I just thought it meant I was special to him. Stupid, I know, because he was engaged to my cousin, but I didn't think he'd never touch me again.

They still tease me for it – jocks and cocks. The joke's gotten so old even *they* don't think it's funny anymore, but they still tease me. The girls don't. Anymore. They just whisper, glance, titter, glance, whisper, titter. Like they've never made a mistake.

But I love him. I fell in love with him because he saw a woman, not a child. But the longer I live the more I've got to wonder – did he? Or was I his version of the stripper: bust a cherry before you get married. It's getting more obvious over time.

So, you can see why I might not be particularly enthused by a guy who opens his laptop and there's two chicks he doesn't know, kissing. Does he like me? Maybe. But how deeply could he possibly like me if *that's* his idea of women? A computer with tits!

What I need is someone who understands women's issues – or just someone who understands that women aren't naked pictures on the internet. And I want some – I don't know – stability? I want someone who's going to want to touch me again. Without spreading it around.

All those fucking guys when I was fourteen. They were all like Bradley.

Guys like to say: "No matter how pretty she is, somebody somewhere is tired of her shit." Well, it's not *my* shit! It's *your* shit and I just happen to be wearing it. 'Cause I didn't even do anything wrong—in fact I did it *right*! And you still never called me, Justin, or Tim, or Andrew, or Max – or Victor.

Victor! Who wouldn't take no for an answer. Day after day with the compliments and the asking and the why-nots.

Why not?

Because I don't want you to make fun of me.

I'm not going to make fun of you.

Well, then, I don't want everyone else to make fun of me.

I won't tell anyone.

Right!

I won't. I promise. You have my word.

Well what good is that?

Well, I'll tell you what good it was, like you don't already know. None! 0! So why wouldn't I be wary of every guy who comes my way?

Maybe Mickey's different – *maybe* – but do I really have the energy to take that risk and find out? Not right now.

But I do wish I could fall in love.

Entry #6: Wednesday, September 15

Today, Mr. Myer assigned the first two acts of Macbeth. I can't say I'm looking forward to it. I would really rather read something cooler than Shakespeare. But there's that pesky discipline as truth thing. I know I'm not supposed to have these thoughts about a teacher, but I really *really* want to call him Sir. There's a creative writing component to this course – about 10%. Not nearly enough for my tastes. But it kind of tries (and fails miserably) to make up for the complete lack of creative writing course in this school period. When I grow up, I'm going to be a freelance creative writing teacher.

Did I just write "When I grow up"? I did too. Oh well. It's there now.

Earlier this week, I decided to bury the hatchet with Mickey. I even decided to apologise to him, which I think is being really generous considering I didn't do anything wrong. So, I'm kinda pissed at him for accepting. Would it have killed him to play the humbled game to my face? He's been playing it for a couple of weeks now to other people. God! Guys are such shits.

Wore my bowler and slacks to school today, and a blazer. People say I look like a guy in that, and I'm like: Really. With the sea of wavy dark hair flowing down my back and the boobs, and the *cinched waist of the blazer* I still look like a guy? Why are people such idiots?

At lunch, Mirella came to sit with us. Well, what she really did was stand there with her tray at the end of the table. She just stood there looking at her food and not moving.

Then, Jeremy looks at me – like I know all about her, right? – and says: "What's she doing?"

"You know, she has a mouth. She'd probably answer you if you spoke to her. Instead of to me about her."

"It's also polite," said Felicity.

"I'm not speaking to that freak!"

"See that?" I said. "That right there? That's not polite."

"Yeah," said Mickey, "faggot."

"Dude! I have asked you to stop calling me that."

"Except this time it's purposeful. Would you prefer 'hypocrite'?"

"Guys!" said Felicity. "Can we not have this conversation right now? Jeremy, if you're so concerned with it, ask her!"

"Fine! Mirella, why are you looming over us like that?"

"I'm waiting."

"Waiting for what? Sit down if you're gonna."

But she didn't. Even when Felicity shifted over to make room for her and said, "Yeah, sweetie, have a seat," she didn't move. She did, however, glance at me and bite her lip.

"What! Sit!"

And she sat. She sat beside me and began picking apart her salad, setting the tomato chunks aside. Everyone exchanged glances. I looked at her out of the corner of my eye. She's really a lot prettier when she smiles. It made me smile, and pretty soon we were all smiling and talking. Goths, and we were actually chatty and convivial.

So, when lunch ended and we all went to our respective washrooms to touch up (because goth boys touch up, too) Mirella came with us. Genevieve Walters was there with her pissy posse and she struck up a very civil conversation.

She said: "Looks like the freaks have another freak."

Alli Davenport was like: "Oh god! They're multiplying. Someone should get them spayed and neutered."

"That would be a human rights violation," said Felicity.

"Human rights only applies to humans," said Gen.

To which I responded: "Well, maybe we should have you put down then, Gen, because you're such a rabid bitch."

"Shut up, horse fucker!" said Alicia McMillan.

Genevieve put out an arm to calm her.

"Oh, a new insult. I haven't heard that one before."

"Yeah? Try this one: baby killer."

"What's that for? Get tired of horse fucker?"

"At least it's true."

"It is not true."

"It is true. I saw you. With my eyes. You were going into an abortion clinic. I was there."

"Getting an abortion of your own?"

"No! I was there picketing that heinous place. With my family. You know? Family? It's what you killed over the summer?"

"I didn't have an abortion over the summer, Genevieve. I don't know what you saw, or who, but it wasn't me."

"I know what you are. You Satan worshiping whore. God will judge you for what you did to that innocent baby."

"Why bother? You've already done it."

Behind her, someone snickered. Her face turned deep red. She snarled, stomped her foot.

"Let's go!" She walked out so quickly, half the posse didn't know what was happening.

"So, Genevieve's caught religion," said Felicity.

"Yeah."

"Because she wasn't mean enough."

"So it goes."

With them gone, we had the place to ourselves, but not for long. Lunch was quickly approaching a close, so we gave the remainder of the time to our makeup. Girls can always get a bathroom break from male teachers. They don't have the mind to be able to keep track of our personal schedules.

Felicity offered Mirella black lipstick, and Mirella looked at me. Why? Why ask my permission?

"What! Don't look at me. Do it if you're gonna." So she did. And we went to chem together, the three of us. But Jeremy and Mick didn't meet us there. They, it turns out, were in the principal's office for fighting. Although, thankfully, not with each other.

As it turns out, they were fighting with other guys in the bathroom at about the same time we were standing off against the pissy posse. And it was over makeup.

"They started it," said Mick as we all left school. "They called him a faggot and started shoving him."

"You broke his nose, man!" said Jeremy. "You got us suspended."

And then Mickey started in on him. "There's gratitude for you! I lay down the first punch so they don't have a head start gay bashing your ass, and you take *their* side?"

"I didn't ask you to be my fucking bodyguard, man! I can handle myself."

"Oh, really!"

"Guys!" I yelled, and Mickey rounded on me.

"What!" he hollered.

"You just got suspended for fighting and we're still on school property. What – do you think!"

Mickey took a deep breath and nodded. He wasn't pleased but he was reasonable again. I'm kinda worried about him. He's never been this angry before. I think he might have been about to hit me.

Mirella seemed to think so too. I don't know when, but at some point during all of the above, she grabbed my hand. I didn't realise her sweaty little bony fingers were grasping my hand until we were off school property. I think the psycho might have a crush on me. It's kinda sweet.

Entry #7: Friday, September 17

What a day! Holy mother! It started two days ago when Mickey broke Genevieve Walters's boyfriend's nose. Isn't that a crazy coincidence? If I were paranoid, I'd think they were trying to start something. I haven't heard the word horse-fucker out of a girl's mouth for at least a year.

Anyway, this afternoon Gen cornered me alone. Except I wasn't alone. I had my shadow with me (i.e. Mirella).

We were just coming out of the library. I had books to return, had a nice talk with Tilly behind the desk. By the time I pulled myself away from her Fascinating-ness, the school was empty. Except for me, Mirella, Tilly, and Gen.

Gen emerged from the shadows of the empty corridor and blocked our way. I'd been expecting this, I suppose, but when school let out and I still hadn't gotten to the library, I thought I'd missed her. No such luck. I don't know what she has against me, but she's become a little obsessed if you ask me.

Anyway! She starts talking trash – which really isn't that far from her ordinary speech – and, like, accusing me. Of what, I'm still not sure. And I'm like: "Okay, sure Gen. Whatever. Can I go now?" And she starts demanding an apology. Well, I'm not going to apologise for something I had absolutely nothing to do with. But she won't let up. She calls me a cunt.

Now, I haven't been in a scrap for years. Not since grade six when Felicity said the hair do I got because she pressured me to get it didn't work for me, "like, in any way at all". Lesson learned. Suspended for two days. Mom spanked me. Three days running.

Anyway! Mirella's got my hand again and I see what she sees – this is going to turn into a fight. So I turn to go back into the library, because it's better to be around Tilly than take my chances outside. But Genevieve grabs me by the hair and yanks me down the hall. Today I wore heeled boots – ball crushers – so balance is a matter of concentration. And I couldn't concentrate on everything. Mirella's hand slipped out of mine, and I fell on the floor and slammed my tailbone.

Mirella shrieks this unholy wail and flies at Gen, toppling her to the ground and she starts pounding on her. Gen's screaming and trying to fight back, but Mirella's too fast. I get to my feet and start hobbling over. Mirella puts her fingers to Gen's lips and Gen tries to bite them, but Mirella's already got a grip on her tongue. Gen tries to pull it back in, but Mirella digs her fingernails in.

By this time I'm standing beside Mirella, looking transfixed at what this girl has done. The library door opens behind me and Tilly steps out. I raise my arm to shoulder height and command, "Go back inside!" And she does. I don't know how that worked, or why I thought to do it, but I did and it did.

"Mistress," says Mirella. She's wide-eyed, and manic.

"Yes, duckling?" You have to understand: I was in a really different headspace. It was really weird. I didn't feel like me.

"Can I take her tongue? Please?"

"If you take her tongue, you could kill her. And then I'd have to cut off your hands. I need those hands, Mirella. Although, if she's not more careful with it in future, we can talk."

As Mirella gets off Gen, Tilly opens the door again and steps out. "What – is going on?" she asks.

"That bitch attacked me! Suspend her!" says Gen.

"Gen threw me down the hall when I tried to go back into the library. Mirella was only protecting me."

Tilly closes her eyes and shakes her head. Then, looking right at Mirella, she says: "It's Friday afternoon, ladies. Go home and enjoy the weekend."

I'm standing beside Gen and Mirella. Mirella gets off Gen. Gen gets off the floor and goes to leave. I start to walk away, a safe distance behind the crazy bitch. But Tilly puts her hand on my shoulder.

"Please step into the library."

Somehow, I don't think she's going to give us the "Into every generation a Slayer is born" speech. And I'm right. It's the "Mirella's in a very delicate position" speech. Apparently, the rumours about Mirella's incarceration are true. Lakeview Institution for Unstable Youth. She's out on probation. If she gets in serious trouble, it's back to the funny farm with her. "They're coming to take me away" and all that. Seriously.

I was looking at Mirella when Tilly told me. She just looked at her hands. And as Tilly went on, she started to cry. And I felt heartbroken. And I heard Mirella last week saying, "I don't see what I see. It's a lie." And I wondered then, and I wonder now if that place wasn't worse for her than better.

There's a reason that I'm writing all this. See, yesterday Mirella called and invited me to spend the night. So, I'm sitting here in her apartment – well, her mother's apartment – with a lamp on low. It's about two in the morning. I tried to sleep but after today – after what I learned—

First – this apartment is tiny! And it's tidy. It's cozy, I guess, but if I had to live here I'd probably go out of my skull. And that's without anyone around. Mirella lives here with her mom.

The two of them live in this one-bedroom apartment. You walk in and practically trip over the fridge. Who puts a kitchen by the front door? Who! It's tiny! And it's separated from the living room (AKA Mirella's bedroom) by a kind of two-way shelf so the sun – when it's up – shines through the living room window into the kitchen. There are two couches in the living room and a shelf for books on the left wall, a small TV in the corner. No cable. And between the living room and the broom closet that greets you opposite the kitchen, there's a hallway. It's the weirdest hallway ever – a dead end. On your left is the bathroom and on your right is Mirella's mother's room. And that's it.

Mirella took me home and we started talking about art and what our parents are like. Mirella's mother has two jobs. She had to work the night shift and the graveyard tonight. So that's why Mirella has me over. She's lonely.

But she's also pretty cool. I mean, once you get past the spacey, she's really smart and crazy intuitive. She says she's on medication and that it evens her out. I wonder what she's like when she's not on them. I wonder what she sees, and how much of it *is* a lie.

See, because there's a plastic box under her desk – the coffee table. She brought it out and showed me her drawings. At first I thought, they're nice. She has some talent. The faces she draws are life-like enough. And I thought she'd make a decent, like, manga artist.

But she said: "They're just derivative. Let me show you."

She dug into the bottom of the box and brought out an old piece of thick yellow paper, heavily folded and a little tattered. I saw a video once of an ancient papyrus being unfolded. For most of the class, it was a snore-fest. For me? Intensely exciting! Better than an action movie. Mirella unfolded the paper with the same care. She put it away, so I can't look at it now but if I could, I'd look forever.

It was me. I was naked, and she had my skin-tone exactly right – brownish grey with that mossy undertone no one seems to notice because it's just a little too odd. Everything else was as exact as that skin-tone: my long nose, high cheek-bones, dark lips, pointed chin, thick neck, pudgy waist. Everything was me – down to my nipples – unmistakeably me. Alive, and deliberate, and me. But that's not even the most amazing part.

It's not the violin in my left hand and the golden book in my right with the silver pen hanging down. It's not my aura, which she'd also drawn – numinous and vibrant, that canvass of green with rays of gold-tipped purple arrows shining towards me and a fuzzy brown inconsistency about it all, a stunningly realistic depiction of everything she talked about including (I don't know how she did this) uneven wavering light refractions, the time anomaly in my aura. Not even *that* is the most amazing part of that drawing, nor is her graphite depiction of her naked and prostrate self – a supplement to the image she worships. Here's the most amazing part:

It's dated five years ago.

She was twelve when she drew that.

You know, it's funny. It's not even in front of me, but I can picture it – I can see it as though it's happening. It's so real and she accomplished it all with pencil crayons. She drew it shortly before she started seeing shrinks. I asked her about how it all happened – with the shrinks and everything.

"The day I got my first period," she told me. "It was gym class. We were running around. Dodge-ball. All of a sudden, every kid in the class has this wavy colour around them and the colours are moving – squirming and writhing – hot and angry, worried and horny.

Everyone! And I could see things – Olivia Garibaldi was being molested by her swimming coach; Adam Front was gay; Tabitha Thibidault was addicted to Ritalin; Tommy Douglas was suicidal. And I ran smack into the wall and got a concussion."

"You ran into the wall? Why?"

"Well, I was distracted. It all happened so fast! One second I'm playing dodge-ball and the next, the world explodes into colours and—"

"Insight?"

"Insight! And I just – I – "

She made a motion with her hand, as if throwing something away from her eyes.

"You were agog."

"Agog! They took me to the hospital and asked me what happened – why I ran into a wall."

"And what did you tell them?"

She sneered ruefully. "The truth."

"Oh. I'm guessing that didn't go over very well."

"Counsellors and therapists and shrinks."

"Oh my."

"What I told them that was right was guess-work. What I told them that was wrong wasn't wrong. It was just stuff that was hidden – stuff they didn't know about themselves or stuff they couldn't admit. One or two believed me, but none of the psychiatrists. Nobody can argue with a doctor. Undifferentiated schizophrenia with delusions of grandeur. One question. Three answers. Unanimous. Tragic."

She shook her head like it hadn't happened to her. Like it happened to somebody else.

"It almost did," she said. They put me on anti-psychotics. I was fourteen. I was blind again but by that time, the voices – faint voices crying out behind a plexiglass wall. Desperate! They told my parents the pills were working."

"The voices?"

"No!" She laughed. "The psychiatrists."

"The pills weren't working?"

"They made the voices sad! But I could concentrate on school again, if I ignored the voices."

Her face cracked and she started to cry. She said: "I'm a horrible person."

"Why?"

"I ignored all those desperate voices and they needed me!"

I didn't know what to say, or even what to believe. Hearing voices isn't a good thing, even in the wizarding world. But there are so many stories about people – girls mostly – who get psychic abilities in their teenage years. And that picture is pretty incredible.

I tried to comfort her. I put my arm around her and she clung to me, but I couldn't get her to stop crying. So I stroked her hair until she fell asleep. Then I came to write this.

You can see why I can't sleep.

Entry #8: Saturday, September 18

Did I ever drop off the edge of the world after I wrote that last night! I don't know what I dreamed, but the front door woke me up at around 9:30.

What I learned last night may have been awkward – even a little creepy – but I realised this morning it's something else too. Mirella sees me that way – in the picture – *that* way. She looks at me and she sees what she's drawn. And if she sees that, she sees all the things I've written in this diary and more. And she sees my run-in with those psychiatrists a couple years back. And she sees *why* I had that run-in with psychiatrists a couple years back. And if she can see all that and still treat me like a normal human being, then I owe her. Not even *I* can treat me like a normal human being.

I was processing this lying down on the couch, and Mirella came out of the kitchen. She said: "Mumma! You'll never believe me! I found the Shining Host!"

Mirella's mother sighed as I reached for my glasses. "That's nice dear," she said. I sat up to see Mrs. Lantigua unzipping her boots. She put a hand on her frizzy, harried head, shook it and said, "I take it back, Mirella. I'm tired of lies. Put the groceries away, please."

"But Mumma!"

"No buts, Mirella. Put the damn groceries away!"

Mrs. Lantigua rose and turned to lock the door. She put her head against it, raised a fist and brought it hard against her hip three times. Then she raised her head heaven-ward. I saw Mirella in the kitchen, dancing a static ballet with the cupboards and the fridge.

"Good morning, Mrs. Lantigua," I said.

She jumped and whirled around.

"Holy Mother! You scared me." Then she got a look at me and she just stared. "You're real!"

"You were expecting, maybe, the tooth fairy?"

"Have you *met* my daughter?" she gestured into the kitchen where another cupboard closed and the fridge opened again.

"Yeah. I have. She told my my aura's inside out."

"She did?" groaned Mrs. Lantigua. "Mirella! What have I told you?"

"No, no. It's cool. It – kind of explains some stuff."

"Oh?"

"Ever read Boccaccio?"

"I don't even know what that is."

"Yeah, you and most of the planet. Let's just say he's not exactly light reading for your average seventeen-year-old."

"Okay. Whatever. If you're comfortable with her, I'm glad you're friendly to her. But keep her out of trouble, okay? She hated Lakeview and I hated to send her there. I'd hate to have to send her back. But if she doesn't—"

"Function?" Because apparently I'm the word mind for the whole family.

"Yeah."

"Don't you hate it when people aren't machines?"

"That's a hell of a thing to say to a woman who just spent sixteen hours in a porn store! I work my ass off for her; I'm stressed up the wazoo over rent because even with child support I can barely feed us. I can't let Mirella do groceries or laundry because she's so spacey I have to worry about her getting lost or kidnapped, or even beaten up; social services threatens to take her back if her grades drop so much as a percent. And on top of all that, she's a high school senior and I have to worry about what life's going to be like for her once she leaves home."

I apologised and she said: "You better be! I kept her off those pills as long as I could. I do love my daughter. I'd hate for her to end up slack-jawed and simple. I do what's best for her."

"I truly am sorry," I said. "It's just, I've seen my share of shrinks. They talked about my mind just like it was everyone else's. When, clearly it's not. It's like they think we're all mass-produced robotic units and they're the mechanics. And some of them are a little more obsessed with sex than others, if you understand me."

By the time I was finished ranting, Mirella was done with the groceries. She stood right by me. I think she would have taken my hand if I'd been a guy. Of course, if I'd been a guy I wouldn't have been nearly as welcome – especially to a mother who'd just spent a double shift at a porn store.

"I didn't lie," she said to her mother. Even just watching her say that, it pissed me off the way she'd constantly been called a liar. It showed in the meek way she insisted – even then – that I was real. That she wasn't a liar. But at least her mom apologised. Not really good enough, considering, but she was so tired. So we made her pancakes and by the time we were done, she was passed out on the couch.

Over breakfast, Mrs. Lantigua told us she had another double shift. I looked at Mirella, but she didn't show any signs of recognition. She just ate. No pouting, no whining, no rolling her eyes. Like she didn't hear. I asked her later – on the bus – what was up with that. I thought she might be numb around her mother. But she just shrugged.

Anyway, I would have offered to stay the night again, but that apartment is damned cramped. My bedroom's bigger. Instead I offered to take her home with me. We spent all day together – on the bus, at coffee, at the bookstore, at the park, at home, dinner. I felt so comfortable with her.

She's drawing now. Lying on my bed with her sketch book. I can see her lanky body and that pretty round head – curly caramel crop – looking thoughtfully at her art. I'm sitting beside my bed looking at her in the mirror. Writing this.

Mirella! Goddess love you, lost like that:
In time, in sight, in this society

That tears apart to look but little sees.
Psychiatrists are all such fucking rats!
How did you keep ahold of your true self,
All locked inside that medic prison cell
Where whitecoats glance and measure if you're
                                    [well
Then say you're not and put you on their shelf.
How will you live a happy life outside?
Iniquity, injustices abound.
They cut you down and sell you pound for pound.
Diminish, demonise, and then deride.
I'll be your friend if you will let me be,
Your lover too, I'm sure that you can see.

Entry #9: Sunday, September 19

I finally kissed a girl! Does that sound desperate? I didn't mean it that way. I'm just super excited! She's *so* sweet. Her lips are so soft! And we were so shy together.

Oh my Gods! I'm still so elated!!

It was last night. I had just finished writing the above Shakespearean sonnet (which I'd originally intended to be Petrarchan), and she looks up from her drawing – right into my eyes in the mirror – and she says: "I can."

In that moment, she looked so clear. There was no glass in her eyes. So, I got up on the bed and I was all prepared to be suave and knowledgeable but she laughed and I knew she saw I didn't have any experience. Bravado wouldn't work on her. It's really humbling to be in the presence of someone who can see into you like that. And a little freeing, in a weird way.

So, the point is I kissed her. Those soft, pink lips! Oh my Gods! If I could just touch them again – just with my fingers. Just look into her eyes and feel my heavy breath in my throat, watch her wet her lips again and lower her eyes.

But here's the best thing ever: it was her first kiss. I mean, I've been around the block a bit. This may have been my first kiss with a girl, but the milestone is somewhat reduced in significance by the many condoms that have been filled in my pussy. Mirella is clean. She's pure.

I have to be extra special careful here. She knows I dwell in darkness, but it doesn't mean she knows how to handle it. And it doesn't mean that I can go do whatever I please.

Entry #10: Monday, September 20

Called to the principal's office with Mirella this morning. Genevieve Walters was there.

"Did you see Miss Lantigua attack Miss Walters?"

"No."

"You didn't?"

"Well, I didn't see the *moment* Miss – Mirella attacked Gen, no." (Honestly! Miss Lantigua? Who does Ladner think he is? A prosecution attorney?) "That's because I was flat on my back with a bruised tailbone. Thanks to your Miss Jones."

"I'm not interested in that at the moment."

"Gee, I feel important. So, what? You're just here to indict my new friend?"

"I'm here, Miss Learner—"

"Lerner."

"Miss – Lerner. I am here to protect the student body of this school. Now, did you or did you not see Mirella Lantigua attacking Genevieve Jones?"

"No."

"No."

"No. I saw them fighting and Mirella winning."

"I see." He wasn't impressed. Don't you love when authority rejects your version of events as semantics?

"And did Mirella threaten to cut out Genevieve's tongue?"

"No."

"No?"

"No." Technically true.

"So, you didn't tell her you'd cut her hands off if she did?"

"What!"

"Did you threaten to cut off Mirella's hands?"

"No."

"No?"

"No."

"No?"

"I didn't threaten to cut off Mirella's hands. Okay? Gross!"

He looked at me, searching for something. Like he could see my aura. Ha-ha! But he's not schizophrenic. Or, at least what passes for schizophrenic.

"You can go back to your class."

I passed Mirella in the hall and projected my memory of her holding Gen's tongue, shaking my head. She nodded. I sat in the hall outside and waited for her.

After school we went to the library and saw Tilly. She was happy to see us, didn't act like she remembered the fight at all. I asked, and she put her fingers to her lips. Winked at me. So I told her about me and Mirella hooking up. She smiled at us and told us that she was happy for us. She thinks it's sweet, but she wants us to be careful.

Then Mirella gasped and covered her mouth. She started giggling and snorting and I had to take her out of there. I asked her about it on the bus, and she said, "One of them told me something about her. I like her."

Entry #11: Thursday, September 23

I used one of the school's violin today. You might think one violin's the same as the other, but you'd be wrong. My tuning was all off! It was miserable. Stupid fiber glass. Doesn't sound anything like wood.

Mickey drove us both home, and helped me up the stairs with my harp. When we got to the top, he put his arm across the door frame. Mirella was about to attack, but I stopped her. We all have to be careful now. We have to protect her.

As gently as I could, I asked Mickey what he wanted.

"I'm *really* sorry about your violin," he said.

I might have stammered, or I might have said, "Okay." In this case, it's the same.

He said: "I'm going to have the money to you, but listen. I – my parents – look, I know I've been more aggressive than I normally am. I – my parents are getting divorced. It's hell at home. Never a moment's peace. Anyway, look, I just wanted you to know that – that I asked you out because I like you. Not because I think you're easy, or slutty, or whatever."

I invited him in so we could talk about it more, but he had to go home for dinner. I could see in his face he didn't want to, but needs must, I suppose. It's our duty as our parents' children to suffer for them.

Before he went, he asked if Mirella and I were together. I took her hand and told him. He said: "That's cool. I mean, you know, it's hot. But it's cool too."

I'm going to call him after I'm done my homework. He and Felicity and Jeremy. We all need to make sure Mirella stays safe – and clear of the likes of Genevieve Walters. The gossip mill is bad enough, but we've scorned the pissy posse worse than ever. They're just inhuman enough to try their hardest to send Mirella back. That can't happen.

Entry #12: Friday, September 24

Well, piss on me! Mirella can't see anyone else's aura except mine. Not even her own. It's the drugs. So, when I tried to get her to tell everyone yesterday what's in their aurae, I ended up embarrassing myself.

I tried to explain to them why it made sense, but they just kinda looked at me. I think they may think I've lost it. Like, I don't know, my desperation to be with a girl has compromised my ability to think clearly? That's bullshit of course, and Jeremy was the first to say it.

"We could take her to a psychic," he suggested. "They can smell their own, or something."

Thanks, Jeremy. But he's right. So, I made the call from school. Tomorrow we've all got an appointment with a psychic. Her name's Thea. Jeremy's mother apparently sees her on a regular basis. We're each going to pitch in $20.

Entry #13: Saturday, September 25

Every time we're away from school, Mirella and I are constantly touching. At tea, on the bus, at the movies. Mostly on the bus. I take her home, or she comes home with me. We go shopping, to the public library, to the park on nice days. Or we will. Maybe Sunday. A picnic. Goths and picnics. Sundays in the Park with Goths?

On our way home, we've been waiting around the school while it empties. In between last period and the end of any practices, we take the buses home so we don't have to put up with any of our classmates – what people call peers – messing with us. Unfortunately, we have to put up with other kinds of messings-with.

Tonight I took Mirella to see that new Indie film, *We*. Not the most romantic movie, I know, but something where we wouldn't be disrupted by kids our own age unless they're A/V freaks, and they're mostly cool with gay stuff. Mostly.

On the way there, Mirella told me she was nervous because she sometimes can't tell the difference between a movie and real life. I told her that even if it wasn't a movie, even if it turned out to be real life, she could hold onto me and know I was real.

She was in the middle of asking what if I were a dream, when the bus door opens and some middle-aged fat man with a clear developmental disability gets on. I mean, he wasn't drooling or anything – nothing so obvious. He was just slow. Like, maybe IQ 80? 75? I don't know. It's a stupid measurement anyway.

See, even now I'm being apologetic. Why?

He gets on the bus, and he sees me with my arm around my girlfriend, talking tenderly to her. Out of the corner of my eye, I see him lick his lips, so I let go of her hand. He lumbers right towards us, stops right in front of us invading our personal space as much as anyone can from an empty bus aisle.

"Evening, ladies," he says.

"Hi!" says Mirella, all smiles.

"You look good together."

"Thanks," says Mirella.

"How long have you two been together?"

You can see what's happening here, right? So, I say, loud enough for everyone to hear: "Gee, Mister Stranger, we'd love to be in your pornographic movie, but we're only seventeen." He got off the bus at the next stop.

I mean, I'm not dead. I know what reality pornography is. And thinking back, it *was* very much like being in front of a camcorder. So I'm thinking, if all it takes is an IQ deficient enough to be uninhibited to not be able to tell the difference between real life and hardcore pornography, how deeply do the rest of us – schizo or not – really understand about the difference between reality and a movie?

I mean, that guy was big and strong. He could have taken us both. But I feel guilty for calling him out because he's slow. Why? I've been scripted to do that. Pity the poor retard who – in a different setting, if we'd known him better – might have raped us?

I didn't have any trouble with Mirella. She understood perfectly that *We* was a movie. Well, maybe not perfectly because she's started calling me A-440, but perfectly enough.

Entry #14: Monday, September 27

What a day! What a mind-blowing day that will compete with all other days for the rest of my life for weirdest day of my life. It started off innocuous enough, but it ended – I really want to get all this down before I get too deep into it. I mean, there's a progression here that – well, it might be important.

We went to the psychic's today, all of us. Thea is a small, lovely woman. I guess you'd call her white, even though her skin's darker than Mirella's. She's got a nice, buoyant pair of breasts – they're like the biggest part of her. Nothing out of proportion, of course, except for that tiny waist of hers. If I see her again – and I'm sure I will – I'll ask her about that waist of hers. I've never seen the like, and I like it. I want to look like her. All in all, she's compact and spindly. Is it weird to be attracted to a woman that much older?

She looked at all of us as we sat on her furniture. It was sparse. Bare hardwood floors, and a few bookshelves. There was some art, but nothing big. A few sketches of animals, one or two fairy drawings. Something that looked like a couple having sex if you turned your head and squinted. The furniture was cozy with a hint of utilitarian. Nothing intensely plush. A couch and a couple of chairs in front of a gas fire place.

The shelves were stacked with books on all kinds of magick, but especially psychic phenomena such as channelling and the Tarot. Here and there, trinkets and magick items dotted the shelves. Silver crescents; a chalice or two; angels and fairies.

She offered us tea. Felicity declined.

When she came back, I had my arm around Mirella again. Thea winced and squinted. She didn't look at us as she delivered our tea. I got to wondering if she had a problem with us together.

She asked us what we wanted, specifically. I told her that I wanted her to tell us if Mirella were schizophrenic or just intensely psychic. She told us the two weren't mutually exclusive, and that she wasn't in any way qualified to comment on schizophrenia, but that she would chat with Mirella and figure some things out. She took Mirella into her office. Alone.

I wanted to go with her, but Thea told me it would be best if I stayed outside. The strength of my aura, apparently, was distracting. I looked at Mirella for any sign of fear – trepidation. She didn't even give me a reassuring smile, just a blank look. Not even confused! Zero.

So, Thea took Mirella off to talk with her and I sat on the couch beside Felicity. She was scowling.

"What?" she said when I looked at her.

"You keep scowling at that coffee table, and we're going to have to pay for a new one."

She rolled her eyes. "At least that'll be a better waste of our money."

"What?"

"This – this, all this? This is ridiculous. She's clearly psychotic, Amy. I like her too and I don't' want her to go back to Lakeview, but this is just nuts! What could we possibly hope to gain from anything she says?"

"Felicity, you don't have to be here if you're not willing to suspend your disbelief for even a second. Go, if you want, and we'll pay you your money back on Monday."

"Look, I'm all for seeing – but shouldn't we be *seeing*?"

"This isn't an opportunity to have your beliefs confirmed or not. This is for Mirella. Besides, you didn't insist on seeing the reports or the notes or the records from her shrink; but you accept their word. You haven't even seen their faces."

"I don't need to see their faces. They're scientists. They work with the scientific method. She's sick, Amy!"

"Okay, first of all: that's my girlfriend you're talking about. And second of all: the scientific method can suck my ass if it's only going to condemn people for seeing things a different way than machines do."

"A stark argument against the industrialization of rural America," Jeremy chimed in.

"What!" we responded in unison.

"Some of us prefer history to literature."

"Look," said Felicity, "all I'm saying is even *if* psychic stuff exists, how do you tell the difference between the real ones and the charlatans."

"Right. There are *no* charlatans in psychiatry. Nobody's out to make a buck, nobody's out to manipulate the process for their own prestige."

"Psychiatrists don't have our money. This woman does."

"She's got my mom's, too," says Jeremy. "Mom swears by this woman."

"Well, no offence Jeremy," said Felicity, "but you're mother's got to be pretty gullible if she believes in this kind of thing."

"What's your problem, Felicity? Why are you still here?"

"Guys!" called Mickey. "This isn't the way! Is it? Bad enough I got parents fighting over money and shit, now I gotta put up with my friends doing it? Not one of us – not in this room, or this town, or this world – knows what the mind is or how it works. Now I know I've been on before about how Irish culture is a sad mess Catholicism, farming poems and hatred but not a day goes by somebody in Ireland doesn't see a fairy. My great aunt Lily saw loads before she died. Did they call her crazy? No. Did they call her psychic? No! They just treated her like normal – them that weren't dickheads. Now, I don't know much about psychiatry and I don't know much about psychics; but I do know something about human decency and it seems to me that whichever treats that poor lost cunt in there with more decency is the clear winner."

I could be self-righteous here, and say that shut Felicity up, but it shut is all up. Even Mickey. I can remember biting my lip and nodding. Felicity snorted and shook her head. Jeremy walked over to Mickey and put a hand on his shoulder, and they nodded at each other. Man-hug.

It's good. Mickey and Jeremy back on friendly terms as they were before Jeremy came out. They even made eye-contact.

Then it was my turn. Thea came out of the office with Mirella, and beckoned me in. I said: "I don't have any more money." She said: "It doesn't matter. If you please?" I went in.

Her office was this amalgam of library and hippy den. At the end of the room, opposite the hallway, there were two yoga mats in a recessed alcove underneath the window. Yellow and orange sarongs hung about her desk, which was turned around facing the wall with the chair pushed in. Above the desk was a dark mirror in a white frame.

Looking into it, I felt lost. My face wavered in front of me, and I almost didn't recognise myself. I thought I saw a fox for a moment and I was reminded, oddly enough, of a sensuous, flowing spring.

Then I became aware of Thea's hand on my wrist. She was smiling when I looked at her. "Please step away from the magick mirror."

Magick mirror. Like: Mirror, mirror on the wall. And I thought, maybe Felicity is right.

Opposite that wall, hung a charcoal sketch of a child hiding behind the arm of an adult. Her hair was a waterfall of black fire. Her tiny hand was clenched around her adult protector's. In her single dark eye, peering out from her shelter, fierce determination fought with vulnerability and fear.

"It's an image," said Thea, still beside me, "of the psychic mind – the intuitive mind – hiding behind the safety of logic. A reminder of the power of psychic abilities and the subsequent vulnerability of the very same. Like a chess queen."

"Funny, I thought it was about child abuse."

"It's about that too. They're not mutually exclusive. The two can exist in the same work of art." Then she said, "Have a seat," and gestured to the bean bag couch below the drawing. I did. She pulled out a bean bag chair from behind the door and sat opposite.

She was seated below her desk, so I could see the three balls on it. I asked about them. She said, moonstone for shifting fortunes; rose quartz for love; and obsidian for the protection of the querant. It was the first time I'd ever heard anyone use the word querant. Querant is a word I learned from the manual of my Tarot deck when I was fifteen. It looked made up. Hearing her say it put a bit of a realistic spin on it. And made her seem more made up.

Then I asked the big question: "Why am I here?"

She smiled, tongue in cheek. But she gave me a serious answer. "Because of your aura. And because you mean so much to that – 'poor, lost cunt' out there."

My upper lip began to sweat. I nodded.

"You heard that?"

"In a manner of speaking."

"Uh-huh."

"She means a lot to you, doesn't she?"

"Do you believe in love at first sight?" I don't know why I said it, because it certainly wasn't anything I'd said to myself.

"No. Love only comes from the second sight," and she tapped her forehead. "How much do you know about Mirella?"

First period; counsellors and therapists and shrinks, oh my; institution. Basically.

Drawing?

Seen it.

Know anything about it?

Just before she was diagnosed.

"You should ask about it," she said, "and if I were you, I'd ask about as much as I could. She's desperate to tell someone who'll believe her."

"Not always easy."

"Well, it won't get any easier if you don't start talking."

"Okay."

"Good. Now, let's talk about your aura."

"Okay."

"What do you think it means?"

"Shouldn't *you* be the one telling *me*?"

"I know what I see, but I don't own your aura."

"I – I don't know."

"Do you ever feel out of place?"

"Do you see what I'm wearing?"

"Even amongst friends?"

"Only all the time."

"Ever feel – out of time?"

"Like I should be living in the Victorian era or something?"

"You wouldn't be at home there, either. Do you have vivid dreams?"

"Not for a while. Years."

"This is going to sound weird but – what do your parents look like?"

Stunned? Oh, yeah. Part of me wanted to get up and leave. I mean, I wasn't about to pass up the opportunity, no matter how bizarre the answer. The question is strange enough. I gave her the short version: not like me; not adopted; faithful mother.

I'm not going to write what she told me. It really is too bizarre! And perhaps bizarrest of all? It makes *way* more sense than switched-at-birth-by-an-evil-nurse.

Maybe I should write it down, though. I mean, right now it's too much to put my head around.

It's not possible – I mean, really not possible – but it's too right to ignore. You think about it – everyone does – but – man!

I don't even want to write it because if anyone ever reads this, they'll think I'm as crazy as my girlfriend!

Changeling.

And you're like, surely they were just autistic children misunderstood by primitive people scared to death of everything they couldn't fix or control so they scorched their own children on spades. But, apparently Merlin was a changeling.

I don't really know what that means, because Merlin was a wizard and as far as I know wizards – much like changelings – don't exist. But fuck! What do I know?

I asked Thea what I should do, and she told me just to continue living the way I always have, like that's even close to possible now. Try to forget it? Please!

But I feel like maybe I should get back on the magick train, and I don't mean Platform 9 ¾. Maybe, but after what happened?

See, about four years ago, Felicity and I started reading about Wicca, and trying our own spells. They were cheesy. I got myself a copy of "The Teen Spell Book", and without really knowing anything about anything, we just started doing some of the spells in there. Felicity wanted to meet the leader of Smashing Pumpkins, which is this band from the '90s her older brother was fond of and he just gave her his CDs to hold onto when he went off to university. So, she built this creepy little teeny-bopper shrine to him, like the book said, and we did spells and chants and whatever. In retrospect, it feels gross, but no harm no foul: she never met him.

I wanted to learn how to fit in, which was another spell in that book. Well, you can see how well that one worked. I mean, I even called on Athene, but nothing. Nothing.

Then, one day, I'm sitting at home alone in the rain during March break. I'm bored, and a little tired, but I'm completely unmotivated to do anything. So, I just sit there, and I'm thinking about magick, and thinking about fitting in, and thinking – in a new way, deeper. I guess that's meditation. And then suddenly I get this image of a girl with these dark eyes and this dark, wet hair. She's holding a mirror and a vase, and she smiles at me and points at me, and puts her finger to her lips.

So, I call up Felicity, and I tell her exactly what happened. It felt like there was someone in the room with me. She felt familiar; she felt real. I told Felicity about it, and she didn't get it. Like, at all. At first, I thought she was making fun of me, but she actually didn't believe me. And then she said that magick is just a hoax, and that there's no such thing as God or gods and that she's giving it up.

Well, I tried to keep it up as long as I could. I tried getting that – I guess – vision back, but she never came. So I stopped believing in magick, and I stopped believing in her. I stopped believing in myself. Kinda.

I mean, there is no Platform 9 ¾, is there? Felicity's kind of right. But, geez! Maybe I *should* try walking through walls. I mean – all bets are off, aren't they? Do vampires really stalk the night? I'm a fairy? That's just stupid!

I mean, the sensible thing would have been just to walk out and demand our money back. The sensible thing would have been to go out and apologise to Felicity right away. What was not particularly sensible was to just sit there with my jaw on my boobs. It was not sensible to believe her, either. Except that it feels right. It feels *so right*.

To be clear, she didn't say I was a changeling, exactly. She said I had fairy blood. But what's the difference, really? Fairies are *real*. And I'm *one of them*!

She told me I should do research into my name. So after this, I'm going to Wiki myself. In fact—

Entry #15: Tuesday, September 28

Amymone. Apparently, there are lots. "The only Danaid not to kill her husband." As if. Nearly raped by satyrs, rescued by Poseidon, seduced by him and shown to the Spring of Lerna. Lerner. Hm.

Suddenly, I'm wondering about the difference between Lerna and learn. They're really simple anagrams of each other. Assailed by satyrs – ugly men with nasty appetites. Saved by Poseidon, God of the Ocean. Loved by the same – protector of women. Educated at the Spring of Lerna – fount of wisdom.

I want to talk to Tilly about this, like I talk to her about everything. After all, she brought me to that GSA meeting last year. Thinking maybe I'll go back so I have at least some support somewhere for something. The problem is, being bi is one thing. Being psychic, still another. Being a fairy? But that's what's burning me. Fairy tales – children's stories. The old shut-up-and-go-to-sleep-or-I'll-sic-the-Yaga-on-you. That's *all* I know: "Some day my prince will come" and "Mirror, Mirror on the wall".

Hey wait. That mirror in Thea's place. That was a *magic mirror!* And I—saw things! The Goddess *is* alive and Magick *is*

afoot!! Why didn't I see it before?? That's not just a kid's story. *I'm*—
not just a kid's story.

I would have told her – Tilly – today. She's the most open-minded person I know. I would have told her today, but what could I say? Whenever anyone gives her a rambling preamble – students, teachers, administrators – she gets this bored, glazed-over look until they get to their point. I don't like that. I couldn't have that. I don't want her to think I'm wasting her time before I tell her. What if she thinks I'm being unreasonable. Imagine! Believing in literal fairies! And that you are one. But if anyone can find some way to understand, it's Tilly. As long as she feels it's worth her time.

But I can't go to her tomorrow. They called today about my violin. It's ready. I'm skipping second period to go and get it. I won't miss anything in Social Justice. It's not like I'm not way ahead of the class anyway. I'll get the money from Mickey at the break tomorrow. I'm not wasting another rehearsal on that cheap fiber glass.

Ordinarily, I'd just walk into school an hour late, but I have Honours English first thing.

Entry #16: Thursday, September 30

Well, that didn't take very long. Two early morning detentions, a second warning, and a call home. First call home of the year. I wonder who'll get the voicemail. I wonder if they'll talk to me about it. I wonder if it'll have any effect on how I lead my life.

But, please understand this, anyone who's reading: I've been punished for being unable to wait for the weekend to reacquaint myself with a family heirloom. If I had taken the first period off, this never would have happened. One detention. Maybe. I would have done the same thing – taken the bus to Anderchuk's, paid for my violin (well, stolen it because I wouldn't have had Mickey's money), and taken the bus to school. But you see, I left school property. Once you're there, you're theirs. So, because I didn't want to leave Mirella high and dry in English, I got detention. I'm beginning to think the Marquis deSade was right: No good deed unpunished.

The violin is perfect, by the way. Mr. Anderchuk says I was very lucky. I told him what happened; he told me not to make men so angry. I laughed and died a little inside. What can I say? The man repaired my violin. I'm not gonna go off on him.

Entry # 17: Saturday, October 2

A conversation with Tilly (largely paraphrased, but spiritually faithful).

"Hello, Amymone." (Tilly always pronounces my name correctly and in full.)

"Hi, Tilly."

"And hello, Mirella." (She was smiling so sweetly. Beneficent. Mirella raised her hand.)

"What can I do for you, dears?"

(And that's when I started stuttering. Got real sweaty. But instead of glossing over, Tilly got a little concerned.)

"Did something happen, Amymone?"

"Ah, no – I guess maybe – you could say that. Yeah."

"Amy's a fairy!" (Of course. Face, meet palm. Tilly looked at her all supercilious.)

"We went to a psychic last weekend. Mirella's been saying my aura's inside out, Thea said I have fairy blood. I just – I've been playing with believing it but—"

Tilly's face *lit up*! She got really excited, breathing deep, stammering herself.

"My office. Tea. Please." She's *so cute* when she's exuberant!

Tilly's office is respectably dusty – not stuffy and old and half-dead with the stuff. She's got books on subjects from the ills of capitalism to the history of abortion law; from autopsy procedure to Renaissance Italian pornography. If the school knew she had half the books she does, they'd fire her and burn her office to the ground. As far as I can tell, I'm the only student she's let into her office. Now, Mirella.

I told Mirella to keep it a secret. Tilly put on the kettle.

"Now tell me," she said. "What did this psychic say?"

"You believe in psychics?"

She looked me in the eye. "I do."

"But – you – books! Science! Reason! Logic!"

She threw her head back and laughed. "When I was – half – your age," she said, "I began having – very intriguing psychic experiences of my own."

"Really? So, you've seen my aura too?"

"Ah, no. I lost the ability. I didn't use it and it faded. Practice, et cetera."

Mirella and I exchanged a worried glance.

"So, now," said Tilly, "this psychic of yours – she told you you have fairy blood? What else did she say?"

"I really – don't remember. Something about Merlin? I really didn't glean much meaning."

"Hm. She was speaking to you in her own language. Forgot – because you have fairy blood – you don't speak it."

"Fairy is a language?"

She chuckled. "You could call it that, I guess. So, she didn't give you any ontological idea what it means?"

"Not that I recall. My mind was kind of—"

"Rather," she interrupted.

"Right. Sorry. My mind was rather—"

"Lost," said Mirella.

"Lost," I conceded, "in that room."

Tilly got a little nervous. She licked her lips, put her tea down.

"Now, dear. This is one of those things I must warn you about. One of those things I am legally obligated *not* to tell you about. And I will remind you that if you do something stupid and irresponsible with what I'm about to tell you, I will deny everything, even so far as ever having met you." She looked at Mirella. "Understood?"

"Understood."

"Good. Now, there is an article by Joseph Campbell about schizophrenia and shamanism. I will Xerox it for you. Amymone, many – many – spiritual leaders from ancient cultures have been said to have the blood of spirits – fairies, *fate*, nymphs. They're heroes in Greek myth – demigods."

"But – we don't – do that – anymore."

"You're right. Our 'post-industrial' society can't find anything in shamanic life that agrees with its philosophies, the 'spirit of capitalism.' There's nothing for it and in a lot of cases, it's for the better. Regardless, you've got an opportunity here. You have to trust yourself – both of you. Trust yourselves, study up, and go inward. Would you like a book?"

"Go inward? Wait. Are we – are we both shamans? I thought shamans were only in Native cultures."

"You mean cultures Indigenous to North America? No. Every culture has a shamanic tradition. Even Christianity."

"I have to say, this is a *lot* easier to swallow than fairy."

"Oh no. Don't misunderstand. This isn't different. This is just a way to deal with it, you know, on an ontological level."

We sat, sipping tea for a few minutes in silence. I looked over at Mirella. She was frowning in consternation with closed eyes. Part of me wanted to get her attention, tell her to be aware and stuff. But another, deeper part of me knew better. Tilly had just told me to trust myself, so I did. I trusted that intuition. Before Mirella opened her eyes again, she nodded.

"I think it's time for us to go," she said.

Tilly nodded. We grabbed our instruments and headed for the door. Mirella stopped and turned to Tilly.

"Gennifer says you must stop blaming yourself."

Tilly put her hand to her mouth and closed her eyes. She looked like she was about to cry.

"Sorry!" whispered Mirella.

She shook her head. "No, dear. It's okay. Thank you."

I wondered out loud who is once we got onto the bus. Mirella shrugged.

"One of them. A new one," she said. "She yelled loud enough. It was über important."

I wanted to kiss her, right then and there. But it was public. Since that ugly asshole accosted us on the bust last week, I've been a little more private in my affection with Mirella. I miss it.

So, as soon as we were off the bus, I planted a kiss on her cheek. She glowed, and brushed up against me.

This may sound stupid and romantic, but I feel like I've got this deep, intimate connection with her. It's too soon to say love, but if nothing goes terribly awry this month, it's safe to say that's what it'll turn into.

Entry #18: Monday, October 4

School is school – big, blocky building that Mussolini would be proud of. Green walls, gaudy tiles, insolent brats, humourless staff. Unimaginative, wholly restrictive, prohibitive, proscriptive. You get punished for being to dumb; you get punished for being too smart. School – is school.

But whatever school is, it has nothing on a shrink's office.

Remember: your psychiatrist is an expert. An *expert*. And you're a kid. You're stupid. Even if you're in the tutoring program for orchestra, and Honours English, you're stupid in comparison to him – and they're *all* hims.

He is a medical doctor, but don't make the mistake of assuming he's a healer. He's a warrior. A warrior against disease. Human disease. Disease of the mind. He has learned "the mind" like a mechanic, and he knows when a mind is not optimized for health – perfect, irreligious calm.

His sword – because he's not a mechanic, remember, he's a warrior – is a *bastard* sword: a big two-handed mother-fucker made of glossy grey steel and dull, meaningless words. As with other medicines, the psychiatrist's battleground is your body – he will colonize it as he pleases. Unlike other medicines – real, beneficial medicines – his enemy is your soul. Athene help you if you try to defend your soul with your emotions. If he doesn't mistake those walls for the enemy itself, he'll call them irrelevant. No Babylon are you – no Troy to his steely grey, deathly dull DSM and his +10 paper armour of banality gilded by dusty old men in dusty old rooms with dusty old tomes containing dusty old theories they can dusty old recite while engaged in a dusty old circle jerk. And the occasional spanking for straying just far enough from the party line.

(Not that there's anything wrong with circle jerks. Or spankings.)

Your psychiatrist will lob burning questions at your soul like so much pitch from a trebuchet. He will tell you there are no "right" answers. Believe him. All your answers are wrong. Insist, and he will dash your face against the mirror of your soul and break it. Then he'll show you his mirror – the One True Mirror – the strange glossy-dull sword, the gold-embossed armour.

Your psychiatrist *may* offer to be your friend. After all his beating on your soul's walls, you're going to trust the gift he bears? He will tie you to the chariot of his thesis and draw you about until the words that are you are broken, beaten, bloody and bad.

For my application to AP English, I wrote a paper on how Romeo and Juliet subverts the love/war analogy. While I was researching, I came to the conclusion that it's really more of a rape/war analogy, wherein men don't take no for an answer. Let that be the lesson of this rant: Your shrink is not the Eros of your Psyche.

And if he is? Holy fuck! It doesn't take an expert to be able to tell: you're fucked!

Wow. I can't believe I wrote all that. It's weird the way I never wrote like that about my own psychiatric rape.

So, last night, Mrs. Lantigua called for me. Well, actually she tried to call for my parents. I picked up expecting Mirella – in a way. The caller ID said, of course, that it was Lantigua, V., meaning Mirella because why would her mom call me? But I hesitated. It didn't feel right. Not that Mirella doesn't do random stuff. Yesterday in class, she studiously unwrapped the metal holding the eraser to her pencil and quietly rejoiced while walking to the window to "free" said eraser. (She's got a thing for freedom.)

Anyway! Mrs. Lantigua. She called for me, but she thought she was calling for my parents.

"Can I speak to your mom or dad?"

"About what?"

"I would – just – like to speak with them, please."

"On the subject of – me, I presume?"

"Would you please just put me on with one of your parents, Amy?"

"If you're going to talk about me behind my back, I'd just as soon not. Whatever you have to say to my parents, you can say to me. I'm sure."

There was a pause, pregnant and awkward. I could practically hear her consider forbidding me to see Mirella again. Instead, she told me what she wanted. I was cordially invited to be examined by Mirella's psychiatrist, thereupon to be reported to her social worker.

Turns out, my interest in neo-Victorian fashions and "Death and the Maiden" may make me a bad influence.

Nah. Who am I kidding? I should never have said anything about psychiatry to her, or my victimisation at the hands of psychobabble. Once again, the truth shall set you on fire.

Anyway, I'm sitting here in the waiting room. I've got about ten minutes to think up some lie that's stupid enough to be believable, but I don't even know what they're going to ask me. Best I can do right now is: my dog ate my reason. What's worse, I have to pretend to be good and respectful. I have to pretend to believe in this trumped up "Defiant" diagnosis. And I have to pretend to be recovered from "it".

Maybe I shouldn't lie. I'm bad at that. It's part of my defiance, oddly enough. The truth is *far* more powerful than the lies that pretend to be. That's why people turn away from it so often.

Watching Mirella as she got up to go into that room behind the frosted glass door – another lie – "you can see through this door." A half-truth. Just like psychiatry.

Supplement:
Fucking hell!! I don't even want to write about it. What happened? That short, silver-haired he-bitch! Fuck! I can't even write it. It's pointless. I refer you to the above rant. Why does *anyone* think it's appropriate for a *doctor* to decide who *anyone's* friends are? Am I *that* dangerous? Do I steal cars? Sleep with older men? For money? Sell drugs to kids? A little truancy, a little hash, a number of indiscretions in my youth, and I could be a monster.

Well, whatever – my life's open to scrutiny by the government. They'll tell Mrs. Lantigua whether or not they'll steal Mirella away from her for being my friend in a week.

Here. Here's the richest part: Dr. Nutzoid warned me about Mirella. "She's very convincing. But it's important you don't believe what she says about your secrets or anyone else's."

"Have you seen her drawing of me?"

"It's an uncanny likeness, I admit. But what else could it be but a coincidence?"

"Magick?"

Raised eye brow.

"It's a joke. I don't believe in magick!" I lied.

"Good," she said over the sound of her note-taking.

What a waste of time. At least Mrs. Lantigua offered to take me for dinner. But I wasn't hungry and the Lantiguas are poor.

I'm tired, but I'm too pissed to sleep. How late is this going to take me?

Entry #19: Tuesday, October 4

I just had an incredibly vivid dream for the first time in years. Not since I was fifteen have I had a dream so powerful. I woke up with tears in my eyes.

First thing I remember, Mirella was standing at my bedroom door. But she didn't' have that scrawny body holding her head up. Instead, she had a lovely, well-fed form: curvy hips and thighs, fullish bust. She was draped in silk, translucent and floating about her body, clinging to her form. And her hair wasn't that greasy caramel colour – it was red as the setting sun and flaming around her face in oranges and yellows. Her eyes were dark and shining—like so much obsidian, no whites. Just the sight of her flooded me with joy and lust.

"Get up," she said to me in this exciting whisper. Her dark eyes shone and shot a bolt through my solar plexus.

I threw the covers off me and rose to find myself draped in the same floating silk. But silk isn't the word for it. I don't even know what it was. It's like it was held aloft by the light. I got up and my hands were radiating purple waves. I looked at her and she smiled. It was like her head filled the room—her shining face. She took my hand and pulled me from the room.

And we were flying! Hand-in-hand – we were flying up over the city, looking down on it. My place, the high rises, the school, the low-rent area, Mirella's place. Then, rich green meadows with blue. And the sky was sunless but blue and cloudless and shot through with greens. It was marshy and warm, fertile and gorgeous. It looked like we could light on it and fall right through.

We lit, however, on a solid knoll where there was a harp in the shape of a butterfly. I was instantly attracted to it. Mirella had her violin. We looked at each other and kissed. Then, she put the violin under her chin and started playing this gorgeous, expansive violin line. I looked out over the marsh, and I saw what she was playing. Blue. Just blue. And I sat down at the harp and started playing. And the sky sparked green through it – veins of vines that hit the ground and spread into the marsh we'd flown over moments ago. We played that expansive miracle, and I wished it would go on forever. I can't really describe it – the music or the feeling. And I'm sure if I tried to write the music down, it would only be a sad vague impression of that glory.

Anyway, maybe I can get more sleep before I have to be up.

Supplement:
I asked Mirella this morning if she'd had a similar dream. She told me, eyes closed, that her medications prevented her from remembering her dreams. I told her that in dreams, she's exactly as radiant as she describes me. She asked me if I could describe her, so instead I read her the whole dream. When I was done, she had her eyes clenched shut and her mouth wide open and she was staring at the ceiling – or not staring I guess, but she would have been. It breaks my heart how badly her medication treats her. I so fucking hate shrinks!

Entry #20: Wednesday, October 5
You know how teachers have this ethical obligation not to molest their students? And you know how being forced to be in the presence of someone from which one or more aspects – especially crucial biological aspects – are forbidden makes the desire all the greater? And you know how tutors aren't really technically held to the same ethical standard as state-managed teachers but the moral implications still apply?

It started with heavy breathing – I noticed, as we were working this morning on tuning those spiccato tri-tones that Mirella was breathing hard. I looked at her and asked if she was okay, thinking the medicine was attacking her systems again. The way she looked at me with hungry lust I knew she was better than okay. My palms were sweaty too, and my heart had been pounding since before

I'd met her this morning. I think that dream yesterday morning really stuck with me.

I put my arm around her and kissed her temple. She snuggled in and we both tried to concentrate on the work; but the feel of her body, bony but soft, and the smell of her – they reminded me of that bronze-faced fire goddess.

Needless to say, we spent most of the morning making out. Strenuously. With – actions. What sheer joy to watch her open-mouthed ecstasy as I pressed against her nipples over the fabric of her camisole! (And the creepy wrongness made it so much sweeter.)

She's got a sweet spot on the right side of her biteable throat. I'm going to give it a hickey when it won't be so obvious that we were wasting our tutoring period.

Well, maybe "wasting" is a bit harsh, but I'm sure that's how the school would see it: as some kind of frivolity. I'm sure that's why we're only paired with people of the same sex – so we don't waste our time making out and worse – fucking.

Ah, fucking! The ultimate frivolity. Intense, pleasurable, dirty, dangerous fucking. So frivolous it's not allowed. So frivolous, we don't want to see it. So frivolous it's harmful to children. So frivolous it's evil, shameful, vile, disgusting. So frivolous it generates life. It's a waste of your time and it will ruin you. It's the dirtiest thing you can do, so only do it to the one you love – your One True Love. (Not family.)

And, while I'm thinking of it, don't forget to be grossed out that your parents fucked. Probably more than once. Probably a lot more than once. Heaven forbid you should feel happy your parents have a loving sex life. Better you should have a Messiah complex because your ma was a virgin when she passed you through her hymenated vagina.

Here's a secret: I *wish* my parents had sex. Loud, noisy, raucous sex instead of the cold silence I hear from them so often. I think if I knew my parents were having sex, it would make me feel like less of a hypocrite for a) having been so active and b) for still wanting to have sex.

And I do. Wow, do I ever! I think of her, and I feel dewdrops in my soul blooming into kaleidoscope mandalas. And I want to be there, I want to protect her and comfort her, and help her blossom. I want to see her shine the way she shone in my dream. I want such great things for her because she's so powerful and so sweet hearted.

Sometimes I wonder if she drew me into existence. I mean, if she's a shaman, she could be that powerful, right? Don't we all create our gods, the same as they create us? And that's where I normally have to stop wondering because the rest is too trippy for me to wrap my head around.

With any luck, the psychiatrist won't banish Mirella from the living world, and I'll be spending the weekend at Mirella's. The laying out? The wondering? Writing music? I feel like if I don't take a risk on something big, we won't have anything to talk about except the pissy posse.

Entry #21: Saturday, October 8

This week, in between groping Mirella instead of studying, keeping Mickey from flying off the handle, and trouncing Matt Jeffries' King's Indian defence – again – I bought a digital sound recorder. Mirella was nervous when I showed her because, of course, the shrinks use it to distort the words of their patients. And so do reporters. But I promised her I'd write it out verbatim, let her read it along with the recording and then delete it from the HD. She agreed to that. What follows is a transcript of our conversation yesterday after school. Written in love.

(It amazes me we've only known each other for a month!)

ML: They didn't let me out of the hospital. They kept me overnight for monitoring. I could see all the stress and all the worry in all the nurses' auras. It was all a jumble – work, home, money, car, facility, legal, whatever. And the nurses would ask me questions and I would answer – or at least I thought I was answering – but what I think now is that I was giving a comparison of what was going on in my head to what I could make out in their lives. And, you know, I think back and I remember this sense of certainty, like, knowing what I was talking about. Except, the nurses all looked at me so worried and sometimes a little angry. So, they scheduled me for a CT scan and an X-ray, and an ultrasound. And a psych evaluation.

The guy. The doctor. People project things. And shrinks –
psychiatrists.

AL: You can say shrinks.

ML: Shrinks. When they examine you, they project the stuff that's
least likeable about themselves, the stuff they hope nobody ever finds
out about them.

AL: Why?

ML: The only thing I can guess is that they need to do it in order to
catch you in a lie or something. Like, they're looking for indicators
that they use themselves? Or something like that? Does that make
sense?

AL: Yeah. It does.

ML: This guy was a masochist. He had an overbearing mother and a
hate-filled, weak-willed father. His sister was a stripper. He had a
thing for his cousin. He masturbated by putting things in his penis and
squeezing his balls too hard.

AL: Not that there's anything wrong with that. The masturbation
thing.

ML: I suppose not. It hurt him, though. And it's kind of gross.

AL: But there's nothing really... I don't know. That's a little extreme
for me, but I don't really like to condemn people, you know?

ML: But—the reason he went into child psychiatry? He had three
kids and he never wanted them to know what a pervert he was, like, in
any way. So he used what he knew about kids to dominate his own
kids, and, like, have them running in mental circles all confused about
who they were and who they were supposed to be. He would use his
knowledge to distract them. He was so worried about fucking up his

own kids, he would experiment on his patients. Like, confuse us and see what happened.

AL: What kinds of things did he do to you?

ML: I don't know anymore. He asked me if I was sexually active – like, it was the first thing he asked, too, after the stuff they all ask. And then he asked what kinds of things I was into. He asked me what I saw in his aura – all of them did – and I lied and said nothing. Because, I could see, when he asked that question – his aura got dark and angry and a little vengeful. And I saw someone else, someone a little older than we are now. He'd been able to hold his own, and figure out what the shrink's problems were, and Mister Shrink hated that. So, I told him nothing, and he knew I was lying. He – I remember – his aura got smoky and he turned red. He said, "I don't like being lied to, Mirella."

AL: Like *he* was psychic.

ML: He said he was only trying to help me, but he took it personally.

AL: I bet you got used to that.

ML: Never quite.

AL: No wonder. Go on.

ML: He accused me of lying and I told him the truth – some of it anyway. And the smoke burled around his aura and it was dark and I could see mad, violent flashes. He wanted to tape my mouth shut and shave my head. He was barely keeping it together! He sat back in his seat, and opened a file folder, and told me that my brainwave activity showed I was schizophrenic, and did I know what schizophrenia was. I told him I didn't, although I probably could have read what it was from his aura. He asked me if anyone was out to get me. I could have told him that he was, but he didn't want to hear that and you have to tell them what they want to hear or they'll lock you away and put electricity in you. But I couldn't lie, because he would know, so I told him it was too soon to tell. And he wrote that down, and this ugly green smoke puked from his pen.

AL: What did that mean?

ML: He was going to give me schizophrenia. And I heard his mother yelling at him. I heard her – I remember – it was something like what a liar he was, and how he'd never get away with it. And I could see how he wished he had strangled his mother himself. And he asked me, right then, if I heard voices. Just like that! Like he knew, but how could I tell him?

AL: What did you say?

ML: He got very stern at me, and he almost yelled. He wanted to strangle me. And I was afraid he would. So I told him yes, that I could hear his mother. And she was yelling at him that he was a horrible son and a failure as a doctor. I felt kinda sorry for him, even though he wanted to hurt me. But then he told me his mother was dead and wrote it all down in his ugly, inky green pen aura. He told me I couldn't hear her voice – it was impossible, an auditory hallucination. He said I shouldn't listen to the voices. That they'd try to hurt me if I did. They would get me in trouble. But they never wanted anything but a little help. Well, most of them never wanted anything but a little help. Anyway, I asked him if the voices were out to get me and he asked me what I thought, and I said it seemed like they were, and he wrote *that* down too, but I only said that because he told me they'd hurt me if I listened to them. By then, I could see this sort of vengeful glee in his aura, a bright shimmering shit-brown-stained gold – I could almost hear the psycho-giggle of an artist on a roll. You know? Like he was making something. Me. You know?

AL: Yeah. I know.

ML: Kind of what you've got right now, but it's much purer. Much shinier.

AL: Well, I'm an artist, and I'm sympathetic to your cause. Shrinks can't be.

ML: No. You're right.

AL: Would you mind talking about Lakeview?

ML: I call it the sanatorium because from what I know of them, they give about the same regard to patients. You know, in Sandman when the angels take over hell and they say they're going to continue the torture and torment but in the spirit of love, and the guy with all the hooks in him says, "But that's even worse!"?

AL: Yeah.

ML: That. They don't dunk you in ice water anymore, but they still use shock therapy. Literally.

AL: They still use electricity?

ML: All the time.

AL: I thought that was illegal.

ML: It probably is.

AL: But they did it to you? How? Why? Like—

ML: Okay, so, you know how you just say your world?

AL: I think I know what you mean, yeah.

ML: Like, all you do is talk your world, and you can't help it when people don't understand?

AL: We see the world not as it is, but as we are?

ML: Maybe. But I was seeing all these things and I was forgetting other people couldn't see them. They didn't know – not even themselves. So I would ask what Andrea was going to do with the social studies test she failed, and suddenly Andrea didn't want to talk to me anymore. And one by one, my friends turned the page on me and I was left alone. No one wanted to read me anymore and I was left alone. Just a blank sheet, with writing all over me. And the worst part – the worst part? I could see how sad it made them. I could see how angry and scared they were of me. I could see which ones really wanted to be my friends and which ones were too afraid to beat me up because they might get in trouble – and that was the only reason they didn't. Those ones started to tease me and the only way I could fight back was by seeing into them and exposing their inner secrets.

AL: I would so love to be able to do that.

ML: It gets you beat up a lot for the first little while. And then you're alone forever. Nobody wants to hang out with someone who can see your sex dreams.

AL: Wait. You can see my sex dreams?

ML: [Does not respond with words.]

AL: Then, you've seen.

ML: The candles, yes. And the blood.

AL: That doesn't scare you?

ML: It – a little. You think about drinking blood a lot.

AL: A lot?

ML: More than you think. And, I mean, sure not a lot of people do it, or think about it, but at least you accept it. You don't stuff it down. At least not all the way. I've seen the candles. Those ones are kind of hot.

AL: Haha. The candles are kind of hot.

ML: [Laughs.] But you don't – what's the word for when you blind yourself to who you really are?

AL: Repressing?

ML: Yeah! Repressing. You don't repressing your – no. You don't repress yourself. So many people do that.

AL: I know.

ML: And it's when you do that – I've seen it so much! – it's when you do that that you end up becoming a horrible person.

AL: Yeah?

ML: Yeah. My psycho analyst[1] at the sanatorium – Uncle Creepy. I called him that because the first thing he said to me was "I have a niece about your age."

AL: Erg.

ML: Yeah, and I could see her. All breasts and backside, with wet blonde hair, and wearing a bikini[2]. He was behind her, untying her top. And then her face changed to mine.

AL: Creepy.

---

[1] Mirella had me change the spelling of this. It was originally psychoanalyst.

[2] I had to change this one too. Mirella originally said, "With wet blonde hair in a bikini," and I didn't want to confuse the issue – the girl was wearing a bikini, not her hair.

ML: Uncle Creepy. Things went downhill from there. He wasn't messing around with his niece. He would have gotten caught. But in the sanatorium –

AL: He had all the power.

ML: No one believes a girl with paranoid delusions. I was projecting and dreaming, hallucinating, fantasising. But if I were fanaticising, why would I cry when I told on him? He had a perfect copy of his niece – and this giant pink hand that was so gentle and so cruel. He had this hymn he used to sing. Wanna hear it?

AL: I guess.

ML: You're a good girl,
A very good girl
Mirella.
Just let me take your hand.
You're a good good girl, sweetie.
Sweet, and loving.
You're a good girl
Mirella.
O sweetie! That's the way.
That's the way.
Mirella.
O yea, sweetheart!
That's my little swimmer.
That's my sweet delight.
O God! Yes!
Charlene!

AL: That's perverse.

ML: I wasn't even anything to him. I wasn't even the girl he was molesting.

AL: I think I need to take a break.

ML: Me too.

AL: Want a tomato?

ML: Yummy nightshade!

[BREAK]

AL: Now, earlier we were talking about school and then we shifted kind of seamlessly into you being in the say – the sanatorium. But – what happened? I mean, they don't just lock kids away for no reason anymore. Kind of.

ML: I tried to kill myself.

AL: How?

ML: [She lifted her sleeves and showed me the marks. They were wide, and jagged, like she'd tried more than once.]

AL: More than once?

ML: No. I – I did some research on the internet. And I found a site that told me how to slit my wrists. It said that to avoid the pain of bleeding out, I should freeze my wrists in ice for an hour. So I did, and I thought it would work – I only wanted to not feel the pain anymore! But they lied. There was barely any blood at all. So, I went again, and again and again. But there was still not very much blood. My mother found me passed out in the bathtub when she came home. I should have locked the door.

AL: No. No, honey. Please, no. [Starts to cry.]

ML: Sorry.

AL: It's okay. Let's go on.

ML: I woke up strapped to a hospital bed.

AL: What? Strapped!

ML: I was a psycho on suicide watch.

AL: Mother Goddess!

ML: [Gasps] She's here!

AL: Oh my – O!

[We both got down on our knees, and basked. She didn't speak; or move; or do anything. It was a tableau. What else can you do in the presence of a Goddess? I don't know if it's appropriate to describe Her. But when She left, we got back on the couch – Mirella's bed – and sat together.]

ML: That was magick.

AL: It sure was. Shall we continue?

ML: I feel blessed now. Let's go on.

AL: You woke up in a hospital bed. You seem to do that a lot.

ML: Too much. This time I was in Lakeview. In a room by myself. And I stayed that way for almost an hour. About ten minutes in, the room started to warp and make sounds. So, of course I tried to get out of the bed. I hoped the rattling would call someone's real attention. But the room just laughed at me. Then it said my name and of course I started screaming. It said it would swallow me, devour me so that no one would remember who I was. And I started screaming and crying and the room made lip-smacking noises and laughed. I shrieked my lungs out, and it said how delicious I looked and how pretty I was when I was panicking. It told me I'd love the doctors, and the doctors would love me and I knew what it meant. By the time the nurses got to me, my bandages were worn to the skin.

AL: They left you in there?

ML: They gave me a sedative and told me I was at Lakeview and that I was safe. I tried to tell them I wasn't, but you already know what came of that.

AL: Sure do.

ML: So, they left me with that smug, vicious room mocking me in slow motion. It was just: I-I-i-i'm-m-m-m g-o-o-o-i-i-i-in-n-ng t-o-o e-e-e-a-a-t-t y-y-o-o-o-u-u-u-u!

AL: That's creepy.

ML: And you weren't even there!

AL: But – it's kind of like I was.

ML: A little.

AL: A little. Like, you're doing a really good job of describing it.

ML: I spent my first night there drugged and crying and begging the walls to stop scaring me. And eventually faces – in the wall. Faces – teenagers and children melting out of the wall – faces trapped forever in the sanatorium. Lost forever. Thrown away and forgotten. I was too sedated to scream, but I couldn't go to sleep. Not in that room!

AL: That's insane!

ML: [snorts]

AL: I guess I should stop saying things like that, eh?

ML: Why?

AL: Because it actually happened, right?

ML: But just because it actually happened doesn't mean it's not insane. It just means nobody wants to hear it.

AL: I heard something once. Something like – I don't know – they out voted me. Oh! Ah, they said I was crazy—

AL & ML: and I said they were crazy and damn them—

ML: they out-voted me. [Starts to cry.]

[End transcript.]

She cried for about an hour. We ordered nightshade pizza: extra sauce, sundried tomatoes, green and red peppers, eggplant, basil. We watched Rocky Horror. I stroked her hair, kissed her temples – she's been taking better care of herself this week. Smells nicer.

Her tomato-y lips, her trusting smile, those hazel eyes that see more of me than I do. Gods! This is murder. Being away from her is so hard! I worry about her. Sometimes when I'm on the brink of sleep it's as if I can feel her presence on me, wriggling and squirming, breathing her hot breath on my throat and kissing. My hands feel her rear and her breasts and the sensations jolt me awake. It happened last night as I was drifting off. I woke up fully, and looked over at her bed. There she was, with her reading lamp on, drawing.

And I watched her, thoroughly engrossed in her activity. She didn't even notice I was as awake as she was. And while I was watching, I was wondering about that drawing, and the difference between that style – that incredible realism versus the manga she draws now. Those anti-psychotics keep her – what? productive at school? -- but they really hinder her artistic voice. I wonder what would happen if she stepped down her dosage.

When I'm at home and I feel her presence on me and around me, just falling off to sleep like that, I wake up and I'm alone in my room. I feel lost, and lonesome, and a little panicked. It is so hard not to call her in the middle of the night and sing my love for her. But I won't. It'd scare her off if I were clingy.

Entry #22: Tuesday, October 12

Today, Anders Espensen came up to me after Social Justice and told me he and Emma Johnson were trying to start a mental health club and did I want to help? I had to tell him the idea of "mental health" isn't really appealing because I think calling someone "ill" for something that might not ultimately be a disease is pretty prejudicial. But on the other hand, being around sympathetic ears for one – ears that aren't tired of hearing my opinionated bullshit – might have its merits. So I asked what I could do. Put up posters, spread the word. I don't know who I'm going to spread the word to, except Mirella, but posters are easy.

"Can we bitch about shrinks?" I asked.

"Oh – yeah!"

"And can we just – be ourselves?"

"You mean, make out with Mirella?"

"Well, maybe not make out, but—"

"For sure. Every sexual orientation will be welcome. Did you know gayness used to be a mental illness?

"Yeah. Did you know you could go to prison for life for it until 1964?"

"I did not."

"So – have you been to a shrink?"

"Yeah."

"What'd they give you?"

"Epival. It evens me out."

"No, I mean – what disease did they give you?"

"Like, going to a shrink makes you crazy?"

"Well, if you're not supposed to know you're crazy, how could you possibly be crazy until someone gives it to you?"

"Ah, I'm not sure that's the way it works."

"Whatever. What'd they give you?"

"They gave me bipolar. You?"

"Heh. Oppositional Defiance Disorder with a side of paranoia."

"Paranoia? You?"

"Yeah. Paranoia."

"You taking anything for that?"

"Fuck that!"

"That would be a no, then."

"That would be a no. I'm not paranoid. The way I look at it, it was either PPD or nymphomania."

"So, the rumours are true?"

"Don't look at me like that."

"Sorry, I—"

"No worries. Are you on anything for yours?"

"Uh, yeah. Epival. If I weren't, I'd be a lot less – manageable."

"Manageable?"

"Y-yeah. A little bit more rage-y? Sometimes? Inconsolable and possibly self-destructive. Unless you just couldn't keep me down and I was, like, singing show-tunes in physics."

"So, you're happy with your diagnosis?"

He shrugged. "The pills – keep me out of the hospital and in school. Everything else – could have been – handled differently."

"Yeah. That's a pretty good way to put it."

I had lunch with him an Emma. Emma's a pudgy girl with pasty skin and dark hair. She's got something called trichotillomania. It put me in mind of that bezoar in Sandman, the one that asshole author pays for Kaliope I tried not to say anything about it, but I didn't know what else to say. She smiled and dropped her hair.

"I've never read that book," she said.

I said: "I can lend them to you. It's a series of ten."

"Oh, I don't have time to read more books."

"No, me neither. Maybe over Yule?"

"Yule?"

"Ah, yeah. Christmas, whatever."

"Trying to take the Christ out of X-mas?" she asked, smiling with those wet pink lips.

"Ah, actually yeah. Do you know what cultural imperialism is?"

She shook her head, started fiddling with her hair again. Put it in her mouth and spat it out.

"So, uh," said Anders, taking Emma's hand, "where's what's-her-name today? What's her name?"

"Mirella. And I called her this morning but she didn't pick up. I thought she might just have slept in. She might be sick."

"So, what's up with her?" asked Emma. "Like, what's – wrong with her?"

"Um, that's not really my place to say. You'll have to ask her. When she's here."

"Are you two in love?" she asked.

"That's not – any of your business."

"Well, you're with her all the time. You seem really buddy-buddy. Close, like."

"I'm her peer tutor. I'm kind of responsible for her. And I like her."

"Like, like her, like her?" asked Anders.

"Yes! Okay? Jesus!" I got up and stormed out. Half-a-plate of food. Wasted.

Anders got up and followed me out the door, took my arm.

"What was that?" he demanded.

"Well, what's with the grilling?"

"Well, you as much as said a while ago."

"Yeah, that – was an empty hallway. Not a crowded cafeteria."

"We were talking confidentially in there. You asked Em about her crazy. What's the difference?"

"I – fuck, I'm sorry. I'm just – the pissy posse keeps trying – if – if Mirella gets into trouble," I murmured, "they'll take her back to the sanatorium. I can't – I don't want to lose her."

He looked at me with hard eyes. Then he cracked a half-smile. "That rumour. About Gen Jones's tongue?"

I blushed. "It was really kinda hot."

"So, you're into crazy."

I laughed. "I guess so."

"Hey," he said, putting his hand on my arm. I jerked back, grabbed the offended appendage. "Whoa! Whoa."

"Sorry. I just. It's –"

"No worries. I think I'm starting to piece you together, Miss Lerner."

"You – pronounced it right."

"I remembered. People's names are important to them."

We went back in and I finished my lunch. Things were relatively peaceful. This crazy club, the psycho squad (it's better than "mental health club" any day) – it's going to be pretty hot!

Supplement

Right in the middle of French class, my cell went off. I don't normally have my cell on during class, but I thought it would be best to keep it on in case Mirella called. It did cross my mind that she could be having a psychotic break and that I might be the only person she'd trust enough to call in that case. So, I sat on it all day – my cell phone. And in French class, it buzzed, shocking me and making the seat vibrate. there was tittering and snickering. I hadn't been exactly prepared for it, but since my cover was blown, there was not reason to pretend any further.

--*Émie,* said Mme. VanderAa. *Sille vous plaît, fermer ta téléphone dans la classe.*

--*Je m'excuse,* Madame. *Je doit accepter.*

Après la leçon.

Mais, Madame. C'est important. Je doit accepter maintenant.

Émie! Ne sortis cette chambre!

Mais, madame! Je doit accepter! C'est très important!

Émie! Non!

Rita! Oui!

And I left.

"Mirella? Where are you?"

"We have to do it, Amy. We have to do it, and we have to win."

"Hold on, sugar. Slow down. Where are you?"

"Home. But, Amy. Listen. There's this demon. And he shows me darkness, and I can't move. We have to take him on and we have to win. You can be Athene and I'll be – I don't know – Mother Theresa? No. That doesn't make sense. Ariadne? No. Arachne! Yeah! You be Athene and I'll be Arachne. Together we can fight the demon, the One-Two, and toss him in to be gored to death. It's dangerous, but it'll be worth it. But we have to win."

Then Mrs. VanderAa comes out of the classroom, crosses her arms and stands in front of me. How's that for *la politesse*?

"Excuse me," I said, "I'm on the phone."

"You should be in class, not talking to your friends. Your cell phone's supposed to be off. *La politesse*?"

"I'm talking," I said, "to my student. I have a responsibility."

"Your responsibility—"

I held up my hand for a moment's silence, because Mirella was still going on. "Sorry, Mirella. Can you give me two minutes? I've got a teacher in front of me. I'll call you back in two minutes, okay?"

She quietened. She trusts me. I hung up and Rita held out her hand.

"What?" I said.

"Give me your phone."

"I have to call her back. Didn't you hear me?

"You shouldn't make promises to break rules, Amy. Give me your phone, now, please."

So, I handed it to her and went back to class. It just boggles me – Mirella's out for the day. No indication of how well she is, and it's business as usual? Does no one understand that a sick day for Mirella could mean something more than a head cold? Doesn't anyone know what a psychotic break is? It's not a vacation! Mirella *trusts* me, which considering all she's been through is astounding. When she was able, she called *me*. Did she call her mom? No. The school? No. Her shrink? Hah! She only called me – as I found out after detention when I went to her place. I have a responsibility to Mirella that does take me well beyond learning French. The language Mirella speaks is far more complicated.

Mrs. VanderAa told me I was on thin ice – like I don't know – and that with a third warning I'd be suspended. She'd already proven it was pointless to defend myself and Mirella against her, so I didn't. Self defense is *not* an acceptable form of expression. So, I toed the line.

"I'm sorry I was rude to you," I told Mrs. VanderAa. "I'm just really worried about Mirella."

"We all are," she lied, "but that's no excuse to walk out of class."

I bit my tongue and nodded. A week's' detention. No third warning. Praise Jesus.

I got home to Mirella at about 4:30, a full two hours after I promised I'd call her. If she were my daughter or even my sister, none of this would have been a problem. Let me put it another way: if I'd been an adult, none of this would have been an issue. Mirella was pissed at me, but I sat her down and told her what happened. It was a hard sell for a half-hour, but then I asked her about the demon. She smiled.

"The angels told me, just after I got my body back, that there's a weakness – his weakness. He tells lies; He's judgmental; He's abusive and irresponsible. The angels told me – nobody like that could save anyone."

Side-swiped. "Are you ... talking about ... God? Take on God? God is weak? I mean, I don't believe in Jesus, but even if that god exists, surely trying to overthrow Him is suicide! "Which—which angels told you?"

"It was Michael. Even Michael's displeased, unsatisfied. It's amazing the way you live in a haze for most of your life, and then something wakes you up."

"What something woke Mickey—I mean, Michael up?"

"He didn't tell me. He said I couldn't understand. Even with my ability, he said he'd blow my mind up if he told me. God's Lucifer, Amy! We have to become our warrior selves and overthrow him. But we have to win!"

'Cause if we don't, we're fucked.

I humoured Mirella while we went for groceries and cooked dinner. I think part of me was so intrigued by the way she was talking, I wanted to give it a shot. In addition to the fact that I didn't want to shut Mirella down without listening to her first. But I can't, can I? We can't! She was talking about the whole world – all of it – and all I could think was I can barely take on a teacher.

"I know what you're thinking," Mirella said to me over the bowtie pasta.

It was funny, because it was true. "What?"

"It's impossible. School, shrinks, the law. Maybe you're right. But how can we rise to ourselves when the God they cry to from the Abyss belongs in the Abyss?"

Seriously. The woman makes sense. Crazy, frightening, nonsensical sense. I can't tell if she's a madwoman, a revolutionary, or a prophet.

Entry #23: Wednesday, October 13

I was thinking about it. Mirella wants us to be Athene and Arachne. I mean, the dressing up to embody the people – Goddesses – we can embody. We can do this on Hallowe'en night.

Besides, I've been looking for someone to dress up with. Felicity would only dress like a prostitute – sexy nurse, sexy maid, sexy red riding hood, you know the type. (Honestly, what right does she have to criticise me for fucking around? At least I dress sensibly and don't let anyone tell me what to wear.) Jeremy – well, it's basically the same thing with him. Except less slutty. He just wants to buy a costume, and I want to make mine. And Mickey? Well, I'm not really ready to build a costume with Mickey, even if he wants to.

I wonder where I can get feathers that look like a tawny owl. Because it's certainly not going to be on-line. I'm not dressing like a slut for Hallowe'en. Besides, Athene was chaste! Every single website I went to to try to find an Athene costume included a tunic so short it would make Aphrodite blush. And some were pink. Pink!

I'll need a shield and a spear. Preferably it'd be a steel one, but I don't think they'd let me into school with it. Plastic for school, and a wooden javelin for afterward, because I don't even think I'd be allowed on the bus with an actual spear. (Those things were long!) I can sharpen a javelin on my own, but where am I going to get a metal shield? Wood will *not* do for that. Maybe I can sub in a mirror or something.

The hardest part of this costume will definitely be the owl wings. And yes, I know owl wings on Athene aren't canonical, but I don't care. Short skirts and pink on Athene are equally non-canonical, the internet, and mine makes more sense.

I wonder if I can get a headpiece to put my hair up with. Something authentically Greek. That one online with the horses. I thought Poseidon got the horse. Shows what I know.

Entry #24: Thursday, October 14

Beware the Ides of October. Somebody set up a webpage devoted to me and Mirella and made sure everyone got the link. No one knows the source for sure, and you can bet they wouldn't tell me if they did know, but would you be surprised to learn it was the pissy posse? I wouldn't. Not really. I mean, I like to call them stupid, but when you actually think about it, they're actually kinda smart. At least one of them understands what a centaur is, even if she doesn't know what it's called. (Bitch!) I know they're just trying to get Mirella to react, but Mirella was defending me, not herself. So, now we have people laughing at us, and guys trying to get us to kiss as we walk down the hall, asking questions about scissors. Ugh!

"What kind of psycho retard would be friends with this goth whore?" [Fig. 1] "Where did she come from and why is she sucking ass with her satanic pimp?" [Fig. 2] "Dykes!" [Fig. 3] (Figure three is an actual video of me making out with Mirella last week in the practice room.)

Why is it, whenever you think you're alone, you're not? And why is it that when you're being watched, it's always by someone evil? And why is it that, with everyone *actually* out to get me, people get to call me paranoid?

It stings. No. It's worse than that. It burns – a heavy, hot lead in the pit of my stomach. I want to lash out. I want to not care. I don't care about popularity. I don't care about – I *do* care about all the people who hate me because it's acceptable. Slut. Goth. Weird name. Kinda masculine. Paranoid and pissed about it. And now Mirella's in the middle and I can't get revenge because I'm already on the authority watch-list. Worse, though, is how Mirella might respond. I mean, how can I be sure that her blank look when she found out – when we both found out – was anything but carefully kept rage, a boiling pot on a secret stove?

So, after class today, I told Mirella to go and visit Tilly. I went to see Mr. Myer. He actually *likes* the way I question everything. I mean, we don't have open discussions in every class, so I'm really active and participatory in the AP English discussions. It's not like he's told me he likes my brain, but you can tell. He's always smiling when he calls on me. It's like he's proud of me, happy to see someone who talks out loud and doesn't worry about being made fun of because she's better than it all.

So, I walk up to him after class and say; "Uh, Mr. Myer? Can I talk, uh, can I ask you – um—"

Without looking up he said, "Take a breath, Miss Lerner. Have a seat and start again." So I did.

"Mr. Myer," I said, "somebody's been baiting me and Mirella."

"Don't take it."

"Direct. But not helpful. I've been not taking bait for years. This – I can't ignore this.

"What is it that you can't ignore?"

"Someone's made a website of me."

"And it's degrading."

"It's worse than that, sir. It might be illegal. I think someone's trying to provoke a fight. Please, sir, I implore you—"

"Implore?"

"I'm desperate, sir. And when I get desperate, I get loquacious."

"So, why come to me? I'm no administrator."

"Precisely the reason, sir. The administration staff is – displeased with me."

He smiled a knowing smile out of the corner of his mouth, but he didn't say anything. "You're asking me to advocate for you?"

"I was hoping you would, sir, yes."

Mr. Myer sat back in his seat and folded his hands on his belly. "Well, Amy," he began, "you haven't ingratiated yourself to many people in the school – students, teachers or administration. You've been disobedient, disruptive, and sometimes downright disrespectful."

"But, sir, that's—"

He put his hand up. "Let me finish. I'll help you, Amymone, but I want you to know why I offer it. Are you ready?"

"Yes, sir."

"I'm scared of you."

"What?"

"You terrify me."

"What!"

"You're elegant, eloquent, sharp as a straight razor, and mean as an alley cat. You know when you're being fed BS and you don't stand for it. People like you have done great and terrible things throughout history, Miss Lerner. But you're young. And young people are stupid. If you're left to your own devices, you'll self destruct and take the rest of us with you."

"That's a bit extreme, don't you think?"

"Perhaps. Are you willing to take that risk? I'm not. So I offer my support. Especially in this. This website is unfair."

"Have you seen it?"

"I have. You work quick magick, Amymone."

"Sir?"

He smiled every time I called him sir. "Mirella – has obvious trust issues among her battery of problems. She's not the kind of girl to kiss someone easily. Especially a girl. Especially a frighteningly austere girl like you."

I heard myself say, "Her mouth is so tasty."

"I didn't hear that," he promised.

"Thank you, sir."

He leant forward on his desk and stared into me. I stared back. "You really do have a disdain for the rules, don't you Miss Lerner?"

"I – just feel so much more capable than what people give me credit for. I wish someone would treat me like an adult. I can almost sign a contract."

"Be that as it may, I don't think any of our peer tutors has ever made out with a schizophrenic student in a practice room before."

The way he said it made my stomach churn and sink into my abdomen. I got cold sweat and a dry mouth. "I know it was wrong, but please believe me. I didn't do it to disdain the rules. I did it because—I'm in love."

He didn't give me the too-young-to-know lecture. He just nodded. If he wanted to say something, he thought better of it. Maybe he is a little scared of me.

"There may be very little I can do to help you, Amy. But I'll do what I can. Now go home."

I don't know what's going to happen.

Athene was a goddess much besought
For wisdom in the bloody field of war;
But for my heart, my ruby lover's core
I'll wager She's not got a stalwart thought.
Arachne, spider lady, was Her child
Who through parthenogenesis was wrought
And who by Lady Distaff was then taught
Humility and went into the wild.
Is this the love a mother shows a girl:
To thrust the wayward child from out her arms?
To send her off? It – truly, it alarms.
She has no family, not in all the world.
Who loves a spider rightly, it is said,
Will have a silken pillow whereupon to rest her head.

Entry #25: Friday, October 15

The Ides of October have been extended for a day. Everyone in Media Arts has seen the website, and sent it on. That is to say, even the instructor, Mrs. Laing has seen it and sent it on. To Mr. Brown the principal. And as a result, I was pulled out of class this morning to go and see said principal. Mr. Myer was there looking somewhat unimpressed. Of course, he commonly looks somewhat unimpressed.

"Hello, Am-I-moan-ee," said Mr. Ladner.

"Amymone," I corrected.

"Miss Lerner," said Mr. Myer, "kindly restrain yourself."

"Yes, sir." I took a seat.

The principal glanced askance between us. I had obeyed a simple command. I couldn't help but feel a little smug at his confusion.

"She responds well to support and respect," said Mr. Myer.

"I see," said Mr. Ladner, dubiously. "Now, Am-I-moan-ee." (I bit my tongue.) "It's come to my attention that you've been using your peer tutoring time period to engage in – homoerotic – activities with Mirella Lantigua."

"I had a moment of weakness, yes."

"Of course you understand, we can't have that."

"No, we can't. It hasn't happened again and it won't. But now, Mr. Ladner—"

"I'd like you to know, Am-I-moan-ee—"

"Please, call me Amy."

"I'd like you to know – Amy – that there are those in this school who think you can't be trusted with a girl so fragile as Mirella Lantigua. They'd be very happy, especially now, if I pulled you from your tutoring responsibilities even though it would mean you didn't graduate on time." (More like *especially* because it would mean I wouldn't graduate on time, but I digress.)

"Who are these people?" I asked.

"That's none of your concern."

"So, you're a gossip monger, then? Talking about people behind their backs with malicious intent and then protecting them when their victims want to respond? Did *you* put up that website?"

"A-mymone!" grunted Mr. Myer behind me.

"What! You have to admit it's suspicious."

"You are on thin ice, Amy!" hollered Mr. Ladner. "You're *that* far from a suspension, and I don`t think I have to tell you what that means for the young woman you've seduced."

"Seduced? With my girlish charm and my winning listening-to-her-instead-of-condemning-her? No. You don't have to tell me what that would mean for her. I know I'm the only one who can protect her."

"That's not true, Amy. This school is doing its level best."

"Really? Letting grown men and women talk shit about a teenager who isn't even there to protect herself? You don't know her! You don't know her and you don't know me! I'm not like anyone else in this school and that –" I said in a moment – a brilliant ray – of inspiration, "that's why I was given Mirella to tutor in the first place, isn't it?"

A pause. Mr. Ladner looked down at his hands, clenched into white knuckles. It would have been awkward if not for all the triumph. Mr. Myer broke the silence.

"I told you she wouldn't take long to figure it out."

"Can we talk about the website, now?" I said. "Seeing as it's a little more ethically suspect than me kissing a girl?"

"That's been taken care of. The culprits have been threatened with punishment if it's not down by the end of the day."

"What kind of punishment?"

"I'm not at liberty to say. But I will say that I need to give you a detention for misusing our practice rooms."

"What!"

"You were wasting time at school, Amy. You were wasting time and you took advantage of a mentally ill student. You're lucky you're only getting a detention."

"But – nothing would be wrong if no one had seen the website that people put up to get us in trouble. You're telling them it worked?"

"Amy, if you're not careful, I'll suspend you for a week. And then where will you be?"

"This is bullshit!" I walked out.

I went into the empty downstairs bathroom and I cried. I actually cried at school. I haven't done that since I was nine and

Lindsay MacKenzie called me a fat ugly lesbian who'd be alone forever. I started crying but she told me crying was weak. So I sucked it up, punched her in the gut, and never cried at school again. Until today.

Mr. Myer caught up with me and Mirella at lunch and told me if I wanted to take the rest of the day off, he'd vouch for my illness. I told him I wanted to but I couldn't leave Mirella. He looked back and forth between us and nodded. After he walked off, Mirella told me that Mr. Myer was sad that the school system keeps putting his most gifted students at risk.

And I just realised now that means Mirella's off her meds. How did I fail to notice that!

Entry #26: Saturday, October 17

Mirella is snuggling up next to me on her futon. She's being really affectionate today – smiling and everything! It's been a rough week for us. I haven't spoken to Felicity one-on-one in a while. We seldom see each other at lunch anymore. I haven't really wanted to talk to her since she was such a bitch at Thea's, and she's been pretty much the same. She looks over to where we're eating, Mirella and me and sometimes Mickey and sometimes Jeremy, and sometimes it's with regret, but other times she gives me this dirty look and shakes her head.

This all amounts to me not wanting to be paranoid. I want to believe that Gen Walters or Patricia Wang or someone else from the pissy posse did it. I don't want to think that Felicity betrayed me like that. I just have to let this rest until I can talk to her. Or want to.

Tonight, after I feed Mirella, we're going down to Dress You to look at costume options. Less than two weeks until the fabled All Souls. I have to say, I'm looking forward to Hallowe'en. With Mirella off her meds (she just curled up into a little ball when she saw me write that – so sweet and affectionate!) she is affectionate, vocal, lucid – in a metaphoric way.

Sometimes, the myth goes by so fast I can't understand it. One second, she's talking gospel, the next Greek myth, and then I'm some Beethoven violin sonata. In a complete circle. In one sentence. One hour I'm the Shining Host (still don't know what that's all about), the next I'm Athene. She's Arachne, then Teresa of Avila – whoever that is – then, Snow White and Rose Red, then she's Alice and I'm Thessaly. But she seems so much more real – metaphorically.

Look, I can't say I'm not worried about her being off her medication. I had a look online, and apparently coming off anti-psychotics can cause a psychotic break. It reminds me of a dam. When the dam wall is removed, there's a flood. Like that, but more dream images. Mirella's holding it together real well, but if she goes crazy I won't know what to do. I know that. Maybe I should tell her mother? Maybe I should tell her doctor? But the thing is, I know what they'd do. Maybe they'd be right?

Entry # 27: Sunday, October 18

Last night's trip downtown was rough on Mirella. Lots of people on the bus; lots of people in the shop. All of them thinking very loudly, apparently. On the way back, Mirella was leaning into me, with an excruciated grimace on her face and her palm pressed over her forehead.

"They're too loud! They're too loud!" she hollered. See, no one was actually saying anything. People looked at us, but I just put my arm around her. I closed my eyes, and imagined the aura she'd drawn of me encompassing us both; then that coppery shimmer hardened to a fine thread – pure metal, gleaming red.

Mirella looked so stunned. She could see the aura, and the change in it. There was a psychotic glee in her face as she exclaimed: "It's gone! I can't hear them at all anymore! Oh, thank you, Mistress! Thank you!" Then she kissed me full on the mouth. We almost missed our stop.

Tomorrow, I'm calling Thea to see if she can train me to control my psychic stuff better.

Entry # 28: Monday, October 19

Spent all day making costumes. Great to have an early start. The more work I get done now, the less I'll have to make up for in a week's time.

Called Thea today. Appointment for Thursday. She's only charging her regular fee: $100/hour, twice a month. And she'll teach us both for that.

"Money is a means to an end, " she said, when I sounded surprised. "You're both young, and you both need training. If I could, I'd do it for free."

"Well, thank you all the same."

And now, the conversation I had with my parents over dinner, after I sent Mirella home by taxi. I sat down to dinner, alone with them for the first Sunday since I met Mirella. We crossed ourselves, started eating.

I looked up.

"Mom, Dad," I said, "I want psychic training."

They looked at me, stunned into a kind of hungry tableau. Dad was the first to speak. Mom facepalmed.

"Why would you want a thing like that, sweetie?"

"I want to help Mirella," I said.

"Oh, honey," said Mom. "You can't. Only a trained professional can help her."

"No, I mean – not like that. I wanna understand her better."

"And you think psychic training will do that for you?" asked Dad.

"I do."

"Why is that?"

"Well, I've been doing some reading, and some people think there's a similarity between, like, I dunno – mystics and schizophrenics."

Dad started nodding in that thoughtful way he has, but Mom is always so full of unhelpful opinions. She said: "Amymone, love, we know better than that now."

"That's just the thing, though – we don't. I mean, this isn't a twenty-five hundred-year-old text I was reading this time. There's a very respectable mythologist named Joseph Campbell who thinks schizophrenia and shamanism are one and the same.

"Oh, but honey," said mom with saccharine pessimism, "Joseph Campbell's not a psychiatrist."

I gritted my teeth, and tried very hard not to launch into a tirade about monolithic narratives and quacks with authority. It gave my mom license to go on.

"I know you want to help Mirella, sweetie, and I for one think you're doing a great job. You're so generous with your time. She seemed so much happier when she left today than she did when we first met her. Didn't she, Rob?"

"For sure," said Dad.

I wasn't very well going to tell them why.

"Please," I said. "I just – I wanna go deeper. I – just—"

Dad put up his hand for silence. "Supposing we believe this cracked theory."

"Kay."

"Where would we find someone to give you this training? How much would it cost? How often would it be? And how would you fit it in with the rest of your responsibilities?"

"Her name's Thea – I've been to see her once before."

"What for?" demanded Mom.

"None of your business. I paid using my own allowance, and it's not illegal. It costs a hundred dollars an hour. She's offering every second Thursday."

"For how long?" asked Dad.

"As long as it takes."

He chuckled. "How long per session?"

"Oh! Oh! One hour each."

He raised his eyebrows and made his "maybe" face. I know better than to be impatient with Dad. We ate dinner in silence.

When we were sated, he leaned back and said: "I'll make you a deal, Amymone."

"Okay."

"You pay for one half of the month, we'll pay for the other. But if your grades slip, it's goodbye crackpot theory. Got it?"

"Rob!" cried Mom.

"It's a hundred bucks a month, Sandra. And whatever the shrinks say, I think my little girl thinks things through. Do you?"

"She's chasing rainbows, Robert!"

"So let her! You're only young once."

Mom made her exasperated I-can't-find-a-good-reason-to-be-against-this sigh. And here I am, about to type up a résumé.

Entry #29: Tuesday, October 20

Why is it that every awesome job requires so much more training than sales clerk? Maybe that's not the way to ask that. I mean, it's fairly obvious. The better question might be: why, in the infancy of the prime of my life, am I being shunted into a profession hawking worthless crap? "Food" with empty calories, flavoured liberally with salt; videos with empty messages flavoured liberally with "artists". Little Death – my funerary fashion home – isn't hiring. I *could* do sales there, but the fact remains, I'd still be doing sales. I prefer to do work for the Women's Centre downtown, or some other shelter, a women's health organisation, something good. Maybe a youth center? But guess what! Those entry-level positions don't pay. Case for social programs much?

Anyway, Graeme at Cherubim Books was able to hire me for eight hours a week. I'm so grateful – I love that store. Graeme is such a nice man.

You know, looking back over the kinds of things I've written about men, I think maybe I've been unfair. Not all men in my life have been absolute cads. But then, come to that, how much of my hatred of men is my own fault? Is all my struggling in vain? Should I just give in and be ashamed I've been a slut? Because I did choose to have sex with a lot of guys and they all hurt me and laughed at me, one after the other, and I still chose to do it. I chose to fuck around, and I didn't stop, thinking I could fuck the pain of being fucked away. Should I just be a nice girl?

"Nice girl" means obedient, quiet, demure, and stupid. How could I help Mirella like that? How could I help myself? People would walk all over me. But I might even be safer for Mirella then. What do I even mean by that?

Ugh! I have so much practicing to do before tomorrow.

Entry #30: Thursday, October 22

Augh! Dress rehearsal tomorrow. Concert on Saturday. Costumes still not done. I want to use hazel wood for the spear –

there's a tree in the park. But I haven't been able to find anything on how Athene feels about it. The tree calls me. It's something Mirella would say, but it feels right. She'd actually talk to it, call back to it from across the street.

For the past week, Mirella's been kind of up and down. She tells me all the thoughts, all the aurae of the people in her classes are distracting. She has trouble focusing on what teachers are saying because it's not what they're thinking.

"People have sexual fantasies at the least appropriate times. And the grosser they are, the brighter they get because people are so worried about them." She looked at me in the eye when she said that. Then she said: "You want my blood. I can see you do. Please. You can have it. I want you to. I trust you. You're the only one who believes in me. And maybe – maybe if you have some of me you can see what I see."

"And," I said, taking the knife from her hand, "maybe if you have some of me, you can protect yourself the way I do. But until we can ask Thea about it, why don't we see if it works with making out?"

She smiled at that. I told her I love her. Finally. And we kissed. She was so excited she said, "The death of me is the life in you and I can feel your pulsing chrome on eh derision of my scorpion. Take me, Beast of Lilith! Transform my modern years into veritable salts of pity and self worth!"

I have *no* idea what most of that means, but she started undressing. I felt kind of guilty watching her, and when I took her hand to stop her, she cried out.

"No, sweet demon! Don't stop me! Please! Slake yourself in my blood, and bind my flesh with your teeth! Your dark loving visage is all I worship – your shining care is all I ever ate!" She gripped my hand tight and jammed it against her groin. "The death of me is the life in you!"

Her eyes were crazy enflamed, desperate. I've never seen her like that. It frightened me.

"Oh no!" she cried, turning from me, putting her hands to her face.

"Mirella! What – what did I do?" I put my hand on her and she fell to her knees bawling.

"I've scared the Dark Mistress of Wisdom! And now she'll send me away to the monstrous dungeon."

"No, Mirella, no!" I wanted to hug her but I didn't want her to freak out more.

"Yes-s-s-s!" she insisted through her tears, "You will! I've frightened you!"

"But, why would I send you away? I love you!"

"*Because* you love me!" she shrieked, and fell forward on her forehead spilling tears from her eyes. This little voice in the side of my head hissed, "She's crazy. This is just the beginning. Leave her, or you'll regret it." But what kind of person would I be if I confirmed her belief that people who love her abandon her? What if she carries that monstrous dungeon around with her and whenever she's alone at night, she returns to it? I do. Kinda.

It took me a while to think of something to say, but here it is: "Mirella, we're not just friends; we're not just girlfriends. Remember, we've seen the Goddess together. She smiled on us, and blessed us. Think how unhappy She'd be if I left you just before we started learning how to fulfill Her blessing."

Mirella looked up at me, teary smile and smudged mascara. She looked at me in awe, then shook her head and said: "You're not Athene."

"I'm not?"

"No."

"Who am I?"

"You're Amymone."

And that was a little weird. Because, that's my name, but that's not what she meant. She clearly thinks I'm the woman from the myth – an incarnation through my own name. But maybe – I don't know – maybe that's how I fit in. Those years ago, on that rainy day, that girl appeared to me. She was carrying a mirror, and that's already part of my costume; and she was carrying a vase. And Amymone, the real one, the one from the story, when she was attacked by satyrs she was retrieving water during a drought. She would have had a vase with her.

Supplement:

It's late, but I have to get this down. We went to Thea's, and she taught us how to manipulate our auras, and open our chakras. She taught us a visualisation exercise to protect ourselves from the bombardment of especially negative psychic energy that people give off without knowing it. Imagine a rich circle of fire encapsulating us, keeping us safe. I prefer the solid metal capsule I've been using because I'm kind of afraid of fire. Mirella likes the fire because she says that the hardened aura one requires an aura and she doesn't have one. Which is patently absurd, of course.

Thea says even dead people have an aura, so someone as potent as Mirella must have an aura. It's just a matter of coaxing it out. Making her feel safe. It was tough to ask about the blood, but I did. I was expecting – I don't know – disgust, maybe? Dismissal? Something. A strong reaction. She looked at me cock-eyed for a moment and then used a word: sanguinarian.

"So, you're otherkin *and* sanguinarian," she said.

"I—guess."

"You're a faery who drinks blood."

"Well, I've never actually drunk anyone else's blood before, but, yeah. I guess."

Most sanguinarians are apparently vampires if they're otherkin, according to Thea. But we know, the three of us, that faeries aren't the lovey-dovey angelic beings of pure Disney-good they pretend they are. Most are sly, deceptive, destructive, dangerous. Faery blessings are always double-edged blades, or ultimately just curses. So, it makes sense that I would feel drawn to that kind of darkness in myself.

"At least you're honest about it," said Thea, "but if you're going to drink blood, you must be very, very careful. Drinking blood is like having sex without a condom. Any blood-borne illness in your victim will obviously become yours. There's a *much* higher risk of infection."

"You're not telling us not to!" Mirella realised out loud.

"No," said Thea. "I wouldn't do that. There's too much in human experience to say definitively that one thing is wrong while another is right, with some very glaring exceptions. All we can do is draw in and accept and, where we see the potential for harm, reduce the risk. Make sense?"

I felt like crying. I felt so much freer when she said that, like a leaden collar had been lifted from my neck. I wanted to thank her, and kneel before her, and pledge my loyalty to her philosophy. But I stopped myself. She's no goddess. And it's not just her philosophy. Tilly's that way too. And maybe even Mr. Myer.

Before we left, Thea offered us a tarot reading. It's so late, though. I wonder if I'll remember it tomorrow. The most important part for me was the near-future and the summary. The near future is the costume ball – represented by the Four of Wands. A harvest festival celebrated by an institution. Gathering, merriment, and dance.

And the summary card was Judgment, which Thea called Aeon. As though, soon we'll be moving into a new world – "a new realm," she said. "A mergence and an emergence."

Something powerful and mystical is going to happen to us – say, on the 31st? – and we're going to be transformed. I can hardly wait!

Entry #31: Friday, October 23

One week till the dance! I can't believe I'm actually going to a school dance, much less excited about it. Probably what excites me most is that no one will know why we're there except us. It's our secret.

Dress rehearsal went off pretty well today. Tuning problems in the damn trombones, but the strings have solved their slow-down issues in the Gypsy Dance, so I'm sold on it. The performance should sound good, if not professional. No one hands out medals for Hallowe'en concerts anyway.

The tour de force will of course be the "Danse Macabre". Mirella – I don't know if it's the fact that she's off her drugs or the conversation we had with Thea last night about vampirism, or what, but she's incredibly inspired. The dark joy in her is infectious, and she's far less timid about her tri-tones.

She told me afterwards: "I just think of being a spider and all the lines – all the strings and the waves – all the celestial dark power that spiders had. That! And I will it through my body and up to my hands. And I'm like, 'Sing, violin, sing!' And it does." Then she giggled about it for a good five minutes.

Right now, we're at my place finishing the last of our costumes. Mirella keeps grinning at me, but when I ask her what she wants, she says, "Nothing," and goes back to her costume. Tonight, I'm going to lay the plaster over her face for the mask. The mandibles are out, but we can still do the eight eyes. Unfortunately, the legs are going to be a little floppy, not sturdy the way we wanted, but that's the pay-off for not spending a small fortune on wiring. They'll still stand, but they won't look like chitin.

Anyway, I'd better get back to my owl feathers.

Entry #32: Saturday, October 24

Oh my gods! Holy music! This orchestra is amazing! I mean, don't get me wrong, we're not the VSO, or the TSO, or the LSO or – well, let's just say we're not going to be playing the Rite of Spring any time soon (and considering we're all graduating this year, soon is all we have.)

"Gypsy Dance" went off without a hitch. It was a great opening. "Un bal"? Syncopation problems in the winds, trouble in the cornet part, and a bit of lag on behalf of the strings. (Fortunately, I was playing the harp, so I'm absolved. Lovely harp, too. Even Mariette DuPont.)

All of which is frankly preamble. When we finished the Berlioz, Mirella ran off-stage. Now, I know what you're thinking. I thought it too. Where the hell is she going! She's got a solo to play in, like, now! But Ms. Baccarat turned without missing a beat and introduced "Danse Macabre." She took her time, too, going into the medieval history of it, and even singing the *Dies Irae*.

When she turned around she looked a little nervous. But she raised her arms and cued Mariette on the harp. As we violins raised our instruments to play, out came a girl with four extra *papier maché* arms wearing a mask with eight eyes on it. She was holding a violin. There were titters and murmurs in the audience. Mirella walked right toward centre stage and put her violin beneath her chin *just* in time for her cue. We're all familiar, of course, with the opening tri-tones that announce Death's presence, but when Mirella bit into that crunchy chord, something happened in the orchestra. I could practically feel it! A thrill ran through me, but it wasn't mine. It was ours.

I don't know how, with all the notes written down the way they are, and with the relative apathy we approached this piece yesterday – I mean, yes it was note-perfect, but it lacked emotion, or understanding – we could play with such refined and morbid darkness. Mirella was on *fucking fire!* Alternately biting and lulling. I half-believed she was a spider.

When the winds came in with their description of the Dies Irae, after the first two statements of the main theme, I almost giggled. When the trumpets echoed them, the new key mocked them, but the theme was a deep agreement, and the appoggiaturas in the oboes reminded us all of the desperate licentiousness – our desire for death.

Then, Mirella. That lulling line, almost pastoral – melancholy comfort. And the low brass brushing it aside when the rest of the violins dared concur. Finally, the low brass understood the coming storm they foretold as we violins danced our colourful scales. A warning, a threat – that violinist was not to be trusted. Remember her biting – remember the vigour with which Death had announced Her presence. And then, we gossiped, the woodwinds and the strings, a note of general agreement. The brass gossiped too, wishing for Mirella's comfort – the spider's comfort – as she arpeggiated ad libitum spiccato.

You'd think – she looked tired and her energy seemed to wane as the music wound down. I watched her and hoped she hadn't lost her will to continue. We needed her – the orchestra and the audience. I don't know how to describe that necessary lull before the musical whirlwind picks the piece of the floor. It's the place where Mirella's had the most trouble, what with all the tri-tones and no open strings. But tonight, it was masterful. Not biting in any way, just floating on the strings so the lulling sonority of her comfort seemed all the truer. And once she'd lulled the audience into the belief they were safe, we the orchestra were free to build implacably to the orgiastic culmination of that lurid dance.

Mirella led the strings in our insistent dominance and we all bit with her. Crunchy bite with more than a hint of the undertones you're not supposed to produce after your first year. The descending appoggiaturas were more like glissandi. It felt more like 20th Century Poland than 19th Century France. Up and down, up and down until even I was wondering, exhausted, if the storm would ever blow itself out. We rose and fell to a tumult and one trombone got lost in the ensuing arpeggio, but nobody cared.

That's. Death. Baby.

I have been known to voice an opinion that the ending of "Danse Macabre" is weak. It just kind of drifts off. It lacks passion. There could a much more pessimistic ending. That kind of thing.

Never again.

The epilogue is afterglow. We've had our collective orgasm and there's that same lulling presence – Death – a cushion to rest your head. Forever.

Entry #33: Sunday, October 25

We did it! Mirella and I made love last night. And it wasn't fucking. It wasn't desperate or anxious or flat. Well, it was by times desperate and anxious but that wasn't the full range of it. In the past, I've felt desperate to be liked, and anxious about my life – my life before and after. It's been like instead of fucking what I've really wanted to be doing is dying.

But last night. Last night was so gentle, so pure – lips on skin, hands on breasts, tongues on hips. Arms, legs, and heavy nightshade-laden breath. It was *making love*!

I can't believe I could be that sappy and then cry over it. But I suppose that's what everyone says about love: it makes you crazy. If that's true, then is it possible that Mirella was made so crazy because of her long-time love for me? She loved me before she'd even set her waking eyes on me.

I had a dream last night. One of the vivid ones – full, bright colours you wish would last even after you wake. There was a spider with a bright white abdomen – the colour of moonstone – and its shininess shifted and swirled in the sunlight. She was crawling on my vulva, attaching strings and testing them. It tickled, then warmed, then cooled and relaxed. I felt honoured to be being covered in her silk, which shimmery-sparkled in the sun like a creamy pool.

And we were swimming, Mirella and I, in deep blue pockets of water – warm like a bed. I stopped holding my breath and realised that only in dreams can you breathe underwater. I told Mirella. She grinned and swam swirly-swift spirals around me.

We were under a tree, clothed in loose-fitting Victorian shifts – undergarments. Birds singing, and I reciting Elizabeth Barrett Browning, which I apparently still have memorised all the way through:

How do I love thee? Let me count the ways!

. . .

I love thee with a passion put to use
In my old griefs, and with my childhood faith.
I love thee with a love I seem to lose
With my lost saints – I love thee with the breath,
Smiles, tears of all my life – and if God choose,
I shall but love thee better after death.

And at "after death" we were floating, flying, falling, through that landscape – the marshy mossy green-blue landscape. We fell to the bottom of the world. And there, we met three-faced Hekate!

Needless to say, that's when I woke up. Mirella's still sleeping, though. It was 4:00 when I woke up. It's not even dawn yet.

I've never watched anyone sleep before. She's so peaceful. The only thing moving is her eyelids. She's dreaming. I wonder what.

Supplement:

When I got up again, Mirella was busy drawing. I snuck a peak over her shoulder to see what she was working on and it was not silly manga outlines. It was a picture – like the one of me – of Three-faced Hekate. And the colours! I didn't know you could get pencil crayons in black-velvet-starless or indigo-flame-lick-pre-dawn. Upon further reflection, I guess it's more of a context thing, and I think the thing about the sharpness of her technique is exactly that. She keeps her pencils so sharp!

I watched, fascinated. this is my girlfriend, jumping from left to right, to center-up-down-corner-opposite-center-left-whatever, pencils making unintelligible marks. And she switched them so often and each time she switched, she sharpened.

Then, suddenly, she stopped. And looked at me.

"Do you know – no – *did* you know someone named Alexander? No! Not Alexander. Alexandroff? Alexandro—?"

"Aleksandros?"

"Yeah, him!"

"He was by grandfather."

"Okay, good. He says, 'Good job last night.'"

"He does?"

"He says you did his violin proud."

"Are you sure he wasn't talking about you?"

"Oh, he liked what I did too. But he's proud of you." She returned to her drawing. "His granddaughter. That makes sense."

I put my hand to my mouth and bit back tears. Two years ago, my grandfather passed away from an aneurism. I wish I'd known him better. He was a terse man, ill-prone to affection. But when I learned of how he fought in the war, and then was subsequently run out of the country by the Americans for being a communist, I realised what a boon it would have been to have spoken to him more, learned more about him. From him.

Mom always says that Grandfather had a special place in his heart for me, but he was always strict and stern. Nothing like Daddy's open, obvious adoration. He barely ever spoke to me, and from the way he touched me – like, he would put his hand on my arm to congratulate me, and he never kissed me – I kind of suspect he'd wished I'd been a boy.

He never said anything by way of being proud of me. So, that he would say that from beyond the grave? I've come used to hearing a lot of weird things, but even so, that was weird to hear. So I asked,

"Was he – did he seem happy?"

"Oh, indeed," said Mirella. "As pleased as anyone in Hades's realm might be expected to be."

"Really?"

"I was surprised you didn't come in. Now, shush. I need to finish this."

So I shushed. And when Mrs. Lantigua came home and she asked for Mirella's help with the groceries, I helped her instead.

While I was making breakfast, Mrs. Lantigua told me that she was surprised I'd become such a close friend to Mirella. I told her freaks and outcasts have to stick together. She seemed to get offended by that but I gave her my look and she nodded.

"I was worried," she said, instead, "that you'd try to manipulate her, use her. You know?"

"Yeah, I do know," I was able to say all-too-honestly. "And that's why I never would."

"What's your story, anyway?"

So I told her. About the sex, and the truancy; the lying, the cutting, the shrink, the diagnosis, the CBT. By then, we'd finished eating. Mrs. Lantigua told me I was a brave girl and that she was happy I'd gotten Mirella drawing again.

Then I had to go to work. But before I left, I asked Mirella if she'd talk to me about her drawing tomorrow. She agreed, so after work tomorrow, I'll be interviewing Mirella Lantigua about art – but especially about her drawing of me. My last furtive look at her, I pressed my finger to my lips. She seemed to understand.

Entry #34: Wednesday, October 28

Spent the night alone last night. It was weird: a Sunday night alone in my own bed. Missed her. Today, Mirella came over after lunch. We went into my bedroom – I almost wrote *our* bedroom! I set up my recorder; we lounged on the bed and she talked. Well, I talked first. Same deal as last time. The sound record has been erased.

AL: When did you do that amazing drawing of me?

ML: It was – the summer of personal grooming. When you realise you can't even go two days without a shower anymore. Cancer. Eight days in. Five, eight, thirteen. Lots of talking to the opposition; but the sight. Vivid. Strange and new. I thought I was learning to control it but every once in a while I'd apparently say something in the dark that would sour their eyes.

AL: Who?

ML: Anyone. I was less by myself than friends, but not that anyone else could see.

AL: Except you.

ML: Except me. One of them told me that my sight was trans-axial. Translatable. That others could see it if I looked the part. You know, with colours. So, I started with crayons. I drew people from their auras. They looked like kids' drawings – random lines and colours. People could barely make out the people. In the middle of June-ini. Gem? Duality. Liar!

AL: Whoa!

ML: Sorry. I switched to sharp objects for a while. Then to pencil crayons.

AL: Sharp objects?

ML: Um.—

AL: No judgement.

ML: More than once I made a drawing with my blood. Secret drawings. For the voices. *Of* the voices.

AL: Whoa.

ML: Well, how else I supposed to do it? I never showed anyone. But I always slew the demons on the blade first, and then an apple skin afterwards. There was no need to worry, but they did. once they found out.

AL: But now, this picture of me.

ML: Right. Five, eight, thirteen. The Shining Host. One morning i had a dream about You[3]. All I remember is You. All I could see was You and when I woke up I had a truck on my head – deadly. All I could remember was my love for You, and the image. I spent all summer trying to get You back, trying to be in Your presence again, but I could never find you. So I drew You. Again and again and again.

AL: Well, okay. So you had a lot of pictures.

ML: [She lifted her head off my shoulder and looked at me. And I mean – she looked me straight in the eyes. It was an incredulous tone in her glare. I'd missed something. I hadn't been paying attention.] They took them. Mom was cleaning my room. She found my drawing of you. I left it on my desk because I liked to look at it. It made me happy and sad. Mom and Dad took me aside and showed me how pleased they were. I could see it all over Dad's face. He was overjoyed by my talent. And Mom was too. They both were. Until they asked why I called You the Shining Host.

AL: Why *do* you call me the Shining Host?

ML: It's not easy – you won't understand.

AL: Keep telling until someone believes you.

ML: Where's that from?

AL: Elementary school. Sex abuse prevention.

ML: It's beautiful.

AL: I think a lot of people forget it. Anyway. Why the Shining Host?

---

[3] Mirella asked me to capitalise this. I didn't want to.

ML: Well, I knew – there would be a turning. I knew that once I met you – and I would meet you – that the voices would be quiet. That the things I see would be – the things I see. You know?

AL: I will always trust your ability, but that doesn't explain the name.

ML: Because you would *host* me. Get it?

AL: But, the Shining Host is a chorus of angels, isn't it? It's not, like, hosting a dinner party.

ML: It can mean what I want it to. Times change. You're my Shining Host and I'm your Legion. We are thousands, just the two of us. Most people are multitudes, but they never see it. Like Uncle Creepy. You'd think with all the whipping and harm the devil did to the angel, he would have realised he was at least three. I mean, there were more but those were the three I saw most often. He had a whole host of devil, all in the employ of his left heart. All weighing heavily on his angel. You could see he got into medicine to do good, but never realised that psychiatry isn't either one.

AL: Good or bad?

ML: Good or medicine. Anyways. I don't know if he thought by taking the images from me he'd take the vision. I was worried about it, and I could see the possibility playing about his mind. He took them and I never saw them again.

AL: Then did you draw that one of me after you got out?

ML: Ah, no. After my parents found my drawing, I hid it. Like, regularly. I even took it to Lakeview with me. I told everyone i burned. That was a month of interrogation. But I kept it. Nurses have reliable routines. Some nurses are even humans. One of them, the Shah'razad – found it out in December. I was in with the eels and she found it on the top shelf. She kept it for a day and watched me go crazy. Then she gave it back and told me she'd do everything she could to help me keep it. I cried. By March, she was fired because being kind to patients countermands the psychiatric process.

AL: [Chuckles]

ML: What?

AL: You speak so simply, and then every once in a while you say something like "countermands the psychiatric process". You surprise me. Relax. I like it. I'm not gonna hurt you. Don't worry. Here. Let me up so I can turn of the sound. Then we can get naughty.

ML: On a Sunday?

AL: Does that bother you? Oh. You're teasing. Brat.

[End Transcript.]

It's late. I congratulated Mariette DuPont on a job well done. She kinda likes me, I think. She said, "Are you really with Mirella Lantigua? She was amazing. I've wanted, like, forever to do something like that. Can you introduce me?"

I'm like: "Introduce yourself. she's just a girl. She's not a superstar."

"But, doesn't – isn't she – is it true she went to a mental hospital?"

I wish people would stop asking me that. It's *so* disrespectful. Anyway, I told her MHC meets for the first time after school next Tuesday. And that's a thing. It happened so fast. I'm looking back to about two weeks ago to when Anders approached me about it. The man can get things done.

Our new pieces for orchestra are: Suite No. 2 from l'Arlésienne (Ms. Baccarat is on about the French stuff this semester.) and Tchaikovsky #1: "Winter Dreams". That finale is going to kill the brass.

School is school. The pissy posse is the pissy posse. Oh yeah! Here's another thing!

Felicity say with Gen today at lunch. The evidence mounts. Tomorrow I'm going to talk to her about the website.

Entry #35: Thursday, October 29

Thursday. Really? Thursday? Couldn't we just skip to Friday? Or Saturday? I don't want to write about what happened – what Felicity said to me. I mean, who does she think she is? Why – how –

DAMMIT!

We've been friends for seven years now. Since grade five! We've had fights and outs before, but this is the meanest thing she's ever done to me. I just don't want to care anymore.

I want to take an Exacto knife to the tub with me. Or hang myself. But where? How could I possibly carry on – I can't even have any friend! I'm just trying to do good, to do right by Mirella. It's my responsibility!

It wouldn't have happened if I'd been a little more available and reasonable. Mirella isn't psychic. She's sick. Schizophrenics. But I've made her so much better. Right? I mean, she's off her meds, walkin' around, bein' psychic. She's not hurting anyone, or crawling into a desperate ball, or staring up at the ceiling with her eyes closed. But if she's sick – if she's ailing – shouldn't I trust the doctors?

All I have to do is think of the way Mirella cried after our first interview. Or about Uncle Creepy and the giant pink hand. Hymn of the perverse? How can I trust *anything* like that? If only I could show Felicity—but I can't. I promised I wouldn't.

Why do I even want to be her friend? She betrayed me! And Mirella.

And she said Mirella should never have been let out of that hell-hole. Like, just because she's different – a "freak" – she should be locked away to be molested and shocked? Where the walls speak to her and devour her? Gods! So she put that shitty website up – with help from Marsha Sinclair – to try to get Mirella to go ballistic. How! Why!

This Friday, I learned today, I've been invited to talk to Mirella's shrink. HAAAATE! (That felt good to write.)

I'm bringing my sound recorder. I can never remember what goes on in a shrink's office. They don't deserve ethical considerations, anyway.

Entry #36: Friday, October 31

Friday. Oh yeah! Best. Friday. Evar! So, today I'm making a concerted effort to ignore every indoctrinating thing they're trying to teach me here. Fortunately, that gives me a lot of opportunity to write while appearing to take notes.

I woke up this morning and the late-October sun was streaming onto my bed. I was so elated by the prospect of the day, I rose smiling and put on Death and the Maiden to make myself up. The usual makeup doesn't jive with the Athene outfit, so I put on the rare absinthe-flavoured eye shadow and a burgundy lipstick.

I went to Tilly to drop off my javelin – nice, thick hawthorn staff. Stares from everyone. No one else wearing a costume – except Mirella. Except Tilly. Her face bloomed when I showed up. Mine must have as well. She was wearing a Catwoman outfit. Looked great on a woman in her thirties. Strangely, that bit of paunch she carries didn't show.

Asked how, she whispered, "Corset."

You know, I never thought that corsets could be practical. I just thought they were the organ-marring iron maiden of the Victorian patriarchy. But if Tilly wears them they can't be all evil.

Second period now. Social justice. Religious freedom, history of. Scandalous wars because someone thinks theirs is the only one right way. I want to put my hand up and say atheists are just as bad as fundies, but it's almost irrelevant – way more important, but too much work to defend out loud. I feel far more comfortable writing it down.

Here it is.

Atheists are as bad as fundies because they insist they're right. I mean, it's not about which facts they're right about – the world is flat and came into being 6000 years ago; the world is round and came into being billions-and-billions of what we now call hears ago. Clearly, I subscribe to the latter because I trust that a global economy wouldn't be possible if the world were flat and because I'm not one to take myths literally and be done with them. Evolution, people. It's in our gestation. We can watch it happen.

But when you turn around and say "We developed because life is conducive to it, not we developed because it is conducive to life; therefore God does not exist, or psychics, or holistic medicine, or anything else that might suggest time is anything but a straight line" – *that's* where I have a problem. Because, then you can get off with saying psychics are mentally ill – you don't *need* to differentiate between autistic and indigo. I'm fine if you want to say we don't know what Gods are. We don't, and the face that we could invert our reasoning on why life is what it is based on that paradox that Joseph Campbell calls the first mystery – that we eat death to gain life – shows that we don't. I would never claim to know what Gods are. I would never deny, though, that I do know, at least to some degree, *who* Gods are. I can be comfortable with that uncertainty and if you can't, you aren't as smart as you think you are.

I just had to read this because Mickey was curious so I passed it to him. Mrs. Nguyen saw, and asked me to read it out. So I did. I've been congratulated but asked to pay attention in class. A strange paradox. Catch-22. If I pay attention in class, I won't write awesome rants. if I don't write awesome rants, I – can't pay attention in class? No. Praise, then scorn. For the same thing. Praise = encouragement. Scorn, discouragement. Do it, just don't do it. (So, it's not a Catch-22. Just stupid.)

I see three options out of this breathless oxymoron. 1. Do more, ignore discouragement. 2. Do less, ignore encouragement. Shit! What was the third one? Maybe there *are* only two.

Oh Goddess! I'm attracted to Mickey. See, after I read that thing out, he leaned over and whispered: "That was brilliant!"

"Really? No one else seemed to get it."

"Well, they're eejits. What did you expect? We're in a league of our own, here. *That* was brilliant."

"Thanks, Mick." If I remember it rightly, I was pretty shy; but the real evidence came when we met Mirella for lunch. Mick made his decision about sitting with me instead of Felicity. As soon as he sat down across from me, Mirella said: "Really?"

"Really, what?"

"Nothing."

"No, what? Really."

She took a second, shrugged her brows, and sighed. "You two are gonna kiss by the end of the day."

"What!" said Mickey. "Don't be daft."

I said: "I wouldn't. I'm not. I won't. I promise."

"Don't – make promises your lips can't keep," she said, biting into a tomato.

I looked at Mickey.

"She's full of it!" he said.

"No," I said, "she's not. That's been the basis of trust in our relationship for a while now. Mirella, I—"

"No, I know. I can see that, too. You still love me. Do whatever you want with your lips." She beckoned to me with a finger. I leaned in and she whispered: "Please don't drink his blood."

"I won't," I said.

"Won't what?" he asked.

I looked at him. "Girl stuff."

"You wouldn't understand," she said.

"Right," he said. "Let's eat."

But Mirella turned toward Mickey. "Look, Monstrous Storm, hurt Her in any way and I won't ask permission. I'll take it."

So, that's a thing. I'm going to try to avoid it. I just feel there would be way more complications than it's worth. But I do kind of like him. I mean, it's not every man who can appreciate a woman for her brains. And it's not like he's put me on a pedestal for it – he's just there with me. I've seen him trying so hard to be upbeat and positive – to do well in school – even though it must be so hard on him this year. And, why this year? Of all years, why this one?

If I look back and read what he said to me in September – he's such a different person when he's saying that. Like he doesn't know me at all. Except he does. So, I can forgive him. Because I could really use a friend.

So, here I sit again, in a waiting room chair that pretends to be comfortable in the waiting room of a "woman" who pretends to be a doctor. Mirella and her mum must have gone in first. Mrs. Lantigua made Mirella take off her costume before going in.

"But, Mom, it's Hallowe'en. They won't care," she protested.

"Mirella, please. Just do this for me?"

I was a hair away from sneering at her that considering all her daughter does for her should she really be asking for more. But I didn't. I guess it's called picking your battles. Basically, Mrs. Lantigua is beyond it. She lives in a demilitarised zone in my head. Diplomatic immunity. In fact, if she'd asked me to take of *my* costume I probably would have, although I don't think she would have liked it considering this is all I'm wearing. And, considering this is all I'm wearing, it's going to be tough to hide this recorder in a place where it's going to record. But Mirella took up the thread.

"Mom, if they're going to put me in a padded cell for wearing a Hallowe'en costume, you cry malpractice. There's nothing wrong with the way I'm dressed." I almost agreed. I almost laughed at the girl wearing four extra arms. I just smiled and put my head in my diary.

Supplement

Well, that was bracing. Mirella's so right. If you trust your intuition, you can tell what shrinks are thinking. I'm beginning to suspect that psychiatry isn't all that hard. You sit down with a list and then give people pills. Anyway!

I've decided to dine with the Lantiguas tonight. They both insisted, so I did. Fast food. When did it get so expensive? How is three combos almost fifty bucks?

Over dinner, Mrs. Lantigua thanked me again for drawing Mirella out of her shell. I wonder if she knows Mirella's off her pills. Doubtful. She'd flip. Instead, she said:

"She's so vibrant again. She's my radiant little girl again."

We both watched as Mirella took a big happy bite out of her chicken burger.

We're on the bus now, headed to the dance. That's why this writing is so spastic. Plan is to arrive as dance starts, dance until it's over – no stopping. Four hours. Mirella has some choreography she wants to go over behind the gym before we go in. She says it's supposed to be Athene and Arachne reunited. Gotta run!

Later:
Off to an after party.

Entry #35: Sunday, November 2

Mirella won't talk to me. Mickey's pissed at me. And God is very far from overthrown. FML! My memory is a hodgepodge of dreams and faces, voices and lights, sighs and signs. But for all the weird, I realise tonight as I write this that I have been missing out. I thought I understood what Mirella sees, but only now do I understand that I don't. I have to get all this down, because it's just crazy!

So, Jeremy shows up last night in a tiara, drag-style makeup and combat fatigues. Or, I guess that was two nights ago. Mirella and I were on hour-two of our trance induction. Mickey was there, too, in a cowboy costume. He watched us dance with our foreheads pressed together, our arms like willow limbs on the ocean. He got us punch and we drank through emergency induction ports; but we didn't stop dancing.

So, Jeremy shows up and he sees us in the middle of the dance floor and he comes right over to us. He tells us about the after party and says to keep it a little hush-hush. I say we're not really here to talk anyway. Then he shows us a stoppered bottle with an eye dropper in it.

"What's that?"
"A potion."
"Really?"
"Oh, yeah."
"We'll talk later. Dance or get out of the way."

So we danced with him for a little while, maybe half-an-hour. Even Mickey got into it. By hour-three I was beginning to see lights and the music was ebbing and flowing about my head, eddying and swirling around. We'd switched to pure water in the middle of hour-two, and by now I was beginning to feel the need to pee. I was torn between dancing and not wetting myself.

Then, I heard Mirella's voice in my head: "Let's leave and go to that party."

I got Jeremy's attention. We went to the bathroom and as I flushed I felt something shift, in me and the world. I was sweating and hearing things. The loud thump of bass and drums made my body shiver and I swore I heard string choirs amid the gossip and laughter.

"Hey, Amy!" said Mariette, dressed in a black body suit and a cat-ear headband. "Great costume. Wicked dancing. Is this your first break?"

I smiled and nodded. "We're leaving."

"No! Aw. Really?"

"It's time. We're dying."

"Death is our friend," said Mirella from behind me. Mariette jumped but I wasn't surprised at all.

"That's true. Death has been kind to us," I said. "Death!"

"Death!" cried Mirella.

"Open your doors so we may walk your halls and find what we don't know we seek!" we prayed in unison.

"Are you two high?" asked Mariette.

"Yeah, I think we are," I said.

"On what?"

"Dan-n-n-c-c-c-e!" grinned Mirella. She started giggling, then I did.

"Come on. Let's get out of here, Arachne."

"Yes, my queen."

We were headed behind the gym. Mirella said: "That potion Jeremy's got is super-potent!"

"Is it? What is it, do you know?"

"Essence of sight. But inward."

We got back there and Jeremy was standing with Mickey, placing drops of the potion onto pills.

"Free of charge," he said.

"What am I doing, Jerms? Seriously."

"It's called a fleur-de-lys. Acid on X. It'll blow your fucking mind! Which is what I hear you want, anyway. Go on. Take it."

I could see. Trace lines and click-pop-boom. They were all over the things. Magick roiling about them. Super-potent. I looked at Mirella.

These are super-potent. And – I'm already having telepathic conversations with you.

And I'm seeing things, too. Wild, amazing things.

"Thanks anyway, Jerms."

"What! I already got three ready!"

"Well, our minds are already blowing – albeit slowly."

"What, from the dancing?"

"Mickey," said Mirella. "Your dragon. Is trying. To down you."

"What's that mean?"

"I don't know!"

"And Jeremy," I said, "you should definitely follow your heart on this one, and see where it goes. But make sure you know what you want. The minotaur won't get any brighter."

"Right," said Jerms. "No drugs for the crazy chicks. What am I gonna do with these?"

"Well, I'll have one," said Mickey. "You can have one."

"This is a twenty-five dollar drug!"

"Well, maybe we can split it. Hang on to it."

They downed their drugs and Jeremy called to the party for a car.

"Man, why not just call a cab?" Mickey asked.

"The location's off the grid."

"What?"

"Dude, I just gave you drugs. What kind of party do you think this is?"

"Guys!" hissed Mirella. "The bushes have ears."

"What!"

"Mariette DuPont is here," I said. "Come on out, Mariette."

Silence.

"We don't bite."

Mirella giggled madly.

"Shush."

She did.

Then she said, "You're invited."

Jeremy hit her arm. They exchanged incredulous glances. But a black kitty cat emerged from the bushes. There was something dark in her shy eyes.

"She's in," I said.

"What does 'off the grid' mean to you people?"

"It means invite the pretty kitty with the loose tongue. Right, Mariette?"

She nodded. I remember her with only her headband on and a collar, lapping at cream on a tile floor but I can't tell if it's a vivid fantasy I had at that moment or it's something that actually happened.

The car arrived. We piled in. Jeremy had shotgun. He kissed the guy on the cheek and we drove off. Even by that point, I felt myself fully into a new world of drugs. Mirella turned to me and said: "You can't control it. Don't try."

So, I whipped out my diary and wrote what I wrote.

"Oh, yeah!" said Jeremy. "Guys, this is August, my boyfriend."

"Have I been that out of touch?" I asked.

"You've been pretty preoccupied," said Mickey. "Nice to meetcha, man. I'm Mick."

"Mick. Hey."

"Yeah," said Jerms, "and that's Mariette, Amy—"

"Amymone."

"Amymone!" said August. "That's a rare name."

"You know it?"

"I'm doing my master's thesis in classical literature."

"I thought you seemed a little older than Jerms, here."

"A bit, yeah. But don't worry, he's within my half-plus-seven."

"What's that?" asked Mariette.

"They youngest a person you can date is half your own age plus seven," I explained, somewhat erratically.

"Is that true?" asked Mirella.

"Socially," I said.

"Then you're lying, August," she said.

"Don't mind her," said Jeremy. "She thinks she's psychic."

"She *is* psychic!"

"It's okay," said August. "What's your name, cutie?"

"Mirella."

"*Ave*, Mirella!"

Mariette and Mirella started giggling. Then Mirella burst out laughing. She caught a moment of lucidity, said, "Hail, Caesar," then dissolved into giggles again. Every once in a while, Mirella will reach a summit of laughter. The joy in her giggles chills and flows away from her in rivulets. Then she starts sobbing. That's what happened, and that's the last thing I remember clearly.

Showing up at a big old heritage home in a part of the city I've never been in. Two storeys and a finished basement. The basement is a dance floor, complete with light effects and DJs. First floor is a lounge. Cuddle puddle. Some dancing, but more sedate. Tarot readings. Once, a blowjob. Who was he? I don't know but he was giving a blowjob.

Upstairs was lit with candles and mirrors. It was less of a hallway and more of an antechamber. I guess the stairs were in the middle of the floor? No, that's not right. A ladder? That makes even less sense. Did I fly?

There were guardians at the candles, prismatic pixies that shone bright dark rainbows across the floor. They make sure the candles don't go out. The candlelight in the mirrors gave the place a nightly, celestial glow.

August: Someone wants to meet you, upstairs.

Mirella: Who?

Me: Whom.

A naked man – lithe and boyish – emerges from a room, waves at us, and tiptoes to the bathroom across the landing.

A woman – fully clothed – opens a door and backs out whispering tearful thanks. Another, taller woman forms at the door before her. She smiles, caresses the woman's cheek, looks at us. The woman turns and walks briskly away.

The statuesque woman at the door is wearing a silken dress, laden with gold and jewels. In the candlelight, I can make out the shape of her thighs. Her arms are decorated. Her nipples are bejeweled. Somehow, her bare breasts don't come as a shock to me. I expected it.

She spreads her arms wide, and says in a hushed, throaty drawl: "Children. Welcome!" And the sound of her voice is liquid home. "Approach, do!"

We do.

Dancing in shadows. The pounding bass has become the thrum of the Earth. Words from a song:

And in the dark I can hear your heartbeat
I tried to find the sound.
But then it stopped and I was in the darkness
A darkness I became.

Mickey in the Middle Earth, trying to get a guy to stop hitting on him. The Priestess descends the stairs for a drink. I rush to be beside her. She smiles at me, kisses my forehead like before. Mariette is singing that song.

"Go help your friend, Hippolyta," says the Priestess.

"Yes, your Highness."

"Sweet child. Where's your spider? But help your friend first."

I get back in the room and that guy has Mickey by the hair and the cock, and he's kissing him. It's in the middle of what was the cuddle puddle. The cuddle puddle has been forcibly divided. Everyone's staring in terrified awe as Mickey struggles against him.

"Hey!" I stomp over and jab the asshole in the side with my hazel wood javelin. "What the hell do you think you're doing!" he growls, releasing Mickey.

"I could ask you the same thing. How dare you set eyes on my boyfriend, let alone hands or lips!"

"I – I'm sorry. He didn't say. You didn't – you're with that crazy chick!"

"Get out of here, unless you want a lesson in respect up your ass!"

He's about to refuse, until someone agrees with me. He looks around at the damage he's wrought: base lead vein in pure gold. He leaves.

"Mickey?" I bend down. "Are you okay?"

The Beneficent Priestess glides into the room as I'm helping Mickey up. She looks upon him with sadness. "Fresh air," she says. We head for the door as she begins to bless the cuddle puddle.

"Should we?"

It's cold – too cold for a tunic.

"Mirella said it was okay."

"Are *you* okay with it?"

Shivery damp wind on goosy arms.

"I'm fine. Are you?"

"I – I want to, but—"

"No pressure, Mick. None at all."

He starts to cry again.

It's cold, but we stay outside for a while longer.

In the basement sits a man. On either side of him, a nude slave kneels. (Is one of them Mariette? Is one of them August? Leather pants?)

How long has Mirella been sitting in the corner? She's content enough. But I want to go upstairs with her. She sees, and we rise together.

The light pixies are making love, rainbow nymphs writing on the floor. A winged serpent with a woman's torso and face comes from a room carrying a baby. She turns to us, smiles. "Make your loving soft and sweet. The Aeon rests."

I lay her out. She lolls her head to the side. Her bronze flesh sparkles in the candlelight – bright, radiant. She's the fiery blonde of the way she's her own dream goddess.

"Oh, Shining Host!" she whispers. I smile the smile of the Beneficent Priestess. Or perhaps I am the Priestess, and she my disciple. I, the Goddess; she, the mortal. Or else, we are both goddesses. I, the moon; She the ocean in which I bathe.

"How young our love is," I murmur, aware how old young love is.

My tunic set on a chair, beside hers. I kneel on the bed over her. Her feet are cold. I cover her shining body – the sea at dusk. Our lips meet as if for the first time.

Hot running blood. Heavy breath. A kiss. Silky lips, dewy and fragrant. A gasp. A sigh. Brilliance in the dark. A lantern.

"Embrace eternity," she says.

The Aeon rests.

Rich, warm incense. Uncomfortable clitoral fluctuations. Undulations. Sex on sex. A murmur. A moan. Nuzzling fingers. Nuzzling a nape. Fingers from behind.

"You've filled out, love."

The Aeon rests.

Floating downstairs. Stupid smiling.
"Is that really the time?"
"Past your bedtime?"
Thought it was later.
Water?
There's someone who wants to see us downstairs.

In the Sunless Land. Bright, but no lights. Magic swirls about the dancers. We are the dancers. Bodies powering the world.

A woman smiles at us, beckons us over. She is dressed in dark clothing and made up with dark shades. It is dark. The bar is open. We sit across from her. She is grave.

"Persephone?"
She smiles. Shakes her head.
"It's time," she says.
"Time for what?"
"The Aeon is resting."
I don't understand.
"Where will the rift occur?" (Mirella.)
"The train yard at dawn." (Me.)

We sing through the earth. Three-faced Hekate. The decay of our Apollonian virtue. (What does that mean?)

I'm exhausted. So is she. We've been dancing for hours? But we can't go home. There's something we still need to find. A truth. A fragment. A call into the Abyss, but where's the Abyss?

The train yard at dawn.

"When the sun rises, it will be red and cold."

No lights. And magick.

"It was only a little weird."
"I'm so crazy!"
"Do you think?"

"Amymone, I love you!"
"I love you too, Mickey."

An ambulance. August lying motionless on the floor, staring up at the ceiling. Jeremy and Mariette stand over him in horror. The cops are on their way! Time to get dressed and go.
"Where shall we go?" (Mickey sounds desperate.)
"The train yard!" says Mirella.
Mariette DuPont lapping milk from a bowl on the floor. Pretty harping hands.

Dressed and ready, but where's Mariette?
"No, we can't leave her!"
"I love her!"

"Geez, Mariette! I never expected you to be so cool with all of this. I thought you were, like, a Jesus freak."
"Jesus can suck my pussy! WOOOOO!"

And we're out the door. Out the back door. Shat onto the street in the pre-dawn hours with the sirens coming up the front street. We run.

A moment of lucidity.
"Amy! Amy!"
"What, Mariette?"
"Did you ever take it up the tailpipe?"
"Not that it's any of your business, but no."

"You know, those chastity pledges are really stupid. I wish I'd been more like you."

"No, you don't."

The sky is pale violet.

The train yard.

At dawn.

Now, the train yard's been abandoned for years. It's a great place to play if you can keep clear of the crazies. But tonight, we *are* the crazies. And I've got a javelin.

Hot blood. A paring knife glistens with isopropyl. It is laser sharp. Flowing down her arm. All that passing – fire red and running. The way she hissed. So familiar. Always so new. That pain. Pain and release from pain.

Hers didn't taste like mine does. I remember that. Copper, iron, salt, estrogen; but different. She's the earth. Liquid, red earth!

That knife tells me to open her. Open her flesh, take her blood. Take her life. If I drink her dry, she'll live on in me. I'll lap up all her juices, and she will flow through me. I'll be the riverbed of her liquid life.

"My blood is free!" she gasps as I suck on her wound.

"I love you, minion!" I hiss.

"The snake!" she hisses back. She clicks her fingers. The knock on the door brings us back to reality.

We're in a bathroom, not a morgue. I am not a vampire; she is not my minion. Yet. We're girls. Naked girls in a stranger's bathroom having kinky sex high on our love, and our dancing.

"Almost done!" I call. A chuckle from outside. Band-aids – apple skins.

"I want to be yours," says Mirella.

The sky is indigo and twilight blue. The old train yard is just down the street. How did we get there? We didn't know where we were.

"Very well, minion Legion. I will allow you to submit to me. It is fitting that the power of Legion should submit to the glory of the Shining Host." She takes my hand. "I like your blood, minion."

"I know," she says.

We get to the fence that keeps everyone out and Mickey lifts the bush that lets everyone in. We all creep through the hole in the fence. With fire in the eastern sky and the majesty of decaying buildings, we all begin twirling. We fall about each other on the cold stones. But we didn't care.

Mickey crawls over to Mirella. She rolled her eyes and sighed. "Yes, I know. You love me. Everyone at that party loves each other. Amy's in love with an Ourobouros."

"That's Miss Lerner to you, minion."

"Yes, Miss Lerner."

"Good girl."

"Why would I trust you to get rich?" she says.

"It's not rich, dear," says I, "it's wealthy. No money, but good fortune."

"Does anyone else feel like we should be on a beach?" said Mariette. "If this were a movie, we'd be on a beach."

Mirella jumped up and ran down the grassy tracks toward the sun. I took off after her. There were rustles in the trees but if might have been the north wind whispering warnings of a chilly winter. It certainly chilled me as I ran.

And as she ran, I watched wings sprout in place of her arms. I watched them unfurl and grow down and then plumage. She spread her wings and soared into the sky.

Not to be outdone, I grew my own pair and flew with her. Toward the sun, red in the low-hanging haze on the horizon. And then I knew why the train yard at dawn. We needed a runway.

I'm not sure I remember this part right, but I think a dragon with red scales gleaming a name that was also a commandment caught us and challenged us to a flying duel. We were both going to refuse but the dragon promised he'd eat both of us if we didn't accept. Well, long story short, we accepted and promptly lost.

His laugh was like the burning of ancient redwoods and the grinding of the gears of war. We hung our heads in shame as he puffed a flame high in the air, a flame that smelled like deaths long forgotten and breaths too slight to be worthwhile.

"How do you expect to defeat the Lord God when a lowly dragon grounds you?" he scoffed.

Our heads hung.

"Help us," squeaked the fiery harpy, now a mouse at my side.

"You will need the help," said the dragon, "but you still won't win. Now, come! Decide which of you will die."

"I will," we both said.

He laughed. "Amusing! But that's not the game and I get so much more pleasure out of watching mortals make choices.":

"Take me!" said the mouse, now a hare at my side.

"Any objection, little fox?" asked the dragon, now a man in front of me.

"Yes. Take me!" I said.

"No, Amy!" said the hare, now a horse beside me. "I've been to the Underworld. They know me there."

"But—"

"Quest for me."

I step into the camp and the satyr beside me puts his arm out. I am – my druid D&D character from two years ago. He whistles a call and soon another of his ilk stands before me. He is tall and muscular, with a Grecian nose and craggy pecs. His fur is jet black, a colour I've never seen on a satyr before. His build is lean, but every curve, every slope, every twist is deliberate. The goat wears a goatee and as he smiles at me, the frame of his face becomes more lovely.

"Ah, so this is the strange visitor your Prinzan was so effusive over? And no wonder. Welcome, wild lady. From where do you hail?

"I am Talii. I come from such-and-such a village to the south."

Behind him, I see the smoke begin to rise again. So it was the smoke of the camp I saw in the distance after noon!

"You were scouting!" I say to my ovine escort, Chorrizei.

He points a finger at me. Affirmative.

"Tali—"

"Talii."

"Talii, what brings you to our camp?"

"I'm looking for one of your number."

Within moments, five more goat-legged men are standing in front of me, eager looks on their faces. The black-legged goat gestures to them.

"Do you see him here?"

"Oh, no! I mean, not of this camp."

"Oh! You want one of us, just not one of us."

"Yes, sir."

"Very well. Enter our camp and be welcome. Do you know the greeting game?"

"I do." Amongst satyrs, the greeting game is an honoured rite. Newcomers are, of course, welcome to refuse; but doing so does not ingratiate. I consider the prospect of not playing, but I need this information. The one I'm after is a slaver. These guys will be more inclined to help me if I play, win or lose.

As the satyrs are forming a straight line, Chorrizei snorts and begins to walk away.

"Not playing, Chorrizei?" calls the black ram.

"What's the point? I won't win anyway!" he calls back.

I walk to the left-most, the black-legged one. The leader. Looking at him preparing to welcome me sparks a strange desire to cheat, but I resolve to play right. I look into his smiling eyes and think maybe I won't *have* to cheat. Maybe I'll lose fair and square.

"Good wildern girl!" he sings. My eyes go wide, my ears back. I will not lose right out of the gate. But that voice is golden! "I, Rikiaveir, leader of this company of sataers, do welcome you to dine amongst our numbaers. Cutie!"

I manage to roll my eyes, keeping my mouth clamped shut and firmly downturned.

"No?"

I shake my head. He steps back and I move on.

"Lady," says the next satyr. "My name is Yskleros. It is a rare delight to meet such a gem, such ineluctable beauty. Ephemeral one, grace us with your beauty this eventide!" For just a moment, I believe him. By times I've seen my face in the water, and I'm almost pleased with what I see there. But I know what I look like. A big ass and a skinny waist don't outweigh the scar that cracks my face in two. My hair's a mess of twigs and mud; my bronzy skin is a marsh of dirty water and fragrant mud. I know what I look like. I'm as wild as the land, and while I may be ineluctable, it's hardly my beauty that knows that quality. What's worse, I can't imagine he doesn't know all this too. Either he's just lied to me to get me in bed, or he's deliberately thrown the game because he doesn't want to.

I bite my lips, and turn sadly aside. Yskleros steps back, and I step before a tall goatboy. His form is lithe, his shoulders slender, and he has breasts. But his beard is full, and his cock hangs low. I've heard of the cross-sexed satyrs, the Baphomets. I consider myself lucky to be meeting one.

"My name is Turvet," says my new opponent.

"You're the dancer."

"I am, indeed."

He is nearly as tall as Rikiaveir, though somewhat younger. His beard's a little overgrown, especially about the sideburns. His physique is exact and he spins about, tromping a deep-earth rhythm with his hooves. He's good – far better than I. He ceases his dancing with a firm stomp on the ground and a fair ripe apple falls from the tree above him.

"Kallisti!" he says, bowing his head and offering the fruit to me. I feel the warm roil of honour in me. Licking my lips, I thank him, but gratefully decline. He steps back and I move on.

Before I make eye contact with the next satyr in line, I collect myself and quiet the simmer in my tummy. His eyes are gray and so's his hair. His barrel chest is full of wiry curls. His arms are thick and so are his hands. He has the Sea God's own beard. The child in me, the *vehalvoll*, is excited. These older types give the best rewards for rare courtesies and the cruelest punishments for refusal. Two *very* good reasons for a *vehalvoll* to smile. But I am no longer *vehalvoll*. The prospect that he might win terrifies me. And it is this terror with which I greet his eyes.

"My name is Korevander, foxy lady," he says. He reaches out and cups my face in his strong, rough-hewn hands.

"No touching, Old Goat! Disqualified," says Rikiaveir. Korevander smiles a knowing smile. I smile back. He's pleased just to touch me; I'm pleased he threw the game. Moving on.

Next comes a young ram – younger even than Chorrizei. He's green. I'd forgotten that satyrs could be green. It throws me and when he raises his two fingers in my direction and says: "How *you* doin'!" I clasp my hand to my mouth.

"She touched her mouth!" he cries. "She touched her mouth! I get to try again this evening!"

"That you do, Tiphten," says Rikiaveir. "That you do."

This evening, he'll have to make me laugh, not just smile.

The next in line is not a satyr. He's a short, squat gnomish man with a wiry black beard and crooked teeth, and he wears only a codpiece held in place by a thong of leather. It almost makes me laugh just to see him. I bet he wins this game a lot.

"I'm Padovaig." He smiles a greasy grin.

"Talii."

"You're one hot piece of tail, Talii."

"Am I? Your scout seems to think I stink."

"Well, I wouldn't throw you out of bed."

"Charming," I say. Fortunately, once you get past the shock, it's not so hard to frown.

As I turn away, Rikiaveir calls an end to the game. He hangs a fig leaf crown on Tiphten 's head. If I'd lost to Tiphten, I'd get a crown of myrtle. Then we'd fuck. I don't want to fuck now, really. But we won't until the game is over anyway. If then.

Tiphten, the singer and leader, asks me if there's a luxury the modest camp can provide.

"A bath," I say. "Chorrizei has me a little self-conscious."

"What did he say?"

"Something about flatfish in the sun for a week."

"That boy's gonna get such a walloping!" says Korevander.

"No." I touch his arm. "Please don't. He's right. I've got swamp water dried all over me. I'm not a rose and I know it. But if I bathe—"

"Allow me to escort you, young lady," says Korevander, holding out his arm.

"By all means, gentle faun." I take his arm and allow him to lead me into the forest. The day is gray and waning. A chill breeze penetrates my fox-fur vestment and I shiver.

"May I say," says Korevander, "you're quite well spoken for a wild woman?"

"Well, Kyrie, I was not born a wild woman. In my youth I was quite tame – well-trained."

"I thought I saw something of the slave in your eyes."

"So be it."

The rustle and tweet of the autumn canopy gives way to a water's rushing babble. The thick forest opens into a lush grove with a large pool. A panther looks up from his repose. Small birds tweet and hop about him. He rises and saunters into the forest. We are alone.

Letting go of Korevander 's arm, I approach the deep blue pool. Nothing feeds it and it empties into nothing, yet the sounds is makes are of a brook or a creek. As I step toward it, I get a peaceful sense of awe.

"This is not where you bathe," I say.

"No, we bathe elsewhere. But this is where you will bathe."

I look into the bright, deep blue. It sparkles, though there is no sunlight. It smiles. I smile back. We know each other.

"This is—"

"It is."

"And you're not—"

"I'm not."

"Then are you—"

"I am."

"And I'm—"

"You are."

"Then that means I owe you—"

"Darling," says Poseidon, "you owe me nothing. Even when I save you, you owe me nothing. I love you, Amymone.

He says it. I hear it. Even *I've* been pronouncing my name wrong. (But I'm still closer to right than most.)

"And I love you, Kyrie."

"I know."

He places his arms about my body. I am engulfed in the scent of sea foam and kelp. I hear sirens call and see the Goddess of Love rise from the ocean's version of ashes. I am nude but warm.

Home.

"Now," says Lovergod, "you must bathe."

Without hesitation, I dive into the Spring of Lerna and swim down, down, down. As deeply as I swim, the water is always bright around me. I can see where I'm going. Trails of gold course through the blue.

Then a whirlpool, an eddy down below. If I escape it, I'll live. But that's not life for me. I quest. And while I quest, there can be no life for me.

The eddy pulls me toward it. I make my body limp and watch the golden trails turn to whorls, spinning about beneath me. Then I too am spinning about, flung and pulled around and downward. Blurs of blue and gold.

Then blackness. The stars and moon have all been blown out. I'm left in the dark, freezing and alone. Except for my feet. My feet are frighteningly warm. I'm lost. Lost to love, and lost to life. Wretched, shamed, alone. And so feverishly cold. I feel myself tremble. My hand – fingers like frost-tipped needles – touch on something metal. It is warm.

Roaming over the contours of it, I feel the familiar space, then a cord of catgut. I pluck the string – a top G – and a tiny light winks into existence above me. It bobs about and begins to dance back and forth. Then it winks out, only to come back moments later and ease my panic.

Excited, and probably delirious, I sit up and pick up my harp. Though it scrapes the ground – cold and smooth and flat like slate – it makes no sound and I realise I can't even hear myself breathe.

That orange light is getting larger, as if it's coming toward me. Trepidation fills my heart. Where am I? What is the light and what does it want? Will this harp – my harp – protect me?

I pluck another string, a low one, and a quiet, low, constant, rumble fills my ears. If I play "The Elements of Glory" will life spring up around me? Light – fire. That rushing noise – water? The ground I'm on – earth. All I need is evidence of my own breath.

That light. Did it just flicker? Bounce off a wall? Or someone's face? Is someone here with me? Making no sound, showing no sign? Why? Why hide from a harpist?

The light is gone. There's someone behind me!

"Hello," says the face in front of me, lit by the light that just disappeared. She is the someone behind me.

"Tilly?" But it's not her. It just looks like her.

"Well, I'm no scarecrow, dear."

"What are you doing here?"

"I'm here to greet you, child."

"Grandmother!" But it isn't her, either. "Where am I?"

My sister answers. Wordless. I am in the Underworld.

I am dead.

My knees are weak in front of my sister. It's not her, but she looks so familiar. She's in that frozen peace that was my last glimpse of her. I want to kiss her again because part of me still believes she's just in a magickal sleep.

I walk up the aisle, my hand in Dad's. Mom's sobbing is loud behind me. Dark pews and plain floors. White walls. An ornate rosewood coffin.

"Lift me." My sister comes into view, all white peace. My heart breaks again.

"Closer," I whisper. Dad hesitates, but when I inhale deeply, about to let out a scream, he moves me in. My sister's lips are cold. She doesn't wake. She doesn't respond.

Dad pulls me back fast, but people have seen. Stunned and grieving, he yanks me back to our seat.

"There we are," says Tilly.

"Come now," says Grandmother, leading me on.

My harp is in a wagon. I am on my way to the Underworld pulling a harp on a wagon. I'd laugh if I could remember how to.

As we walk, the lady with the light and I, the rumbling, thrumming noise becomes louder. We are approaching, I presume, the River Styx – the famed crossing point upon which the gods make unbreakable oaths. I know I will have to play to cross.

The lady – Hekate by name – stops and I beside her. The river shimmers beneath Her light. I glance at the Goddess beside me. She is the Goddess we bowed to, Mirella and I, when we were alone in that apartment.

Without looking at me, Hekate puts a finger to Her lips. I realise I was about to say something. At that moment, I understand how important silence is here. Nonsound.

I hear it before I see it. The sound of paddling in the river. The sound of the river parting for the boat. Perhaps the last sound the dead ever hear. Then I see Him, shrouded and steady, the little boat with the tall, slender boatman.

Hekate recedes and I know it is time. I sit at the harp and play. It is soft and low. The sound of the water accompanies and intertwines. Then, unbidden, I start to sing in my chesty contralto. It is a song of a lost love, and no way to find her, a yearning, a wishing. For death.

When I finish, I notice eyes peering at me from dark places – namely, all around me. Charon's light glints off them. A small harpy sits beside me. Her visage is not repulsive. She sheds a tear and as Charon docks, I bend to speak with her.

"Your song is music!" she rasps.

"It is."

"I will trade you a tear for a chord. Three for three."

"Very well."

She perches on my head and places the tears on my forehead, then flutters back to the earth. The Underworld is better lit for me now. The bird-woman opens her heart, a dull shine. I play a shining C major arpeggio, then d minor, then G^7, and watch her heart take on the glimmer. Tears flow from her eyes freely. She limps away.

"You will play," says Charon.

"Of course, Kyrie."

I pack my harp on His boat and seat myself before it. I can't rightly remember what song I played, but it seemed to please the boatman.

Even from far off I could see the forms on the shore of the Sunless Land. Hundreds of millions of pallid, drawn, persony ghosts milling about. They gave off a collective glimmer, a pale blue. As we got closer, I could make out faces. I became more curious. The faces weren't drawn or hollow. They weren't despairing or dying of ennui. They were peaceful, placid.

Downstream, I saw at least seven other ferries dock on the shore. They too were carrying passengers. I looked harder, deeper into the blackness, and thought I could see millions along the coast.

Having arrived, I disembarked with my harp. The dead-peace gaze that the ghosts fixed on me gave me shivers. The moment I set foot on that sand – the Sands of Time perhaps – all eyes were on me. My harp was on a wagon behind me again, and as I stepped through the throng, they reached for both me and the harp. I realised that I was making sound. I didn't even need the harp. Even if I stayed stock still, I'd still be making sounds because I was alive – though I still had no evidence of my breath.

When their fingers reached me, I felt chilled. It was not a physical sensation. It's like if your body poured cold water on your brain and it trickled down your spine, but even that analogy is like trying to describe red to someone who's never seen colours. And as they met with the harp, they passed right through the strings. They could not make a sound.

I was sure of where I was going and I wanted the straightest path. I didn't want to spend more time there in the Underworld than absolutely necessary. As I cast about, the harpy's tear on my forehead began to grow warm. I carried on in that direction.

It led me down a darkening corridor. I could make out the walls, but nothing else. Or else, there wasn't anything else. I wasn't sure, because everything there is silent, but I think I'd taken a path through some kind of punishment zone – like hell, except with a very different purpose. Or, like, not like hell at all. Like a holding chamber. They weren't being punished.

See, here's the thing and the thing is this: I came across these women in a recessed alcove along the corridor. There were twenty-seven of them. Three-by-three-by-three. And those were the only ghosts I saw there, in that corridor. The light they gave off was dull and red, not blue like the ghosts on the shore. Also, where the others had form in a memorial sense – vague and unreal and somewhat generic – these women had what I would dare to call bodies. But because of that, they were horrific. They looked like they'd been stitched together, these women, haphazardly and carelessly. Their graying, decaying skin was broken along specific straight lines but the lines seemed to be in random places on their bodies.

They howled. How I know they howled, I don't know, but they did. And the howling, the moaning, the crying wasn't just coming from their reconstituted mouths. It came from every split, every line, every crack in their poorly stitched bodies. And I knew then – these women were the Missing Women – the lost, the wretched, the ignored. They were invisible, yet I could see them. And I wondered what the harpy was doing with my chords if she thought her true-seeing tears were fair recompense.

My third eye felt that pressure, that warmth. This was my path. I sat at my harp and, feeling like a lost little girl myself, began to play.

Those crystalline chords cast a countercurse on the silence and soon their weeping and crying almost overwhelmed me. Though my heart was breaking, I kept playing. Though my harp seemed inappropriate accompaniment, I kept playing. The dissonant chorus would have made a serialist blush, but I kept playing. And when the Pendereckian wall of sound threatened to overwhelm me, threatened to consume me with grief and despair, the song ceased.

It just did. It was over.

They had all gathered around me. I'd like to say they were smiling, or more back-together, or even that they had more peace in their eyes. None of those things were true. But their wailing had ceased and that meant something.

They sat on the ground and began sleeping. All but one. Blood dripped from her mouth and her vulva, both of which had been sewn shut. She was missing her right hand and her left eye. With the other, she gazed at me, yearning. She was about my age, but so much older.

I looked at the hand she reached out for me. I wanted to take it but I was worried she would drain me. One of the sleeping Missing Women stirred and I grabbed the girl's hand. She led me through a door I hadn't even seen.

Beyond the door where scads and scads of women – mothers, daughters, cooks, typists, writers, singers, models, actresses, wives, seneschals, High Priestesses – prostitutes all. I knew this on just a glance. And there were children too. Scads. Zombies, not ghosts. Too real to be spirits, too dead to be alive, too slighted to lie still.

They worked at a gigantic loom, moving about on rebuilt bodies like chitinous masses tumbling over each other. The tapestry above them, enormous and awesome, is dark. There are grays and reds, oranges and blacks, and deep colours I've never even dreamed. But what are they weaving? It's anyone's guess. Streaks and lines, like sorrow and vengeance, but nothing a storyteller would be proud of, particularly. On the other hand, there are abstract artists that could only ever dream of the dark silver fantasy this tapestry seems to suggest. And I still can't make any meaning of it. Is it just a make-work project? Why would the dead need a make-work project?

I held the Broken Child's only hand as she led me amongst that sea of spectators, who stopped what they were doing and watched – heard – the living, whole girl cross through their workplace. If I thought the stares of the placid newcomers were unnerving, these ones were – is there even a word for the willies that's not stupid? Has anyone ever looked at you wanting your skin, and despaired because they didn't have it? Is so, you know how I felt; but probably not. If I felt out of place for being alive and sounding on the Shores of Night, I felt guilty about it here. Which is weird, because these women were definitely sounding.

The Broken Child led me to a tightrope over the Abyss. She let go of my hand and held hers over my eyes. I closed them and let the harpy's tear guide me across.

It was narrow, and my living heart raced at the prospect that without my looking in, the Abyss was staring into me. It could swallow me for my own folly, and then who would I be?

"Amy," said a familiar comforting voice. I opened my eyes.

"Mirella!"

She had wings, not arms. And she was smiling a big, broad grin. We embraced and I felt music playing.

"Have you enjoyed your time in the Underworld?"

"I feel more out of place here than in the Overworld."

"Middle World. The Overworld is Heaven."

"Well, I feel out of place. What's with the wings?"

"Oh, that's my form in the Underworld – harpy."

"And my form is – Amymone?"

"Ah, no. You have to earn your form."

"So, were you the harpy that traded me the tear for the chord?"

"You're from Canada. Do you know Charlotte from Nova Scotia?"

"Fair point. Can we leave now?"

"Ah, well, yes. But—"

"There's a but?"

"Oh, there is. You're doing Orpheus."

"What?"

"You have your harp. You're doing Orpheus."

"Of course!"

"Right, so you have to lead me out of here without looking back."

"Sounds easy enough."

"Amy, not even Ishtar got out of the Underworld with her love."

"But, you're not really dead, Mirella."

"It's your quest, Amy."

So, we started up the spiraling stone stairs. They jutted out from the cavern in precise, smooth arcs. My footing was sure, but it was the only sound. There was nothing ahead of me, and nothing behind me. Even at the beginning I wanted to turn to make sure she was following. I stopped and shook my head. It wasn't going to be an easy climb.

It was dark. I could make out the stair I was standing on and nothing else. A strain from a song at the party last night began running through my head:

No dawn
No day
I'm always in this twilight
In the shadow of your heart

And as if kept repeating and I stood on stair after endless stair, nothing else around me and I just wondered: Am I even going anywhere? Is this just the one step? Am I in some kind of cruel limbo? Why isn't Mirella making any noise? Is this going to end? What about the red dragon? Can we really escape the Underworld?

The stars
The moon
They have all been blown out
You left me in the dark

Always in this twilight? Am I stuck here forever? How did Mirella know so much about the Underworld? But she knows. She's not dead, so what does it matter if I turn around? But I'd better trust her.

All of this was going through my mind when the sound came back, a flood of light. I could see the stairs and I heard fluttering behind me. I turned to see.

The look on Mirella's face was shocked indignity. She started flapping madly and flew off her crumbling stair. I turned back around and just made it to the next stair as it started to decay. I gained the flat ground of the train yard before she did.

Behind me she screamed. I turned around and saw her feathers give way to flesh. She was in flight and her fall threatened to take her all the way down, into the Abyss. She grasped the gravel ledge and I bent down to help her up.

That's when I woke up. In the train yard. Lying on my back. I hadn't moved since we'd laid down. Mirella woke beside me. My feet were tangled in something. I turned over.

"You two are really fucking weird, you know that?" asked Mickey. He sounded exhausted. "Get up and give me my coat back." There was a tugging at my feet.

"What time is it?" I asked.

"Time to go home."

"Seriously, Mickey. I have to work today. What time is it?"

"Noon."

"Shit. Mirella. Do you want to come to work with me today?"

But Mirella was asleep.

"Mirella?"

She lay on her back, covered in my trench coat, still as marble.

"Mirella!"

I crawled over to her and shook her by the shoulders. Her head bobbled around on her shoulders.

"What! Fuck!"

"I thought you were dead."

"You're an idiot. I hate you."

Like being struck in the chest. I fell backward.

"Failure."

"I – what did I do?"

She glared at me. "Traitor!"

"Mirella—"

"Don't talk to me. You abandoned me. You left me to die."

"I'm sorry. I didn't mean to. I wasn't thinking."

"Fat lot of good that does me."

"I really have to get to work, Mirella. Do you want to come?"

"Not even a little. Monster."

"What? You're the harpy."

She lashed out and struck me across the face.

"You and your big mouth. No one's supposed to know. You speak like a man – without end, and about what don't know anything about."

She got up then and tossed my coat off her. Love was not in the air.

"Mirella! Come back!" called Mickey.

"I can make it home on my own!"

I was too stunned to do anything. Mickey stayed with me.

Entry #36: Thursday, November 7

Mirella's still despondent. Fortunately she did make it home. I wish I could figure out what's wrong, but I don't know where to begin talking with her. Mickey wants to talk a lot, too, but I really don't feel like explaining everything to him. I mean, to be honest, Mirella's right. There's just stuff Mickey wouldn't understand, or Felicity. Like, not even if they wanted to. Which they kind of don't. And there's stuff even I don't understand, and I can't very well start explaining what I don't understand to people who don't understand what I'm already explaining. I don't know what about being a harpy is so gods-awful to tell about, but clearly it's something and I did wrong.

I mean, the only thing I can think of that Mirella's so pissed at is the dream, and I fulfilled the cycle of that myth so should she really be that pissed? But, I guess, because I did fulfill that cycle it means I can't have Mirella. Doesn't it? So, it's really her who's fulfilled the cycle. This is so confusing. First she starts off by worshiping me, and now I'm nothing to her. She feels more like the priestess, and I feel more like the little graphite figure in my own picture, kneeling naked before grandeur.

First meeting of Crazy Club was today. Kind of awkward. There are a lot of people there. Way more than I thought would be there. Lots with AD(H)D and ODD. It's just words meant to control us. Some people do have legitimate problems, but most of us? Most of our problems can be put down to one thing: lack of blind obedience. Anxiety? Look at the wide range of things I went through last week, and none of it acceptable, and all of it real and all of it necessary. Who wouldn't have anxiety? Depression? See above, re: anxiety. Society fucking hates us. It hates to watch us improve; it hates to see us change; it wants us to die or shut up.

We're made to feel dumb; we're made to feel weak; we're made to feel like if we don't do it right the first time, there's no other time left. They say that everyone's crazy, and I suppose if you look deep enough, everyone is. But mental health is a huge, huge problem. It's running rampant, and it's no wonder. And no one's doing anything about it. The inmates run the asylum, as they say, and those of us who see clearly what the problem is or have been forced to turn away from seeing clearly what the problem is and blame ourselves?

When it got to my turn to speak, Mirella glared at me. I had to be really careful not to talk about things too specifically. And I had to be careful not to cry. I've been feeling far less snarky in the past week. Less talkative; less sure of myself. My throat is tight, and under my eyelids it feels like I've been crying for hours. I try to make myself, but nothing comes. It's like faking dry heaving into a toilet. You want release, and you hope that simulating it will become that release, but it doesn't. So you feel like an idiot.

I tried to talk about it, what had happened, how I've been living this past – Jesus! It's only two months! I still can't get over that. But the point is, I can't say anything. I look around me, and I see a bunch of people who have to accept what I tell them, and humour me, but they're all atheists. They don't believe in dreams. Or, even if they do, I'm not really prepared to take that risk. I can't tell anyone about the bizarre synchronicities that have led me to this point. I can't talk about the drugs especially, and I can't talk about the dreams, or the visitation by the Goddess last month. (When was that even?)

The last thing I want to be told is that I should be on medication. Or, even have it suggested to me. No. These deep, ephemeral, nuanced things are too important and much too real to risk speaking out loud to – I used to call them plebs before I knew I was one. I thought I knew what Mirella went through on the regs, but I'm only now coming into it.

The worst part is, I can't even talk to Tilly. This is exactly the kind of thing she told me not to do with the forbidden knowledge she gave me.

Entry #37: Tuesday, November 13

Happy birthday to me. What's the fucking point?

Entry #38: Thursday, November 14

Why am I even writing in a diary? I can't think of anything to put into it that I haven't already said or that doesn't seem über-mundane.

Entry #39: Thursday, November 21

It's like I've been in a haze since Hallowe'en. I've just been playing it over and over in my mind: Hear fluttering, look back, crumble walls, angry Mirella. How do I make it right? How do I get her back? She barely looks at me. I abandoned her at a crucial point. She was right. I acted *just* like her mother.

But that's the end of the myth! Orpheus goes on and lives forever and Eurydice dies. And that's *it!* Curse my ancestors and their insistence on suffering!

I have to talk to Tilly. I'll die if I don't.

Entry #40: Friday, November 22

Finally worked up the courage to even go into the library, today. Tilly saw it immediately, and drew me into her office. I told her everything without making eye contact – barely had my eyes open. When I looked up, she looked worried. I apologised and she bit her lips. A tear drizzled down her face.

"What do I do?"

"I don't know."

"Well, there must be some myth, isn't there?"

"Amymone, myths are not solutions to problems. Myths are –"

"Myths are quests. Tasks. Obedience. Seeking. Atonement. I have to do something. I'm going crazy. Please!"

"I – don't think so. I think I've already caused too much trouble already."

"Show me, please!"

Tilly let out a sigh. "Have patience."

"There's no time for that."

"You just had a fight. Let this blow over."

"It was more than that, Tilly. We didn't exchange words. We didn't shout at each other. I woke Mirella up and she's hated me ever since. It was a dream, but it was real. I need to resolve this dissonance. And you're the only person I can turn to."

"I see," she said, softly. "You're right. I'm in the middle of this now, with you. I regret even having guided you this far."

"But if you hadn't done that, I would be failing peer tutoring right now. This is meant to happen!"

She sighed again and leaned back, looking at the ceiling. "Very well. Cupid and Psyche."

"What about them?"

"Find out."

So, I did. I never understood why Psyche wasn't allowed to see Cupid. She lived with him, and slept with him, but she couldn't see him. So, when her sisters convinced her to sneak a peek while he was sleeping, and she dropped hot wax on him, he grew angry and flew off. And that's where the story ends, or so I used to think.

As it turns out, Venus sets Psyche four impossible tasks to win back her son. So, I mean, I don't know exactly what those would entail in the real world, but if I figure the role of Venus in my life is being played by someone who blesses love. Which means I need to get back to that party house.

A transcript of a call to Jeremy Zhao I just made (unrecorded):

JZ: What do you want, Amy?

AL: To apologise.

JZ: Apology accepted. Goodbye.

AL: Jeremy, wait! Jeremy?

JZ: I'm here.

AL: Look. I could make a bunch of excuses about the way I acted, but that would just make this so much worse. I – was out of my depth. Totally, totally. I shouldn't have run and left you.

JZ: You would have gotten a warning, too. I should have run.

AL: Yeah. How's August?

JZ: Fine. And a douche.

AL: Really? What happened?

JZ: Oh, you know, he's one of these moderate white guys. How's Mariette?

AL: Quiet. Nervous and scared. She thinks she's attracted to me.

JZ: She's not?

AL: She's attracted to rebellion. She's attracted to sin.

JZ: I see. So nothing will come of it?

AL: I'm trying to put things back together with Mirella. I may be collecting a harem, but now is not the time to expand.

JZ: Harem, eh?

AL: Mirella and Mickey. Mariette. A har-em-m.

JZ: [chuckles]

AL: And speaking of freaky sex shit, uh, where did we go to that party?

JZ: Why?

AL: I just really need to know, okay? Please?

JZ: I'm not – supposed to say.

AL: Please, I just – I need to get back there.

JZ: Why?

AL: I need to make amends.

JZ: I'm sure they've seen freakier shit than what you two did. They loved you!

AL: Were – we really walking around naked?

JZ: Ah, no. But everyone was pretty fucked up. And happy about it.

AL: Are you sure?

JZ: There's a reason the party was off the grid. A lot of things went on there. You were really awesome when you poked that guy. Sally spent the entire party bare-breasted.

AL: What about Mariette?

JZ: What about Mariette?

AL: Was she ... cuffed and collared and naked lapping at milk on the floor?

JZ: What?

AL: You heard me.

JZ: No, she was nothing like that. You didn't even have any drugs and you hallucinated like that?

AL: I couldn't remember if it was a dream, or a memory, or a fantasy I had suddenly and vividly when she came out of the woods before we invited her.

JZ: Well, I didn't see anything. But I wasn't always clear and present. I'm sure you're fine, Amy.

AL: Thanks, but it's actually for Mirella.

JZ: Did she leave something?

AL: No. No. I just – I need – I need to get a quest.

JZ: A quest. Amy. Are you okay?

AL: No. I fucked up with Mirella and she lives on myth and it *happened* in myth and I just don't know what else to do.

JZ: That's – kinda crazy.

AL: I am sick and tired of that word. I don't know what else to do. Just please help me, okay? Please?

JZ: You're really in love with her, aren't you?

AL: So deeply. *So* deeply!

JZ: Okay. Okay. I'll take you tomorrow, okay?

AL: Jeremy. Thank you. Thank you!

JZ: Hey, girl. All in the name of love.

Entry #41: Saturday, November 23

Anyway. Jeremy and I went to the place where that party had been. It didn't look anything like the way I remembered it. It was just a house, with dirty floors and cluttered books. The dishes were piled up and there was no music. In the living room, we sat on a couch I distinctly remember not having been there.

I knocked on the door and a woman opened it. I remembered her having the body of a serpent and the wings of a rainbow. And I thought she'd been, like, at least six feet tall. But she was a slender 5'6" at most.

"Jeremy," she said. Her welcome was cool and nervous.

"Hi, Mackenzie."

"And—" She pointed at me.

"Amymone," I said.

"Amymone. Right. What do you want?"

"Amy's looking for Sally."

"Sally. Come on in."

We stepped in. Home. It smelled like a home. There was something bubbling in the kitchen. That was probably the cause of it. Broth.

"Sal!" called Mackenzie up the stairs. "There are more consequences here to see you! Can I get you some tea?" she asked us.

"Do you have chamomile?" I asked.

"Sure do. Honey?"

"No thanks."

"You, Jeremy?"

"No, thank you."

We sat on the couch for what seemed an eternity. Mackenzie came back with my tea, but didn't stay to chat, and didn't make any excuses. I wanted to ask her how the Aeon was, but I couldn't be sure that I remembered that rightly. After all, Mackenzie looked *very* different. Which is not to say she didn't retain some of her serpentine features. Her jaw line was pronounced, but high. Her cheekbones had an odd curve to them that framed her eyes in as much a way as to make her small nose seem streamlined. And the under-pronounced overbite added just the perfect touch of fang.

I'm not describing this very well at all. Look. If a serpent could have a human face, it would be hers.

Finally, Sally came downstairs. She was wearing a pair of jeans and a black sweater. I guess part of me was hoping she'd be wearing her bare-breasted goddess garb, and that disappointed me. But the moment I saw her gorgeous round face and considerable hips, a memory smacked me in the face. Kneeling before her, the two of us, and she puts some kind of oil on our foreheads. Kisses the crown.

"Amymone, love!" she beamed, hand on her chest. "I was hoping you'd make it back. Where's your spider companion?"

"She's – that's why I'm here."

"Is she lost?"

"No. I am. Without her."

"Oh. Did you two have a fight?"

So, I explained what happened as best I could. She didn't ever stop smiling, but she did get a bit concerned once or twice. (Jeremy, on the other hand, had his chin on his chest the entire time.) When I was done, Sally took a moment to think.

"Well," she said. "That's weird."

We all laughed. Then she said, "I've never been asked to give a quest before. And, really, I suppose, rationally, there's nothing I can give you that would have any bearing on your relationship. Are you seeing a counselor?"

"No!"

"We're not all bad."

"Are—you?"

"Studying to be."

"Then you must think I'm crazy."

"No. I don't. I think you're deep. But I think you're a little out of your depth. I think you'll make it, though. A mother bird throws her baby out of the nest to teach her to fly." Then she looked at me askance. "I've never met anyone like you."

"Me neither," said Jeremy.

Well, that made me blush. Which brings me to this point: Where did all these awesome women start coming from? Last year, all I had was Tilly and then Mirella steps into my life – shoved by fate and secret bureaucracy – and suddenly my life is a magick goddess extravaganza! And can I just say that when I'm surrounded by magick, I feel like I'm surrounded by love? It was a great comfort just to look at this Sally again.

She had us for dinner: chicken soup and bread. Homemade. And after dinner over cranberry tarts – also homemade – she said to me: "Amy, I don't think I can help you. The quest idea is a okay, but I just met you and Mirella. I don't know much about you, and I know even less about her. I don't know anything about your relationship, and even if I did I wouldn't know where to begin. So, sorry but I'm afraid you'll have to seek elsewhere. Why don't you try her mother?"

Yeah. That's right. I'll just call her up and say: "Mrs. Lantigua? Can you give me a quest to get Mirella to love me again?" Oh, no. Wait. I can't do that because Mirella's not answering my calls. And Mrs. Lantigua isn't exactly quest-positive. I'd risk losing everything. But I didn't say that. I just looked down at my empty dessert plate and nodded.

Entry 42: Sunday, November 24

Well, this morning I woke up bound and determined to find someone else to give me that quest. I thought Tilly would be better than Sally. She knows me; she knows Mirella; she's seen our relationship in action. She's even psychic. (Well, ex-psychic, but still...) If anyone can help me get Mirella back, I thought, it's Tilly.

So, I went to see her after school; but she was in a rush, packing things up for the day. She handed me a pile of books and we went into the stacks together.

"So, how's your quest coming, dear?" she asked in librarian.

"As I don't have one? Not well."

"Well, keep at it," she said. "I'm sure someone will be willing to task you with something important.

"Yeah, about that. I was hoping you could actually give me the quest."

"Haha! I started you on this path. Would you like me to do the rest for you?" She shook her head and put another book back.

"Well, you know so much about us, I just thought you'd have – I don't know – insight?"

"That, I may be able to help you with." She stopped and turned to me. I stood there, looking down at her. She rolled her eyes a little, smiling, then said: "What myth do you find yourself enmeshed in?"

"Psyche and Eros."

"Psyche and Cupid. And who are you?"

"Psyche."

"And who is Mirella?"

"Cupid."

"Who does Psyche ask for help getting Cupid back?"

"Aphro—Venus, I guess."

"And who is Venus to Cupid?"

I pursed my lips.

"So," she continued, "there's no better person to speak to than Mrs. Lantigua. I'm sure she'll have plenty of stuff for you to do. Now, let's get these books re-shelved. I have a hot date, tonight." We were silent until we said our goodbyes.

Entry #43: Monday, November 25

This is not going to be easy. Mirella *lives* with her mother. How am I going to visit – because I have to because Mirella won't answer the phone – without Mirella knowing I'm there? I mean, how can I even be sure I'll get Mrs. Lantigua if I visit? She works two jobs.

She did say something about a porn store in September when I met her, and I know she normally works night shift. I don't know when that starts, but there are only so many porn stores in this city. Even if I included all the adult toy stores, I think it's about six.

She's gone almost every day. Odds are good if I don't find her tomorrow, I'll find her the day after, but I have psychic lessons that day, so better find her tomorrow.

Entry #44: Tuesday, November 26

Welp! I found her. She was in a lonely room with windows so black even the fluorescent lights struggled. I stepped in and she barely said a word to me – wasn't looking.

I'd tried four stores beforehand, hoping she worked in one of the better lit ones, and I would get one of two reactions, if not both. Either I'd be asked for ID, or the clerk would watch me closely. Or both. I mean, I'm not dead. If I walk into a formerly forbidden place I'm going to take a look. I never thought I'd be so angry, sickened, saddened, and aroused at the same time. I didn't even think it was possible! But looking at all those girls with all those cocks in all those places? People who defend porn make noise about freedom of choice. Where does your life need to take you so *that's* a desirable choice? I mean, I like sex and I understand exhibitionism, but this is – it's not either one of them. But it's *so* hot! How?

Oh, man! Even just remembering it gets me going in the worst way. And I mean that – the *worst* way. But here's the kicker, the thing that makes me most disgusted by my own arousal: No one was smiling. I mean, the corners of some of the girls' mouths were turned up and their teeth were showing, but their eyes were all sad. No one was smiling.

So, at porn store number five, I'd had my fill of porn. I wanted it to be over. Was I ever relieved to see Mrs. Lantigua!

"Thank Gods it's you!" I said once I was sure it was her.

"Amy!" she cried. "What are you doing here? Are you old enough to be in here?"

"Yes. And I was hoping you could help me."

She looked at me, wary and concerned. "I – am not sure that I should be –"

"Oh, I don't want to buy anything. It's about Mirella."

"Oh, thank God! What do you need?"

"Well, maybe you've noticed I haven't been over lately?"

She nodded.

"And maybe Mirella's gotten a little listless or whatever?"

"You two fought."

"Not – not really. We went to a party and I did something. I'm not proud of it, and Mirella's pretty pissed at me. I'm just wondering if there's anything I could do – if – you could help?"

"You want me to speak to her? She doesn't listen to me."

"No. I want to talk to her myself."

"But she won't talk to you."

"No."

"So, what can I do?"

"Maybe – you can – I don't know – what do *you* do when she's pissed at you?"

"I wait. But she lives with me. She's my little girl. She *has* to speak to me."

"No, I mean – it has to be something I should be doing. Something active. A quest."

Fuck, of course. Fuck fuck fuck! I tried not to say it, but it just slid its way onto my tongue. Of course, how far would I have gotten if I'd never said the word? How do you ask for a quest without asking for a quest? And just writing that, I'm noticing just how crazy it sounds.

Mrs. Lantigua looked at me with growing disbelief. I could see her thinking – I've been leaving my child in the hands of a lunatic! When I bit my lips and shrugged, she sighed and put her hand to her face.

"Ai-yi-yi, Amy!"

"Look, I know you don't appreciate the way I treat your daughter like she's normal, and deserves to be taken at face value, but I really do need your help. I haven't been able to sleep or eat or concentrate on school. I'm just so in love with her!" I said that. All of it. Even the last part.

But Mrs. Lantigua just shrugged. She was tired.

"Ai, Mirella. I mean, Amy. This is not good news for me. How long?"

"Since – late September."

"Where have I been!"

"Here, mostly."

"Yes, thank you Amy, I know that."

"Look, I'm sorry, Mrs. Lantigua. I don't want to be confrontational. I'm just really desperate. Please! Give me something."

Mrs. Lantigua looked me in the eye. She was angry and scared. And so tired. She sighed and I thought she was going to ask me to leave. But instead, she said: "Sort your life out, Amy. Be sure you want what you think you want."

"I'm pretty good at that."

She said: "Really? You break rules left and right; you enable Mirella's psychosis; you dress like a prostitute at a funeral; you – you yell and scream at psychiatrists. And now you tell me you're in love with my daughter?"

I opened my mouth to say something snarky about hypocrisy: her working in a porn store and never being around for her daughter, locking her up in a sanatorium, making her a zombie with pharmaceuticals. But she silenced me with a look. She does what she has to. I know that.

Then she said: "Do you know what they call girls like you in this industry? 'Barely Legal.' There are entire series of pornos devoted to exploiting girls your age – just days after they've turned eighteen. Sometimes I think that's all the industry's for. And I'm here eight hours a day. I have to sell men images of girls my daughter's age – your age, Amy – to whack off to all day. That's my job – one of them. It's how I support my child. So where do you get off telling me you mean my daughter well when there's a million girls your age making the worst decisions of their lives?"

I stood there with my mouth closed, without the courage to tell her I'd already made that decision, and I've learned from it. If I'm honest, I haven't stopped learning from it. That's kind of why I'm with Mirella. Rather.

But is it? That haunting picture of me. Am I with Mirella for friendship? Courtship? Worship? All of the above? Am I with Mirella because she drew me? Reality's rather slipping away from me. But knowing reality? How much do I really want it around?

"Sort your life out, Amy," said Mrs. Lantigua. "I didn't. And look where I am today."

I held it together pretty much until I got home. The four blocks from the bus stop to our walk-up were murder – I was barely there for any of it – and when I opened the door, my parents told me I was late for dinner and where had I been, but I was already in tears.

I wanted to be self righteous at Mrs. Lantigua for lording it over me, but that wasn't true. I wanted to be pissed at myself for being such a stupid slut, but that wasn't the matter either. I tried Mickey, Mirella, Mariette, Sally, even Tilly! But the tears kept coming and no one I landed on felt right. My mom and dad wrapped me up in a big hug after their futile attempts to get me to talk. This huge grief overwhelmed me, bigger than me. Bigger than all of us. Even now, as I write this, hours later, I still feel the tears behind my eyes.

I'm lost in woods as black as starless night.
There is no path, just grim tree after tree.
No leaves, no buds, no hope for me sans thee.
No golden orb to teach me left from right.
What strange beguiling light these stark nude trees
Give off – a nimbus cloak of dun despair.
What lives they must have lived in Springtime fair,
But now they're rigid, barren with unease.
Don't leave me here, Mirella, with neglect!
Don't cast aside the joys of what we've done!
Don't say I'm not your beloved one!
Don't let the melancholia infect.

The Underworld must see me yet again,
Alive or dead. The question is: But when?

Is that melo-dramatic? That volta sucks. I feel so empty.

Entry #45: Wednesday, November 27

Someone plastered the word SLUT all over my locker. I'd go and talk to someone about it, but no one who cares would do anything. Mr. Meyer might, but I've already asked him for a favour like that this semester. The last thing I need is to find out that he can't help me because I get myself into these situations. I don't need another talk about how people don't like the way I'm such a know-it-all like I got last summer. Fuck. That. I am not in the mood.

So, instead, I'm sitting here in front of my locker. The word SLUT looks like a title. My title. People walk by and giggle, but people always do that.

I'm skipping French class. I've got to wonder if I want to marry Mirella, and I can't do that in French because I don't have the vocabulary. I'd be correcting myself, and wondering if that's the right way to say that, even though I'm just thinking it. So, here's what I'm thinking.

Mirella is a sweet girl. She fills me with joy. Every time I think things like that, I'm hard on myself for thinking in clichés and platitudes, but how else do people think about the way they love their lovers? I would give a definitive answer: yes. But I can't. That would be irresponsible of me. I want Mirella back so badly, I'm willing to say basically anything.

She's so erratic sometimes, though. I mean, her mother's right to worry. That thing, with the guy on the bus in September? If I hadn't been there, what would have happened? Can I have a full-time career and an ostensibly schizophrenic wife? And if I can't, which do I want more? I mean, I never even suspected I wanted a wife until last month, and now it's all I can think about. *She's* all I can think about. And I don't even know what I want to do with the rest of my life. Although, these days, I'm starting to think I could be a decent psychologist. Better than most. And if I have a psychic-psycho partner for the rest of my life and a job dealing with other people's problems? That's a lot of shit to worry about every single day.

Everyone seems to think I'm doing Mirella wrong by listening to her and trying to understand. I think I started humouring her because it was easier than trying to get her to explain what she meant by the metaphors she used, because she doesn't really see metaphors as these, like, distant comparisons. It was just easier to lean into the whorl. I never thought anything like this would happen, and, like, I don't see it hurting her.

Lots of people think she's violent because Gen and the pissy posse didn't stop talking about that fight for, like, a month. Thing is, though, Gen started it. Gen hurt me. Mirella just scared Gen. She wasn't violent or anything. Just creative.

And this trouble we're having now? I mean, if it weren't for the myths and the quests, it'd just be relationship problems, like normal. Neither of us are normal, though, so how surprising is it that this fight between us is weird? You don't have to be psychotic to give someone the silent treatment.

Fuck! I have *got* to stop calling Mirella psychotic. Even if it's true, and schizophrenia is shamanism presenting itself to a world that doesn't respect shamanism, psychotic is the wrong word for what Mirella is. I cannot continue to use the words of her oppressors. *My* oppressors.

And I think that, more than anything, *that's* the greatest gift I can give Mirella. I believe in *her* like no other person ever has. I can't explain it. I look back over this diary, and I'm almost appalled with how easily I overcame my rank cynicism. I *totally* cried psychic even while I was saying I wasn't the type. Yet, here we are.

I mean, I could be wrong. But I hate being wrong. Being wrong makes me unhappy. It makes others unhappy. Is it right to oppress people for their own good? Is that a thing that's possible?

Look, I know what I see when I look in Mirella's eyes. I see depth. And a weird kind of worldliness. I see worry and anxiety. And when I look into her eyes while I'm taking her seriously, I see relief. Gratitude.

So, yeah. I guess, if it's the only way I'm going to be with Mirella, and the only way I can keep her out of prison, and the only way – the only way. Yes. I will marry her.

Supplement:
As I sat here writing, a contemplative wave rolled over me. I felt calm and aware, like when I'm meditating. Thea's been teaching us clairaudience, of course, so naturally I checked out what I could hear. It was mostly classes droning on, and a bored whisper here and there, but then I found myself in an echo chamber with running water. Yup, you guessed it: guys' bathroom.

Suddenly, I had an opportunity I assume no one else would even take: what do guys really say in there? So, I listened in and what I heard – well, I'm sure it's not in any way representative of what guys really actually talk about. At least I hope. I mean, I don't really know, do I? And guys make rape jokes all the time. This sounded serious though. Here's what I heard:

"Is everything ready for Friday?"

"Yeah, I guess."

"Good. I know another guy who might be interested. Man, I'm so stoked for this! What about you?"

"Yeah, I guess."

"You're not gonna pussy out on me, are you, man?"

"No. No!"

"Because I'd hate to have to hurt you, bro."

"No. I'm – good. I just – Is it too far? Like, we could really get in trouble. I don't want a record."

"You're not gonna get a record, man. Nobody fucking cares about two sluts who can't keep their clothes on for ten seconds. And they're both batshit insane! No one's gonna believe them."

I mean, what am I supposed to think here? Are they coming after me, or Mirella, or no one, or someone else? Is it just some kind of twisted fantasy they've got going? Or have they done this shit before? Is this the entire point of those two videos? I don't even know who these dickheads are! What am I supposed to do?

Later:

I went to see Tilly. It was weird. Very weird. I told her what I happened and she looked at me ruefully and didn't say anything for a long time.

"I would help you, Amymone," she said. "I'd say, 'Get Mirella and I'll take you both home that day.' But, I won't be here."

"You won't?" I tried not to be terrified.

"No. Amber will be covering for me. But, listen, Amymone – whatever this turns out to be, I'm sure you can handle it."

"Even if they rape us?"

"Yes, worst-case scenario in the world, yes. I'm sure you can handle that. But I have every confidence in you that you won't need to. You're resourceful and careful."

Still Later:

I'm having some catnip tea tonight, that I've asked Morpheus to bless. With a black-handled kitchen knife I've drawn an invoking pentagram on my pillow. It's not much, but I think it'll do.

Entry #46: Thursday, November 28

Matt Jeffries! I knew I recognised that damn voice!

I had a dream last night that I was playing strip chess with a faceless stranger. We were both relatively naked, but I was down a rook. My scorched earth policy had failed me. The queens had just been exchanged and I couldn't remember half the game. I was panicking and making stupid moves. Worst of all, I couldn't see his half of the board. I took his first rook with my last, and got flanked by an invisible bishop. Off came the bra and I felt empty. I moved my own bishop back to defend, but with only that piece and three pawns to his five, I felt thoroughly disadvantaged. I played it out to the bitter end but he won, and I had to be his puppet.

In the clear light of day, I realised I generally only use my scorched earth policy against one man because of his propensity for a specific opening. It's Matt Jeffries. Matt Jeffries is planning to rape my girlfriend. Maybe.

I mean, it's not like strategy isn't strategy, and Matt likes to talk a good game. Lots of guys talk about beating someone in chess – or anything really – as raping that person. But if I look back over the things they said, they were definitely talking about fucking. I just can't be sure if they're being serious. So I have to talk to Matt. Gods! That's not going to be fun.

Supplement:

Had a game with Matt today. Deliberately blundered. Lost. The first time his King's Indian has defeated my scorched earth. He was elated. When I knocked my king over, he jumped up and whooped.

Then he pointed at me and yelled: "I just totally fucking r—" and he trailed off. I could see the cold triumph in his eyes. The pride. The undressing of me. (Why had I never noticed his attraction to me before?)

"Congratulations, Matt."

"I think you mean, 'con-Matt-ulations'."

"Yeah, okay, alright, fine. Con-Matt-ulations."

"Fuck yeah, bitch! Oops. Sorry, Amy." But he wasn't.

The thing is, that should have been a more hollow victory for him. I mean, yeah he won, but it wasn't due to any superior strategy, or even superior tactics. It was my blunder.

Anyway, I asked him: "Hey, Matt. What are you doing Friday?"

I think I caught him off his guard, because he got all red-faced and started stuttering.

"Hot date?" I asked.

"Uh, no. Why?—Do you want to know?"

"Oh, ah, just – a couple friends and I are going to a movie. I thought you might like to come."

"I, uh, I would. But I do have plans. Uh, with friends."

"Oh, really? What are you doing? Can I come?"

"I thought you have plans."

"Eh, it's a movie."

"Oh, well, I guess, if you're interested, uh, maybe we could, uh, get together? Just the two of us? Maybe?"

"Oh." I sucked my teeth. "I don't know if you'll understand this, but I don't really like to 'get together just the two of us' until I know someone in a group setting."

"Oh, uh, well, maybe – some other time, then?"

"Oh – sure," sounding disappointed, "just let me know, okay?" I smiled into his eyes. He looked down and walked away.

Hopefully if he is planning anything, the prospect of being with me legit gives him pause. Regardless, I managed to snag one of his pawns while he was gloating and I was packing his set away, so hopefully I can overhear something if the plan continues.

Further supplement:

Home now. Parents working for three more hours, so I can do mad magicks. I'm going to use elements from my costume to inform the Watchtowers: feathers for air; spear for fire; mirror for water; horsey headdress for earth. I've drawn a pentagram in my own blood on a piece of printer paper, upon which I've placed the black pawn. And I'm about to call on Apollo for oracular visions. My meditation will use the mantra ISIS, as Thea taught me, for clairvoyance. I'll be gazing into the mirror, holding the pawn.

Should I do something to the pawn? I mean, here's my chance to do some real malevolent magick, especially if it turns out he is going to rape Mirella. Still, I should be conscious of the three-fold rule.

I know! I should name the pawn. The pawn's name is Matt Jeffries. Now, please excuse me while I begin my invocation.

Later:

I should be doing my homework now, but I just had to get this down. I could barely eat supper because I was so knocked sideways by what I witnessed.

See, I *became* Matt Jeffries. It was *so* bizarre. I, like, fell through the looking glass and walked around *as* Matt. I mean, it wasn't as clear and vivid as a dream, so it took me a while to realise what I was experiencing. I couldn't hear what he heard, but I saw what he saw and I felt what he felt. I entered his head at the moment of orgasm. He'd been masturbating to a gang rape fantasy, so my thoughts were kind of overloaded with those images. When the haze cleared, I realised it was an online video, still playing. I—he—we looked up, and we saw the woman crying. We were scared, anxious. He reached for a tissue. Then he cleared hid browser history.

That anxiety reduced inside him, but it lingered, fighting with the post-orgasmic calm. It was like a fear or a shame, or something? But fear or shame of what exactly, I wasn't privy to.

Once he'd zipped up and flushed his tissues, he went to check his texts. There was one from Foster Genkins – a skater I used to get used by.

still in?

yeah, i guess
gr8! nu guy brns' bud
name?
idk
legit?
call n ask
nah
fri aft sch?
yep
bitch wont no ass fr mouth!
lol

Matt was not laughing out loud. In fact, he got so much more nervous, started pacing. After he erased the texts on his phone he went to his bookshelf where, on the bottom shelf, he had a binder labelled "Subject 0". He picked it up and opened it.

It was a dossier on Mirella, with pictures of her building, behaviour reports on her and her mother. There were only two entries: one from Monday, the other from Tuesday. He seemed flustered, placing his fingers below the Tuesday entry and breathing heavy. After pacing for a while, he went to his computer again. I worried then, because I wasn't sure how I'd get out of his head if he started looking at rape porn again. But I hung on, and watched him check his e-mail. Whoever's message he was waiting for wasn't there, so he clicked on the URL and typed in another website – obviously a porn site. I panicked and screamed in his head. He started and looked around and I felt myself lifted, swept from his mind out the top of his head and returned firmly to mine, disoriented but grateful.

How has Mirella not noticed she's being stalked? Has she noticed? Does she know what's going on? What's her plan? I need to talk to her.

Entry #47: Friday, November 29

I spoke to Mirella today about the whole thing. "I overheard a bunch of guys talking about – kidnapping you. And – doing awful stuff to you."

"Mm," she said.

"So look, I'm going to take you to my place on Friday to throw them off the scent. You can spend the night, and we can talk."

She looked at me. Looked through me.

"You're not her. You are *not* the Shining Host! It's so uncanny – all the detail. The aura. Her voice. Demon!"

She shoved me. I grabbed her hands.

"Mirella!"

She looked in my eyes. Neither of us breathed. She was as lost as I was. I could guess where.

"How did you get down here? Why are you here?" she asked.

"I – had to come." Then, looking about. "There's a group of – incubi after you down here."

"Incubi? How did they get into the Underworld?"

I hadn't seen incubi there, I just assumed they were there. You know: demons in hell. But I guess the Underworld isn't Hell and Hell does exist. Whatever. It was a guess, and I made it and I was right. "You're not in the Underworld, Mirella."

"I'm – I'm not?"

"Not this time, no."

"Oh – God. I thought – I thought you were a shade – a bright, bright shade. What are you doing, *here*, Mistress? Take me with you!"

"I wish I could. I'm trying. But I'm here to protect you. Because you need protection. There's a group of incubi going to kidnap you when you get home on Friday."

"I – have I angered you? Why send me to Hell, Mistress?"

"I couldn't have known that's what would happen, darkling. I'm working to get you back, though. Okay? We'll reunite, sweet, and soon. But for now, let me offer you protection."

"You're not a shade? Having a few laughs at my expense? Looking to look naked at me?"

(I've taught her too well.)

"Falpala, no. I'm here to help you."

"But why?"

"Because I love you. And because I'm sorry I looked back. I'm not perfection, Nachla. And I regret that."

"You're working to get me back?"

"Oh, deerheart. I am."

"Because you could be the shade of an incubus."

I raised my head, looking for guidance. "Mirella, lovelust, I have the better of these demons. I've had one before. His name is Foster. He's mean. Sadistic. And he's on board. And two others. At the same time."

"You're stronger than me," she whispered.

"I don't know about that. But they are. And I would never – never – do that to you."

"Rape."

"What?"

"Rape. Say it. So I can see it."

"Rape."

"Say the vow."

"The vow?"

"What you just said. Say it. Say you wouldn't."

"Oh. I would never – *never* – rape you, Mirella."

She nodded.

"Let me take you home on Friday. You can sleep on the couch, if need be. Can I call you tonight so we can coordinate?"

She shook her head.

"Please?"

"We don't have one. There were demons in the phone jack, so I filled it with salt."

"I – see. Okay. Well, we can't talk again until –"

"Bitch!" she cried, and shoved me again. Then she turned around and walked away. I don't know what that was about. I don't know if she suddenly decided I couldn't be trusted or what, but I'm going to go about my business as though that didn't happen.

Entry #46: Monday, December 2

My stupid parents! They're having a party tomorrow night and they've neglected to tell me and because it's people from Dad's work, I can't bring my girlfriend. I mean, it's not like we have to make out. Or hold hands. Or be in the damn room. But apparently we're too lez for rich people.

So, I have to got to her place on Friday. This was going to be so simple. We could have called the cops; Mom and Dad would have been there. I can only hope the people in the other apartments are busy bodies. That old place – the walls are practically see-through. But everyone there is up to something questionable, and would prefer not to know who's up to what.

My stupid parents! At least they gave me the car.

Entry #47: Friday, December 6

Last night was perhaps the weirdest night I've spent with Mirella. First, the getting there. I was hurrying to meet up with Mirella after class and James Gilmore from the rugby team steps right in front of me. I wasn't sure if I recognised him from the gang, but I was willing to bet. People think he's a dog. I'm sure they're not wrong. He stepped right in front of me, blocked half the hallway with his bulk – arm on wall, body in space.

"Hey, Amy, right?"

"Yep. Excuse me. I have somewhere to be."

"Whoa, whoa, whoa! Just, allow yourself to relax for a second." I gawked at him.

"Do you realise," he continued, "you're always in a hurry? It makes you look like an ant or something."

"An ant?"

"Yeah."

"I'm not an ant. Ants live in hives and do everything they're told and act as a unit, though they're individuals. You're more like an ant because you're on a team. Can I go, please?"

"See," he said, moving to block. "That's what I like about you. You're smart *and* you're pretty."

"Um. Y—wait. What?"

"Does that surprise you? That I like you?"

"A little, yes. But I really do have –"

"A person can relax, Amy, and still make it everywhere on time."

"Yes, well, that may be true, but this is really pretty urgent."

"Okay," he said, finally stepping aside. "Can I at least have your number?"

You know? For a second, I considered giving it to him. He seemed kinda sweet somehow.

"Nine." (The disaster number.)

"What?"

"It's the number you dial to get out of the building." I brushed by him and scurried down the hall.

When I got out to the parking lot, there were a bunch of guys crowded in a kind of huddle. I raced over there as fast as I could. Ridiculous to wear heels on such an important day, but I did. So, "racing" was a bad word choice, but I got there.

"Get away from her!" She wasn't there.

"What!" said one of them. "What are you doing?"

"What did you do with her?"

They started laughing, called me a crazy bitch. I looked around at their faces, to see if I recognised any of them. Yup.

"Hey! You're that bitch who's always talking in class."

"I'm a girl, not a bitch, and it's called participating. And right now, I'm looking for my gi—my friend. So, please excuse me."

And I left with horrific images of her bound and gagged in the trunk of a car. Suddenly certain of my solution, I turned and raced back toward the school accompanied by the jeers and catcalls of the rapists behind me. I got to the door just as James was coming out. He blocked me again, pretending to try to get around me, but it turned into a dance. Then he put his hands on my waist and moved me aside. I squirmed and hit him, and he dropped me, laughing. His chest was so hard and muscled, and all I could think was that if they could plan to rape someone in her home, it's only a hop-skip-jump to dragging me into a dark, disused corner of the school.

He laughed at me. He laughed at my helplessness. He wasn't even phased by my jab to his chest. He could have done anything with me that he wanted to. Anything.

And, for that matter, how do men stay hard when a woman is crying and struggling and begging? I mean, I guess a lot of girls must hold it all in, but not that many. Mirella wouldn't and I'm not sure I would. Jeremy wouldn't. Mickey didn't. So, what's the deal? Do men have some kind of universal sadistic streak that's wired directly to their penises? I mean, you'd think one of them – just one! – would have had a major attack of conscience and I suppose I don't really know if one of them didn't. But if one did, doesn't that increase the likelihood that others would? Instead, it was four in the morning before they shut up. Where was everyone! They were utterly pornographic, yelling in the hallway through the night like that!

At about midnight, I started suspecting that Mirella might be right. That they were, in fact, incubi. We were in a room in Hell looking starkly like Mirella's apartment room. We were alone, and angry men were pounding on the door, slathering all over themselves with sexual depravity. What goes on in men's minds? How is there that much evil in so many people? I really want to think that I was hallucinating, that I was psychotic with Mirella. I would take "I'm going crazy" over "that really happened."

I went up to the library, heart pounding, hallway spinning. Amber was still taking care of things. Tilly was still out. Mirella was reading quietly at a study table. I went up to her, and without looking up, she said: "They're after you too."

"Come on, Golden Fleece," I said, "let's get out of here."

The school was deathly when we left. Even the parking lot was empty, save for my mother's little Honda Civic. It was all very eerie, and I was looking over my shoulder all the way to the car. I could see straight, but my mouth was dry, and my heart was still pounding. Finding my keys was an exercise in French farce. Mirella was just her numb self. Maybe she *wouldn't* cry.

I left the parking lot and drove toward Mirella's place. There was nowhere else we could go. I thought about taking her for coffee, and I thought about taking her to Cherubim Books; but the longer I was away from her place, the more I could envision those guys being in front of her apartment door. If we got there fast enough, I thought we'd have time to get in the back and up to the apartment before they could. All I could hope was that they'd gotten lost.

Why didn't I call the cops? Why didn't I just tell *someone* what was going on? But when I think about who I'd tell, Tilly's the only real answer for me. She wasn't there. And she couldn't do anything but tell me to tell someone else, or do it herself. And what would the cops have done? We weren't being followed. We weren't being raped at that moment. All I heard was a plan, a conspiracy, psychically, and one that – who does that kind of thing!!

So, anyway, we get to Mirella's complex, and I park around

back. Mirella gets her keys out before we leave the car, and we open the doors together. Doors shut, but there are more than two of them shutting. They're in another car. They were lying in wait for us! We *race* up the stairs as fast as we can. (Stupid heels!) The sound of us pounding up the stairs and the sound of them so close behind made us indistinguishable from each other. I knew if they caught us in the staircase, we were sunk because everyone uses the elevator. Again, racing up the stairs, heart blaring like a siren, my vision gets blurry and skewed. And in heels, that's not a good thing at all. Mirella grabs my hand and bursts through the third-story door.

It felt like ten minutes waiting for Mirella to find and be able to use her keys. They were practically on our backs, coming down the hall at us. Time just slowed. Mirella fumbled at the lock. I almost fainted. She got it. We slipped in the door, and locked all three locks and that was the safest I felt all night.

I'm so tired, but I have to make it to Cherubim today. I've got a six-hour shift. I'd love to call in, but I need that money. If I have to ask Dad for it, I'll have to tell him, and then he'll be pissed at me.

Supplement:

This is just turning into the weirdest weekend ever. It's four in the morning again and I'm in a bookstore. There's a sluice of snow blowing against the window. Graeme's asleep on the floor. He asked me if I was on drugs today. But I couldn't tell him why I was really being bad at my job.

It was snowing when I came to work today. I haven't slept since two nights ago. I'm really tired. The store was packed today. There was barely time to take a breath that didn't end in an explanation of some sort. You know the saying, "The customer is always right?" The customer is always stupid. I'd go into it, but I'm too tired. Neither of us noticed that the storm had turned into something dangerous until someone came in – this beautiful androgyne. Never seen the like. Man? Woman? Who cares. Just beautiful. Anyway, they come in and buy a small anthology of Nietzsche. They look out the window and say: "Do you know if they've stopped running the buses yet?" Graeme and I looked at each other. We both use the bus. He called. We'd missed it. But he had some blankets and pillows in the back just in case. I called home.

I don't want to be here. And I don't want to be awake. And I *really* don't want to be as afraid of Graeme as I am today. Tonight. Whenever. And I don't think I can come in to work tomorrow. The snow's kind of lightening up. If I see a bus go by, I'm going home. Except I can't because I don't have a key. Graeme would hear me leave. And then he'd yell at me and I'd cry.

I need to talk to someone, and I have no idea who that is. Fuck it. If the buses start running, I'm waking Graeme up and going home. I need some rest.

Entry #48: Saturday, December 7

I'm sitting in my bedroom, writing. It's 11:30. I should be sleeping, but try telling that to my body. I lie there, and just lie and my mind is racing, but I don't know what I'm thinking. My heart is pounding but I'm not sure why. It hurts in my chest. How did those guys just get away with that, and do I remember that the door held shut because I can't stand remembering that Mirella and I got gang raped on Friday night?

"Death and the Maiden" is supposed to be about the comfort of death on the weary and the sick, but honestly, it makes a great soundtrack for crying. Especially the second movement. I've been listening to that movement since I got home, and bawling myself into sand. If I make it through this crazy quest thing, I'm starting a string quartet just to play "Death and the Maiden" next semester. Hopefully I can get Mirella to play first, no matter what happens.

Anyway, I've been putting something off for too long. I've got fairy blood, and it can't only be me. I need to find out who else does. Am I alone in this overwhelming sexuality and foolhardy belief in magick even though I never do any? Does that only happen to me?

So, that was fruitless. I signed up for a forum, but when I tried to sign in, I was told my account was inactive. I waited for a while, checked my e-mail, nothing. Tried logging in again, same message. Tried contacting an administrator – but you have to be signed in for that. Clicked on the re-send activation e-mail button. Checked to see if e-mail address was spelled right. Checked to see if forum still active. No e-mail. And yes – forum still active.

And the thought comes to me: maybe I should be seeing a therapist. But what good would that do me? After that psycho bitch Jocelyn Bankman demanded I show her my self-harm scars, that was the final straw. What has a therapist ever done for me? Nothing. Why would I think that could change in my favour? But I don't want to be alone. I just need someone to talk to.

Fuck it! I'm going for coffee. Maybe that'll wake me up.

Supplement:

Side-tracked by my wandering brain, I found myself walking down a street I seldom – well, I guess never – have been on. It's bad, really, that I've been here my whole life and I've never been to this quaint little out-of-the-way village.

There's a salon, and a piercing parlour, a toy store (for kids), art gallery, and music gallery, and a nifty little cafe and bookstore. Oh, village whose name I don't yet know, where have you been all my life? There's even a playground two blocks down and it's got swings!

I'm actually giddy! After all the shit I've been through over the past month-and-a-half, I'm giddy as a clam!

So, I order myself a nice, sinful eggnog latte and a cinnamon coffee cake from this plump silver-haired darling of a lady. She looks like she could be a hundred-and-two, except for those smiling eyes. They were younger than me. I don't know what overcame me – I'm usually so quiet to strangers – but I introduced myself. Her name's Isobel.

I said: "How have I lived here my whole life and never known about this place?"

She clucked her tongue and said: "Must be magick!"

"Is it?"

"Well, you're an adventuresome girl, aren't you, Amy?"

I laughed out loud. "I suppose you could say that, yes."

She patted my hand. "Just relax, pet. You're here now."

"Am I dreaming?"

"It's not beyond the realm of possibility." She smiled and handed me my comfort food.

I sat down and opened a graphic novel about the ghost of a black teenager who works with his living Choctaw-Jamaican girlfriend to terrorise corrupt cops with black magick. And I guess the skeptical part of my brain was turned off, because I found myself wondering if it were based on a true story. It was riveting and heart breaking. I took a sip of my latte and in walked this guy with a cane. He was about twenty, I guess, and he leaned heavily on that cane as he stumped over to the counter. Long curly waves down his back and a truly full beard, all black and shiny. He had a thick body, and smiling eyes, but his right foot was shrivelled.

This guy walks up to the counter and I'm torn between him and the book in my hand. But he opens his mouth, and the book in my hand dissolves in his baritone. It's a dark, rich chocolate that would make the Swiss jealous. I wanna suck the words off his tongue. And it scares me.

Isobel says something, then points my way. "And she is too."

He looks my way, does a double take. "Now how did I miss her?" He smiles at me, takes his coffee and starts walking toward me. I blush, and bite my lip, lowering my eyes.

"Do you mind if I sit down here for a moment?"

"Ah," I breathed. My heart was pounding and I could only think of sex. It was confusing and scary. Because I really don't know how to feel about guys right now.

"If not, feel free to say so. I don't want to make you feel unsafe. Just wanna welcome you home."

I glanced into his eyes. He looked a little concerned.

"I see you like my books," he said.

I looked down at the comic in my hand. It was getting fibrous from all the sweat. I set it down.

"This is you?" I asked.

"Indeed, it is."

"I – want more."

"That's what they all say." He chuckled, and watched me blush, embarrassed by my own shame. My heart raced and my lace felt scratchy. I took a sip of latte.

"Hey," he said. "I know what you're feeling right now. A lot of girls and a number of guys feel that way around me. It's a bit of a curse. Best thing you can do is just relax into it. Let it suffuse you and be comfortable in your arousal. No pressure to act."

"I – I can't," I said.

"No? Why would that be?"

I looked up at him – way up – and I told him about what happened Friday night. All of it. Every vile detail.

"*Io Evoe!*" he breathed, crossing himself. "No wonder! Well, never you fear, dear. I'll take my java and go elsewhere."

"No. No! It's fine now." And it was. In that moment it was. I could tell him what happened, and he could respond like that, in that gentle way. It was fine. I mean, it's not now. Now, I'm panicking inside my head, wondering what the fuck is wrong with me, how could I let a man do that, how could I put myself in such a dangerous position. But then? Then it was fine. Stupid.

He looked at me, brow furrowed. Then he shrugged and sat down.

"So you know my name," he said. "Shall I guess at yours?"

"Oh, I'm sorry. I guess I should have told—"

"No no. I really want to guess it."

"Oh, um, well. Okay. You won't, but go for it."

"Ah. It's obscure. You're not a Naomi or an Elizabeth, that's for sure. Are you, perhaps, a Simone?"

"Wow! You are good."

"Amy – I mean, am I? Right?"

"N-no. No. Not technically. It's my middle name."

"Ah, your middle name. Let's see, then. I'm catching a Greek air. Is it – Penelope?"

It struck me like an arrow to the chest. "That's my sister."

"Are you two close?"

"No. Well. Kind of. She's dead."

"Oh. I'm very sorry. Maybe I should stop?"

"No. No, no. Carry on. This is amazing!"

"Am I right about the Greek part?"

"Yeah. You're good on that account."

"Can I get a letter?"

"Upsilon."

"Upsilon. You don't make it easy, do you?"

"I used to. But I got burned."

"Ha. But upsilon isn't the first letter, is it? No. You're an alpha. Makes sense. Ai. Wow, this is obscure. Amu. Amumoa? Amymone! Amymone?"

Eyes bugging: "That's incredible. Yes!"

He wiped imaginary sweat from his brow and reclined in his chair. I took another sip of latté.

"Amymone," he said. "I've never heard that name before. It's lovely."

"Thank you."

Now, this Mirella of yours. Is she your *belle*?"

"Sorry?"

"Your lady love?"

I sighed. "I hope so. I love her desperately."

My heart pounded so hard and I was struck like lightning by the thought of my face buried in the gooshy flesh between her legs. It made me want to cry.

"I can see," he said, "you've got a lot on your plate."

"If only I was sharing this with her. She's *way* cooler than I am."

And then, I really did cry. I couldn't hold on any longer. I just started   blubbering.

"Oh, dear," said Ricky (that's his name).

"What will I do without her?"

Just then, a girl and a boy joined us. They were thin-limbed, pale-skinned.

"Is this stag bothering you, Miss?" asked the girl.

"I thought your days of making ladies cry was over, Ricky," said the boy.

"Don't look at me, man. She did this all on her own."

"I did," I sobbed. "It's all my fault!"

"Can we help in any way?" asked the girl.

"She looks weary," said the boy.

The girl gasped. "Her heart is breaking. Am I right?"

I nodded. They began to sing. I saw my heart – cracked and chipped and limping – start to repair its form. The girl reached out her hand to touch mine. I looked into her dark, smiling eyes and let her

---

and her masculine counterpart vibrate me with their song. The intervals between their voices were crystalline with perfection.

The weight of my sleepiness seemed to bear down on me. I yawned. Their song faded. Ricky stood and half-carried me to his car. I think I must have told him where I live, because the next thing I remember I was in my room writing this. I'm not sure, but I don't think I slept. It's twilight now, and I'm still exhausted – weary – but I don't know if I'll be sleeping again tonight.

Entry #49: Sunday, December 8
That was the worst exam ever. Fucking chemistry!

Anyway, Jeremy was waiting for me when I got out. He looked rather nervous and a little unhappy.

"I've been asked to get a message to you," he said as we walked down the echoing empty hallway. "What's that?" I asked.

"You've been invited to dinner with Sally. She says something about timing and a vision quest? I don't know. Anyway, August gave me her number."

"I thought you weren't seeing August anymore."

"I'm not!" He was not happy. "He called me last night with the message. I might have to change my number. He wants to get back together with me."

"Don't let him," I said. "What did he do?"

"Cheated. With a girl. Lied about it. You know."

"Dick things."

"Yeah, I guess. You're so lucky, Amy."

"How am *I* lucky?"

"You can swear off guys."

Or can I? That Ricky! If I hadn't been in such a state, I would have gone home with him.

I invited Jeremy to come with me back to that sweet cafe – whose name I can't remember – but he said he had to study. Not all of us can be geniuses, apparently. Even though I probably didn't do very well on that exam. (I should probably stick to my strengths.)

He left me in the parking lot. I went home, had lunch, then remembered something: How long has it been since I've seen my

---

audio recorder? I bet Mirella has it. But if she has it, why didn't she give it back to me on Friday?

Mrs. Lantigua told me I yell and scream at shrinks. I may have raised my voice a little, but I can't remember what I said, or what she said. It was a month-and-a-half ago. I would really like to know what I said, because I'm pretty sure Mrs. Lantigua's comment would have had less to do with volume and more to do with tone, but I can't be sure if I don't have that recording.

And I have to call Sally, of course.

But while I was rummaging through my satchel, I found an address scrawled on a sticky note with the message "Seek and ye shall find" scrawled beneath it, with a big R. underneath that. I wonder why he wouldn't give me his number or email or something. But I guess I'll get to that address. Maybe go right now. I can't help but think that maybe, despite the fear I feel over the idea of going to his address, I'm supposed to. Seek and ye shall find. Find what? Does he know something I don't? Or is he just trying to lure me to his place so he can kidnap me? And I feel drawn to find out? That's kind of sick. Except I'm torn between that fear and a need to be around more people like me. He seemed to have some kind of psychic capacity, and Isobel believed in magick. Dare I call those two who sang to me yesterday faith healers? But I can't say I have enough money to return to that cafe everyday for the rest of my life.

I'll call Sally first, though.

Supplement:

I'm so ridiculously tired. It's half-past midnight. I've been looking for that recording for three hours. No idea where it is.

Later:

I've been lying in bed for about two hours. I'm tired as hell, but sleep is so bloody elusive these days. I keep thinking there's something I should be doing, and it's keeping me awake, but I can't figure out what it is. And every time I close my eyes, and try to relax, I hear loud noises in my heads: banging, and pornographic shouting. So, I'm awake now. I should say something about the day, because I've got a new picture of me.

Let's see. After I called Sally, I went to see if I could find that address. And just let me say, Sally wouldn't give me the first sweet clue about the vision quest. She just told me she'd been contacted by an entity who'd told her it was important. I am *highly* skeptical. But we set a time and date. Dinner and a vision quest. But that's all I know.

So, I went to that address I had from the cafe. I don't even remember taking it. Or getting it. And I thought if I mightn't have fallen asleep in his car. And I fantacised – not worried, mind, fanticised – that he'd touched me. But of course, I would have felt it when I woke up but those long spindly fingers? And then when I started thinking about his fingers – as now – I started thinking about Mirella's. You'd think they'd be uncomfortable because they're kind of knobby and a little crooked but, as it turns out, they're really good. Mirella's are. I don't know about Ricky's, because, like I say, I'm trying to get my girlfriend back.

I was walking and thinking this, and I almost had to sit down and cry but that would have been cold and wet. When I got there, Ricky let me in to his second floor loft, painted all black and stars, and hung with cords and masks, and some animal skulls and the like. He introduced me to his blind girlfriend, Spider. He offered me tea and while he was preparing it, Spider watched me with her milky eyes. Then she said, "The fairy lover."

I said: "What?"

"The blessed one will always love you. But it's good you seek her."

Yeah. Only a little creepy. And Ricky came back in the room with our tea.

"I'm happy you came," he said.

"Um, yeah, thanks." I blushed, thinking of coming. Spider giggled. It sounded quietly maniacal. "Thanks for inviting me."

"Not at all, though I did have an ulterior motive."

Panic! That mixture of fear and inexplicable lust coursing through me. Why can't lust ever just stand on its own? Spider laughed.

"He's not going to hurt you, morsel," she said, and threw a savage grin at her brother. "Not with me here."

He smiled, thinly. "I'd never hurt you, Amymone. I'm not trying to seduce you. I want to draw you."

"I'm not taking off my clothes."

They both laughed. I smoldered. "That would defeat the purpose," he said. "It's your style I want to capture – the way you express you."

But I couldn't help imagining myself reclining on a satin divan, hand lazing on my collar bone, come-hither opium-smoke eyes, hair curled about my shoulders and tummy, completely bare for him to draw. It made me blush, and smile.

"Sit for me this afternoon? I'll do a still-life and give it to you to take home."

"You can give it to your blessed girl, but it won't compare," said Spider.

"Please," said Ricky, "don't mind her."

Spider stuck her tongue out.

He took me up to his studio and asked me to make myself comfortable. I took my e-reader from my satchel and opened a book on magick I downloaded. Then I sat in the half-lotus, with my skirts splayed out over my knees. I started reading, but that didn't last long. My mind kept wandering to Mirella, so I gave up reading and thought about her. But it wasn't anything specific. I was vibrating the mantra *ISIS* that Thea taught us to open our third-eye. And I was focused on my breathing to keep myself still and calm. I could hear my heart beat. And that feeling of longing that I get when I think of her now, just kind of went numb. It almost made me smile. And then my heartbeat felt as though it were being accompanied by another. Like I had two heartbeats – two breaths. I was more than one person.

My third eye pounded open. I closed my eyes and it was like I could still see, but, like, energetic outlines of things. Not the actual things. I knew where my e-reader was, for example, but I couldn't read the words. And there was a presence. A tall, dark, feminine presence draped in the light of the moon. I couldn't see her exactly, but I knew she was there and I asked her what my life would be like if I married Mirella. And I saw.

We weren't rich. We lived in a comfortable kind of poverty. Mirella drew all day, and sold some of her pictures. We had few friends, and our families were uncomfortable with our union. Sometimes people would come to us for advice, or healing. We were vegetarian; we performed lots of magick; and we were happy together.

The only problem is, I really want to kiss Ricky. On the penis. And I feel like if I can't get that under control; if I can't control my attraction to Mickey; if Mariette duPont doesn't lay off that's going to cause a lot of problems.

I was awakened from my reverie by the sound of Ricky's voice. "All done." I looked up in surprise.

"Already?"

"How long do you think it's been?"

"I don't know."

"You've been sitting for almost two hours."

"Holy cats!"

"You're a very good model."

I blushed. "Thank you." The way he makes me feel so innocent scares me.

Then he showed me the picture. It was alive with sensuality. I didn't think I'd posed with such lugubrious inquisitiveness, but who knows what you yourself look like when you're asking the universe for guidance? I've never seen. Ironically.

"It's lovely," I said.

"It's yours. I'd love to do a colour portrait of you sometime. And, actually, I'd love to use your likeness in a graphic novel."

"Really?"

"You're a stunning creature, Amy."

"Uh, thanks." Fucking blushing! I'm stronger than that!

"I don't want to intrude, but you've got such a unique skin tone. Do you mind if I ask your ethnic background?"

"Well, my mother's Celtic and Scandinavian. My father's Greek."

"But you're so dark!"

"I don't look like either of them."

"Hm. And where does that mossy undertone come from?"

"Fairy blood?"

"Ah, you're a nymph!"

"I – suppose."

"Fancy that. Well, I'm stag-like, as you know, and my sister is an arachnid."

"Is Spider her real name?"

"Real, yes. Given? No. Will you stay for dinner, dear nymph of the olive grove?"

"Thank you, no. I have to be home for my parents. My mother thinks she's overprotective – takes pride in it, really. She'd flip if she knew I was posing for a strange man in his bedroom studio. And, to be honest, I think she might be right."

"I see. Well, I'll try not to be so strange in the future."

I looked ruefully at him. He winked. I smiled.

"Let's get you home."

So, here I am; home, sweet home. It's about four in the morning – *again* – and I still can't sleep. I'm worried about Mirella; I'm worried about myself. That recorder is still missing. That rant Mrs. Lantigua went on is still raving in my head when the horrific visions of gang rape aren't dancing satanically through it. I don't think I'll ever have those fantasies again. And I have a sensuous picture of myself drawn by a man I just met and already want to hump. And the thing is I want to want to hump him but Mirella, and Barely Legal, and gang rape. If I stop being a slut, do the terrorists win? (Not that Mirella's any kind of terrorist.) I've got to keep myself safe, but does that mean being what everyone wants me to be?

I'm so ashamed of myself!

I can't even sleep. I'm lost! I wish I would just die. But that wouldn't do any good, would it? I'd just go to the Land of Missing Women and work on that abstract tapestry for all eternity. I'd be the source of pity and statistics forever until they forgot about me. It's hopeless. I'm trapped here, and there's nothing I can do.

I wish something would happen. I wish something would change.

Bjork??

Only if a ship would sail in
Or just somebody came
And knocked on my door

Or just—
Or just
Something!

Oh look! It's started to snow again.

Entry # 49: Monday, December 9

    I just spent the morning in a place I never thought I'd end up. Jail. And it's all because I started yelling instead of "helping." It all went down like this:

    I went out into the snow. It didn't take long for me to get to the edge of town. Since the blizzard, the snow's pretty thick when the trees aren't. I trudged through it, though, into the piney woods, my feet sinking well above the ankle. It didn't take long for me to realise that women's winter walking shoes aren't really built for – you know, winter walking. I thought about going back to change, but the only boots I have that are above ankle height are heels and they're even worse for snow. Dad's wouldn't fit, and Mom's got the same problem. So, on I went with snow melting into my socks.

    I know now why I went, but then I had no idea. I just went aimlessly about the woods futilely wiggling my toes against the cold warm snow. I remembered a trick I learned in, like, third grade about covering my head to keep my feet warm, so I put up the hood of my cloak. That, and the uphill trip seemed to keep my toes nice and attached to my feet.

    So, with all my appendages in place, I stalked the snowy forest. I don't know how long I was out there, but I had this impression that I was out there to die, and considering all the bullshit I wrote about last night, it was a comforting though. Fear and comfort, together at last. I felt like my toes felt and that brought a, shall we say "chilling", reality to my consciousness. It was like I was aware of every snowflake drifting in front of my nose, every squeaky crunch of my feet in the snow.

    Of course, the deeper I got into the thick of the forest, the easier it was to walk, the fewer snowflakes fell before me. I was even walking on semi-hard chilly moss and other terra firma for a while.

Never before have I been that deep into the undeveloped woods not ten blocks from our walk-up. I thought I'd feel free. I didn't.

Eventually, the path evened out, and the trees cleared. There were snow drifts piled up on the banks of a sweet little pond. The big moon in the sky reflected off the glassy ice and every once in a while an ice pixie would dance across it. I watched for a while, in awe, like a child coming across a butterfly face to face. And then I stepped out onto the ice.

I thought how perfect it would be if the ice gave out beneath me and I froze to death in a mysterious spring, preserved till spring. What a fitting end for Amymone. Yet, here I am, writing this, fresh from the drunk tank. And, come to think of it, it was kind of miraculous that the ice did hold, as it were. It hasn't been that cold for that long, and this pond wasn't exactly a puddle.

When I'd gotten to about the middle, I heard a voice, and saw a woman's form rise out of the snow wisps on the other side. They were here: a white lady. A snow maiden.

"Welcome, Living Thing," she said. "Your life drum is hot with trouble."

"How – do you know that?"

"My Father is the Rhythm of the Earth. My Mother is the Queen of the Dead. I know rhythm, and I know keening. Besides, why else would you seek out my pool?"

"I do want to die," I said. "Everyone at school wants me dead or ruined and they're allowed to. Even my friends abandon me. I thought I had a love of my life but even she is gone – she won't speak to me. Why should I go on?"

The snow spirit began to approach me. I watched the wisps blow through her, around her, behind her, in front of us. She looked sad.

"My Father says that all times change. He says that I shall pass on and be renewed. Perhaps this is what you seek?"

"No. I just want to end. Can't it just be over?"

"No." The word was icy on my face, like a gentle breeze from the ninth plane of hell. Despair overwhelmed me. I sank to my knees, tears streaming down my cheeks – hot and salty, like rivers. I don't even remember breathing, let alone sobbing.

Around me, the ice began to wear through. I could see the rivulets under the ice through the rivulets in my eyes. I was so exhausted that I couldn't stop the tears and they ate away at the ice until the ice broke free and I fell into the pond and down. But there was no water. Just falling.

Around me, I heard the voice of a man. It sounded like the booming of a bass drum, and the low strumming, pulsing of a didgeridoo. He spoke to my soul so my head couldn't understand. But I was fine – calm and weeping and kind of aroused. The falling became a kind of floating, and before I knew it, I was on the ground. Or something.

And there was my sister, Penelope. She was pale and thin, like the last time in the hospital. And just like the last time in the hospital, she smiled at me. I wanted to hug her to me, but she seemed too insubstantial. I wanted to take her back with me.

"I missed you," I said.

"I haven't," she said. Yet she smiled. "Come. Your last visit was too short, too single-minded. You left something behind. It should have been yours."

She took my hand and led me out of the blackness into the strange sunless light. I knew there were lights, there had to be, but no sun obviously and no fire. Weird.

Pen led me to a room with a double helix spiralled up – way up – a mix of beige and white stone. It felt like a desert. There was a crystal blue pool sparkling in the centre and people reclining like they were at a resort. The only blessedly missing element was the scantily-clad sex pots delivering drinks to rich men who would then molest them – the sex pots, not the drinks. So, I guess what I'm saying is that death is better than the upland. I mean, look at it! Who wouldn't rather be dead?

But the strange thing was, nice as it was, it was scary.

There was no music.

There was no sound. Not even that high-pitched sound you get when the power goes out. In fact, thinking about it now, I'm not sure I wasn't staring at a still-life I could walk through.

Pen took me up the helix on the right side. I felt like there should have been sun there, but there wasn't any. And anyway, that big round crystal pool? That might even just have been a window on the sky, but I can't be certain. Regardless, we went up and there were divets, caves in the wall. Caves where people live. Or – I guess – reside. And there was one where Popoulos Aleksandros was.

He greeted us with a grunt. We sat.

"Amymone," he said. "Welcome. Your friend – Mirella, is it? – speaks very highly of you. And – I am proud of how you play my violin."

"Um, thank you Pappous. Do—do you like it here?"

He lifted his head and said: "That is irrelevant. I am here and that is all there is."

It was okay. He seemed content.

"Where's Grandmother?" I asked.

"I'm alone, here, and for the better," he answered. "Perhaps one time I will seek her out, but we are separate at the moment, and we prefer it that way."

Then he took up his violin, and looked at it. Then at me. "It doesn't play anymore. I can't play anymore." He held it out to me. "Take it."

I hesitated.

"Go! Do! Take it!"

I did.

"Now, play," he commanded, huskily.

I played. I played the only thing that came to mind: the Canzonetta from the Tchaikovsky Concerto. When I was done, Poppous was in tears. Tears! I brought him to tears with his own violin. Which I own. But I've never played it like that before. Pen put her hand on my arm.

"You'll find your harpy," she said.

Poppous Aleksandros regained himself. He rose, and I with him. He held out his hand and I took it. With a firm grasp, he looked me right in the eyes. I saw everything there: his love, his pride, his pain, his music – his heart. He put his hand on my arm where Pen had placed hers – where, after every chess game with my father, he'd placed his hand, win or lose. His grip was firm. It held me steady. Then he nodded, a curt nod; but the waves coming off it were like a shockwave.

Then, Pen and I were on our way, his violin still tucked under my arm, and I knew that I would forever dedicate the sound I produced – cherry wood vibrating in sympathy with the nylon and horsehair, my heart, and now the memory of the Underworld – to Aleksandros Lerner.

We travelled from the light place into the dark. It was a frightening transition, and quick. The dark was lit around corners, but at the corners, the light went dark. And it was bright light, too, casting contrasts against the stone walls – blues and violets and darker colours that have no name – where once there was white and beige. Maybe.

We floated down hallways and corridors. Down one to my right, I caught a brief bright glint of the Missing Women. Silent though they were, and sad, there was fondness in their light and I felt fondness for them in return. Pen and I passed on by.

"One day," said Pen, "The Missing Women will thank you."

"For bringing sound to them?"

"No. For keeping one of them in the realm of the living."

"Oh."

She stopped and turned to me. Her dark, beetle-y eyes shone bright in the unlight. She looked hungry to say something, opened her mouth, closed it, looked shy.

"Come on!" I whispered, whining like when we were kids and she kept secrets from me. Secrets she thought I'd never believe. But a childish faith in your parents has nothing on the strength of faith from meeting with your long-dead sister in the Underworld while seeking something – anything – a reason to live.

She looked back in my eyes, saw me there, smiled. "One day, Amymone, those women will be yours to command."

I wanted to balk at it, like I'd balked at the fact that I'd bleed every month till I stopped; or that boys who like boys do it in the bum; or that sometimes girls take money for sex. My sister had always told me the truth – well, not always, but the cruel rivalry had been stripped from her eyes. But why would I be leading an army of undead women?

"This way, Shining Host."

Thinking about it now, it feels kind of creepy. I mean, really, with Mirella it's bad enough. Does everyone in the Underworld know what I'm thinking? Who else knows me as the Shining Host? But I didn't care, then. Then, I was just eager to find my piece of beauty and get living again.

So we walked, and the deeper we walked, the darker it got. The lights around corners waned and soon the corners and other corridors stopped. The walls got narrow, and I got less, somehow. No light, but I kept going, following the spirit of my sister until there were no walls.

And then, there were spirits – grays – standing stock still. Dead eyes, mouths closed, unclothed. Still as life. In such a wide open expanse, there were millions crowded around, not awkward and not moving, but not at rest. Just still.

Pen's spirit was gone. I couldn't find her. So I made my way patiently forward, trying as best I could not to touch any of them – it seemed only respectful, somehow.

I came upon a woman as tall as the sky in amongst the spirits. She saw my motion and picked me out of the crop. When I was at height with Her, she spoke.

WHAT DOES THE WANDERING LIFE AMONGST THE UNBORN?

Realising Whom I was speaking to, I bowed low, my forehead on Her palm.

PRETTY THING, She said. SOMETIMES I DESPAIR EVEN THE DEAD DO NOT KNOW ME. RISE AMYMONE OF THE SPRING OF LERNA, LOVER OF MY HUSBAND'S BROTHER.

I had no right to rise, but She'd told me to, so I did. We were in Her chambers, I on black marble floor veined blue, She reclining on a settee.

"Your Majesty, Queen Persephone of the Dead, Daughter of the Green Lady, Mother of Winter—" there was another one. I knew, it but not to speak it.

"Midwife to the Reborn," She finished for me.

"I am humbled and honoured to meet You," I said.

"And I am pleased to make your acquaintance again, as well," She said, "and simply charmed that you would greet me as a mortal should."

"I – am – mortal."

"And yet you come and go blithely from my and my husband's realm? I think not. Please, sit. Eat."

I sat on a similar settee behind me. A loaf of bread appeared before me on a capitol. I looked at it, looked at Her, back at it. She chuckled.

"Would you prefer a pomegranate?" She asked.

"Ah, no, Mistress. Thank you."

"I would not keep you here, Amymone. It is perfectly safe to eat that bread."

I picked it up, nibbled at it, then decided I was very hungry. She smiled and watched me eat. When I'd finished, I reclined *à la Renaissance*, feeling much less anxious.

"So, my dear, it has been quite a while. I see you've become a questress, yes?"

"Yes, I suppose I have."

"Living in the way of the mortals does strange things to one, does it not?"

"It does, indeed," I replied, because by that time I could remember knowing Her, having met Her before. I don't remember how or when or why, now; but I did then. I knew Her like an in-law. We reminisced – something else I can't remember – and then She got down to brass tacks.

"I suppose you'll be wanting a bit of my beauty?"

I admit it – She was blindingly beautiful. I mean, if I saw Her on earth sometime, I'd maybe go blind or forget to breathe or something. But in the Underworld, neither of those things matter.

"If You would be so generous," I said.

"Sweet, humble nymph. For a sister-in-arms, anything at all. Did I never tell you how outraged your beloved was at my rape, and at the way Olympos would not budge on the matter?"

"I – You never – no."

"I would not need to ask, if they'd recorded it. But what can one do?"

"Mistress, if I may?"

"By all means, Amymone."

"He raped You. He stole You. Have You forgiven Him?"

Queen Persephone got sad. She said nothing for a long time.

"There are days – aeons, perhaps – when I hate Him. And He is humble enough to see that He has done wrong, and wise enough to know that an angry wife makes for a restless home. Have I forgiven Him? By times. Am I happy in the Underworld? Yes. I am."

"Sounds complicated."

"Love always is."

"You love Him?"

"I love the dead, Amymone."

"Oh."

"Now, let me present you with a sweet ornate box containing my beauty."

She did, and sent me on my way, rebirthing me into my abandoned body.

I was freezing and disoriented. I have no idea where the pool went. The trip down the hill in the snow, with frost-bitten feet was unpleasant to say the least. I got turned around and worried I'd meet Persephone again much sooner than I wanted to. The snow was coming down hard by the time I found my way back into town. I barely recognised it. It was anguished. And accompanied by a violin.

I hurried toward it, and found Mirella screeching incoherently, playing something bizarre. She was standing on the stoop of St. Paul's Catholic Church. I don't even know what language she was shrieking in, and sometimes it sounded more like song. I grabbed her, and yelled her name, but she was lost. She didn't even see me, much less feel or hear me. And I began to get overwhelmed by her sound – the loudest thing I'd heard since stepping out into the night. I could tell what she meant, but not what she was saying. I wanted to protect her, to get her off the street at Gods-know-what-time before dawn. But there was no one who could help me. So I turned and started screaming at the church in English.

"You loved us so much You sent Your son to suffer torture in our name? For all the evils we do? You subjected Your own flesh and blood to that? What kind of love is that? And how could we help but do evil when You gave us that knowledge – and in a way, I might add, that allowed You to be an asshole to us forever more! What kind of love is *that*! And then – then! – You expect *us* to beg *you* for forgiveness? Why should we! You so-called created this; You gave us knowledge of good and evil. And then You swept God-hood out from under us. And why? Because You're a jealous boyfriend! Because You can't deal with the idea that we might just do a better job than You! Well, no more! You're goin' down!"

And that's when the cops showed up.

Entry #50: Tuesday, December 10

One exam to go, and I still haven't slept. Mirella – last night – yesterday after our parents bailed us out of jail. We went to school in separate cars. We got to school once, once we were inside she slammed into me with a big hug and cooed, "I love you!"

Someone was standing by, and yelled, "Kiss!" in this maniacal, vicious voice. I think. Maybe. Who knows anymore? Who cares?

I've got my Mirella back – my crazy, sweet-loveable, psychic sidekick – and we played music together and it was sweet and beautiful. I think Mirella thinks I saved her from hell. It's kind of heartbreaking if one assumes she's right. Who would have thought hell would be so easy to get into. It wasn't even her fault. But when we were alone in the practice room, she bowed before me again with her forehead on the floor. She offered me a prayer. My memory is a jumble of distracted dreamstuff, but I think I can remember close to what she said:

Shining Host
Oh, embodiment of Goddesses
Oh, demon slayer, mouse purveyor
This humble creature offers you her deepest gratitude
And her most gracious, humble apology
Fairykin!
How ruinous is my heart,
Lying all in tatters for your love,
And how unspoken my terrible acts have been!

Dear bright and shining beacon,
Traverser of the Underworld,
Take me back, I beg you.
Take me in your arms and never let me go.

I was so moved, I didn't even care if anyone recorded us. I took her in my arms, and held her close.

Which, of course, we're forbidden to do, now that we've been arrested together. So, whereas once our homes were safe places to make out and make love, even just to hang out, now we have to find somewhere else. This isn't a big city, but we went looking for places after school, separately of course. Neither of us really found a secluded spot. I mean, they have spies everywhere.

I still haven't slept. (Have I mentioned that?) It's two in the morning. I have an exam tomorrow afternoon – or, *this* afternoon, I guess. Fortunately, Mirella's on the same sleep schedule, too. We went up to the school at around 11:00. I know it's illegal, but there was no one there so we could make out quite easily.

Tomorrow I'm going to ask Sally and Ricky if we can invade their places for a little privacy. Maybe not Ricky. I should wait till after the vision quest to ask Sally.

Oh, I'm so fucked up! I hope I can write a coherent essay for my English exam tommorrow.

Oh! Here's a thing: Mirella gave me my recorder back. She stole it from me in November before she left. I didn't even see her take it. I'm gonna lie down and try to sleep for an hour. I probably won't, so then I'll transcribe what's on it.

Oh, but before I go to sleep, let me give you a reminder of what my parents were like. They sat me down in the living room last night, and they spoke to me with really serious looks on their faces.

Mom said: "You're eighteen now, Amy, and if you get in trouble no one's going to treat you like a kid anymore. Those days are over – you're an adult now, in the eyes of the law. It's time to start acting like one. If you get a criminal record, that's it – it will be with you for life. It doesn't matter what it is." You know – stuff I'd already had ample time to think about in jail while the overcast was brightening through the window.

Dad, who's always a little more real, said: "You've changed, Amymone, sugar. You used to be all about your music. Now, you're going to psychics, yelling at churches, you come home crying and won't tell us why. This girl – Mirella – she's taken over your life. I don't even recognise you anymore."

So, irresponsible brat gets guilt tripped by father. I swear I'm moving so far away from this place as soon as I can. I – will just run as – far-away-as-I-can. Oh Goddess! And I'll take Mirella with me. The second she turns 18, I'm taking her and we're going far, far away. Maybe we'll even change our names. I can be Simone Hyksakolos and she can be Carmelita Peres-Hyksokolos – or whatever she wants. We'll get married, and we'll hitch-hike across the country playing our violins for cash. If we get enough, we'll settle down – or even move to Europe.

I hate them so much! Working hours and hours, and leaving me alone sometimes twelve hours a day, then complaining that I yell at churches? They don't even know me! How can they pretend to be interested in my well being? All nostalgic for when I was perfectly dependent on them. Maybe I should start shitting myself again, or forget how to fucking talk.

Holy shit! I'm so damn tired! What's wrong with me! I mean, they're right. Mirella's changed me, and while I'm kinda comfortable with it, it's only been since September. That was fast! I just feel like I haven't been able to talk to them for years.

When I was fourteen, I had to secretly have an abortion. I didn't tell anyone about it, because I couldn't tell anyone about Bradley and the sex we had. And you know what? I've been retelling this story so that I'm consenting. But I didn't. I didn't want to have sex with my cousin's fiancé. He was strong and he smelled good and he cornered me against the barn door. He raped me. And I had to have an abortion I couldn't tell anyone about. (Oh, that hurts!)

It was exactly at that moment that I realised I couldn't count on my parents to protect me from everything. And I resented them for that, and I do, and it sucks because they still try to protect me, but they're hardly ever around and they don't know about, like, men's rights activists and pick-up artists. They don't know about the video that circulates around the school even to this day. Maybe I could have told them about Bradley and the abortion, but I was so ashamed and I didn't need them piling guilt and fear on my own. I couldn't take the risk that they wouldn't believe me. Because – I didn't believe me. So, I stopped taking risks.

Then, Mirella comes along, and everything is a risk – everything. I don't know what to do from here on out. I know I love Mirella, but I don't know what that means. I know I want to do well in this peer tutoring course, but I don't know what that means. I know I've been pretty self-destructive and I want to stop, but I don't know what it means that I will be a different person.

All I really know the meaning of right now is that I want to sleep but I'm too tired.

So, here's the transcript of that psychiatrist's appointment.

Shrink: How are you today, Am-I-moan-ee?

Me: Fine.

S: And *who* are you today? [So clever. You could hear "her" voice drip with pride at her "wit".]

M: Athene.

S: Ah, I see. The feathers are—

M: Owls'.

S: And the spear is, of course, but the mirror?

M: Lighter than a shield.

S: Mm-hmm. (Note-taking.) So, you're Athene. Mirella's Arachne.

M: Yup.

S: What made you decide to do that?

M: Mirella suggested it. It seemed like fun.

S: But doesn't Athene hate Arachne?

M: That's one way of looking at it.

S: Okay. What's another way?

M: That Athene's the mother of spiders.

S: The mother of spiders. So, you would be Mirella's mother?

M: No. That would be Mrs. Lantigua. I'm the girl who dressed up as Athene for Hallowe'en.

S: And Mirella's dressed up as a spider – the first spider, your – Athene's – daughter. You want to be her mother.

M: Fine. That makes three of us, doesn't it?

S: Sorry?

M: Well, I mean, you've chosen a profession that gives you intimate care-taker access to people and you've chosen a specialty that puts you close to children. You've chosen Mirella's case – I assume it was a choice – so there must be something in you that wants to be Mirella's mother.

S: (pause)

M: See? Psychiatry. It's not that difficult.

S: I see. (Note-taking.) How has your relationship with Mirella been progressing?

M: Fantastic! We had a great concert. She's brilliant.

S: And you're taking her to the dance tonight?

M: That's the idea.

S: Why not go with a boy?

M: I don't want to, really. Besides, my costume goes with Mirella's.

S: You don't want to?

M: I want Mirella to have a good time.

S: Wouldn't she have a better time with a boy?

M: What are you getting at?

S: Do you have sex with Mirella?

M: Why is that your business?

S: I have to make sure Mirella is making responsible decisions with her life.

M: Oh. You mean because you locked her away in an asylum for the three years she was supposed to be developing romantic and sexual relationships? That?

S: Well, I didn't do that.

M: Well, it wasn't her choice.

S: No, her choice was suicide. Would you have preferred that?

M: No, but—

S: Then maybe you should spend less time and effort criticising and more time answering my questions. Do you have sex with Mirella?

M: Which is the good answer?

S: (sighs) There are no right or wrong answers, Am-I-moan-ee.

M: (sighs) That's why I didn't ask that. Which one's the *good* answer? Which one lets me continue being Mirella's friend?

S: If you're interested in being Mirella's friend, then I suggest you answer all my questions fully and honestly. Do you have sex with Mirella?

M: I see how it is. No. I do not *have sex with* Mirella.

S: Then, what *is* the full nature of your relationship?

M: (pause) [I remember this point clearly. I hear it, and I feel what I felt then, which is the same way I felt in grade nine when people would ask me if I'd slept with him or him or him. "Then why do you hang around him so much, if you're not having sex with him?" The answer was the same too. There's only one answer you can give to that kind of interrogation.] We're friends.

S: I see. (Note-taking.) [And, of course, that's the stock answer, complete with note-taking.]

M: What are you writing?

S: I'm wondering again why you're taking her to the dance.

M: If I'm not going to fuck her afterwards? Is that it?

S: Well, you couldn't, really.

M: Sorry, what?

S: You couldn't do that to her. Not without a penis.

M: Are you sure I don't have one?

S: (Note-taking) What does that mean?

M: Do you know what the expression finger-fucking means?

S: Yes. But without a penis, you can't really.

M: Is this actually medicine?

S: It's basic anatomy, yes.

M: How does this help you determine if Mirella's making responsible choices?

S: That's not your concern.

M: Look. Mirella and I are close friends. Fast friends. One might even say "bosom friends". I look out for Mirella's safety and do my best to help her out in the *real* world. And in the real world? Finger fucking is just as intimate as penis fucking. And it can hurt *way* more.

S: Really? (note-taking) And, how many men have you had sex with?

M: One.

S: One?

M: [faux-Transylvanian accent] One. One man! Ah-ah-ah!

S: (note-taking) And how many women?

M: None.

S: None?

M: No. None!

S: (frantic scribbling) Then how have you had so many digitally insti
gated orgasms?

M: I can finger fuck myself!!
[How about that. I really do yell and scream at psychiatrists. That
can't be good.]

S: Calm down, please. Has Mirella been sexually active since you've
known her?

M: Not that I know of, no.

S: I thought you said you look out for her.

M: I'm not around her all the time!

S: How much time do you spend with her?

M: As much as I care to.

S: But how many hours a week, would you say?

M: A lot. She's my student, I sit beside her in class; I help her with
her homework; we made these costumes together. We spend a lot of
time together.

S: So, upwards of thirty?

M: Sure, why not.

S: (scribbling) Does she have the opportunity to develop friendships
outside the bond you two have formed?

M: I certainly wouldn't stop her if she wanted to. I don't want to monopolise her time.

S: Would you know for sure if you were?

M: I like to think so, yes.

S: What would that look like?

M: Well, for one thing, I think she'd stop holding my hand. She'd turn from me. She'd be colder. She'd smile less at my presence. She probably wouldn't do as much art.

S: Okay. (note-taking) Now, one last question. Has Mirella performed any acts of worship to you?

M: Acts of worship?

S: Sacrifice, prayers, protestation, exaltation, protective acts? Acts of worship.

M: No. Not at all. None.

S: (scribbling) I see. Well, if she ever starts, it's up to you to discourage it. Understood?

M: Yes.

S: Thank you for your time, Miss Learner. Enjoy the dance.

[End Transcript.]

I'm not entirely sure anymore that all those questions were bad.

Entry #51: Thursday, December 12
Finally slept last night. Felt so good to wake up! What a gruelling semester! These better not be the best years of my life!

Looking over this journal reveals some pretty bizarre circumstances. I almost don't recognise myself. Dad's right, I have changed. Thank Gods!

So, I think if I can get Mickey and Jeremy interested, I'd like to do something for the Solstice. A little dream magick, maybe. I'd say, "Let's do a vigil!" but, honestly, the idea of staying up all night again doesn't sit well with me at the moment. What can I say? I'm a diurnal creature.

Anyway, I'm going to relax with a glass of wine. I'm very curious to hear what Mirella's said to me while I was away.

Supplement:

You know? Sometimes I can let my anger and jealousy get the better of me. When I got there, Mirella was there, sitting on his couch. I felt dead inside, or dying. The front room was strewn with all kinds of paper, clothes, and old electric gadgets. I had the sense – the very real sense – that I'd been terribly wrong. But I wasn't about to let that stop me. Oh, no!

"What the hell is going on here?" I gesticulated toward Mirella.

"She showed up out of the blue," said Mickey. "And then you did. I should be asking you that question."

"You rapist asshole!"

"What!"

"How dare you treat her that way!"

"Miss Lerner!"

"Call me Amy, Mirella. I'm no better than you."

"Wait. Treat her what way? She was gagging for it! Maybe if you hadn't been such an eejit, I wouldn't have had to comfort her!"

"Oh, Shining Lady! Please!"

"Call me Amy, Mirella. And you. You comforted her by raping her virginity away?"

"Amy!!" screeched Mirella. We both started at her. Silence – thick like awkward. "Sorry," she whispered. "He didn't rape me. And, he didn't comfort me. I comforted him. It was my idea."

I looked between them both for a moment, Mirella's recorded words ringing in my head. Mickey really loves me? Impossible!

"Just like a fucking feminist!" muttered Mickey.

"You shut up!" growled Mirella, rising from the couch, finger pointed like a dagger. "I did you a favour because I could see your pain. I did you a favour because I thought I was doing *her* a favour because I thought if she could see your pain at that moment – just that moment, right then – she would have done the same thing. Don't you *dare* badmouth the Black Sun Goddess! And You!" She rounded on me. "I'm seventeen, and you've taught me well. You've taught me *very fucking well*! I can fuck anyone I want, and I can do it in your honour if I want to. I am insulted – insulted! – that you would assume, even after you told me I could, that I couldn't consent to sex. And besides, *you* got my virginity, not him! Fuck!"

I looked at Mickey, and saw my violin splayed out on the road. I heard the chirp of his tires leaving the driveway. I saw him about to hit me after he'd been suspended for fighting. And I realised:

"I'm quite afraid of you."

"What? Why?"

"Because when I said no to you last September in my driveway, you yelled at me, and kicked me out and you drove away angry. If I'd been in front of your car, you might have killed me. You broke my violin. You got really, really pissed and all I did was say no."

Mickey nodded. He'd actually listened. It felt good to say it to non-deaf ears.

"Two things," he said. "First, I already apologised for all that shit. It was shitty of me and I'm sorry. Second, you did not just say no."

"I did too! I said, 'I don't think that would be appropriate.'"

"And you laughed while you said it."

"I did?"

"Yeah, you did. Fuck! Do you even know what the guys say about you at school?"

"Slut, mostly."

"You know what that's guy-code for?"

"What?"

"Heartbreaker."

"It means a lot more than that."

"No. Especially not in your case. You're a heartbreaker, Amymone."

Stunned. No response. Clichéd quip about guys not having hearts inappropriate.

"You've gotta learn, Amy," he continued, "guys have feelings too. And whatever sense of entitlement we feel and however that fucks us up, we still feel hurt when you laugh at us."

"But—you know I'm like this. Why – why even bother?"

Mickey looked at Mirella. Mirella looked rueful. "Gotta tell her sometime."

"Tell me what?"

Mickey looked back at me. He took a deep breath and then let it out toward the ceiling. Then he looked at me again. "I love you."

"What!" I snickered.

"See? See? There you go again!"

I put my hand to my mouth and tried to stop laughing. A bubble appeared in my throat and I tried, but failed, to sound calm when I said what follows: "Why would you love me?"

"What?" said Mirella from behind me.

"Because," said Mickey, "you're everything that a strong man should want in a woman. You're fucking brilliant, and infuriating and frustrating and beautiful, and fucking brilliant – did I mention that? – and right *way* too much for your own good. You bring out the best and the worst in me. I'm a total fucking mess when I'm not around you and for the past three years, everything I've thought about has involved you somehow. Why do I love you? I can't do anything else!"

I dropped to my knees, right there, tasting something bitter in my mouth. My breathing was heavy, my vision was fuzzy. I heard blood rushing, felt hot and cold. The room spun.

"But—no man could ever love me."

"Well, then I'm no man," said Mickey.

Mirella was beside me, stroking my hair and whispering, "Princess? Princess? Princess?"

And that's when I puked on Mickey O'Malley's carpet.

Entry #52: Friday, December 13

Here I lie, bed-ridden with the stomach flu that pounced on me yesterday at Mickey's. I've got nothing better to do, so I'm going to transcribe Mirella's words to me. Prayers, she calls them. This is verbatim, and untainted by my questions. I don't think I'll even put dates to them. She didn't.

I'm sorry. I'm so sorry! Miss Lerner, I'm so-o-o sorry. O, Great and Wonderful Shining Host, my love! My own personal saviour! How could I do this to you? There can be no doubt why you turn me back! That man – the space man, the bad man, the Mickey man. Oh, that man. I betrayed you, Mistress! I'm so sorry! O that I might lie in front of you nude, Falpala! O that you might take burning knitting needles to my flesh and boil the blood of me! O that you would bind my wicked womanhood shut with barbed wire! Drain me of my blood and slake your needy thirst, my Mistress Bathoria! Anything – anything! – but exile.

What overtook me? It's because I'm crazy for sure. Everything's because I'm crazy – everything bad. You're the only good because I'm crazy and now you're gone because craziness is wicked. He was only doing his manly duty. A man is but a man, but a woman is the guardian of virtue.

His kiss, so sweet and cloying
So desperately boying
His fingers in my hair,
He stripped me bare
I could have told him no
I could have! I could have
I wanted to but
You finish what you start!

That's what Papi always said. And he was always so kind to me. So kind! He didn't want to throw me away. But Mumma insisted I couldn't be of his family line. And he insisted if I weren't she were a lying, cheating slut. Even Abuela said it must be so but the doctors all agreed – she's as luney as her nieta – so my parents got divorced and I could never be my Daddy's girl again. They made it that way. He can't talk to me or see me because a man is but a man but a woman is virtue's guardian. Then I must guard against the crazy, but there's so much virtue in the crazy, and I'm a woman – I should know. But they

183

wouldn't listen, not even Mumma, so I slit my wrists but they punished me for that because that's no virtue either! And neither was cheating on you! Oh Mistress! Am I my Daddy's girl or a lying, cheating slut! (sobbing) Come back for me! Please!!

***

There's a ghost in my lung and it sighs in my sleep. It wraps itself around my tongue as it softly speaks. Then it walks – then walks – with my legs, to fall, to fall, to fall at your feet. There but for the grace of God go I. And when you kiss me, I am happy enough to die. Do you remember that song? It played while you drank my blood. I don't belong here. I don't belong anywhere. The voices tell me I'll go back to the sanatorium. I tell them I won't hurt myself. I try my hardest. But they tell me it's not good. I'm no good. Well, it's no good. I'll drink an alchemy of willow bark and potatoes. There is no E in potatoes. Look Amy, Lamp of Life, Heroine of the Dark in my Soul. I slept with Josh – er, Ricky – Victor, Bradley. Augh! What's his name? Mickey. I let him fuck me. I don't know why exactly, but I did. The day he took me home. Some days, I think about not coming to school. I don't speak to you because you cast me from you. But I never wronged you, Amymone! I never harmed you or disobeyed you. I bled for you, blood magick, and oh, how you shone!

I have a confession. I picture us married. I get gooshy thinking of it. I kneel before you and someone pronounces us Goddess and minion, bound to each other. You carve your sigil into my thigh, lick the blood, kiss me, call me yours. I dream I can taste my blood on your lips. I dream you love me. I kneel before you. So now when I cut myself, I lick the wound and pretend it's your lips. Last night, against my better judging voices, I carved your sigil into my thigh in the hopes it would transport you to my side. Today, it burns. It itches a little. But you are nowhere to be seen. I feel blind and naked at once. I'm going to masturbate with a pen now. I want you to know that I honour your wish – I do not masturbate anymore with knives. It makes me smile to know that you have my best (gasp) Did you cast me out to teach me? Did you want to show me? Did you feel you had wronged me? You have my best interests at heart, Falpala, you've

---

never said my crazy is wicked. You—cast me from you so I would learn, but what shall I learn for you Mistress of my hope!

***

The sigil on my thigh is itchier today. Does that mean it's working? Oh, Dark Mistress of Light! I prayed for you till night was day for years and even though I see you every day, I can't help but wonder – is it you? How can I be close to you, day after day if just moments ago you cast me away? So, I wonder if it's you. You may be some shade disguised as you. Or you may have forgotten who I am – or you. I speak to you where you've put my voice. It's your memory. I'm talking to you now, but you won't know it until later. My voice goes into the box and stays there – a little piece of me anyone can hear without me even knowing: and they say I'm crazy for hearing voices.

***

I forgot I had this. I've been sleeping with it under my pillow every night. Miss Lerner? Please believe me when I tell you: I only want to please you. No boy has ever been passionate about me. The real me. But Mickey: Look. You've got to understand something about Amymone. She's cold, sometimes, heartless. She really means well, maybe. It's just, no one really comes before Amymone. You know? And in that moment, I saw. And I knew – because I do know you a little – that if you could see what he meant, you'd want to stop his heart – he really does love you, mistress, in his sobby, lanky way. So I did my best, but he only felt worse. I tried to tell him I acted on your behalf, in honour of you. I do my best not to scratch the sigil. It's starting to burn and feel uncomfortable. I'm not sure if it's supposed to do that. Do you think the magick might have gone sour? I hope I haven't killed you.

***

"Hey there, girl. Mirella, right?"

"And you're the Big Bad Wolf."

"No. Ah, nope. Unless you mean that I huff and I puff and I bring the house down. 'Cause I am a singer in a band. Maybe you've heard of us? My Sister My Bride?

"Song of Songs 4:7. I met the man who wrote it."

"That's me."

"Is it? You look different. Almost like it's not you. And where's your beard? No, no. Nice try."

"I's just teasin' you. But seriously, I do have a band."

"Sorry. What?!"

"Uh—"

"That's disgusting! Old enough to bleed, old enough to breed. Antiochus, shut up! Sorry, you were saying?"

"Oh. Uh. I just wanted to, you know, say hi. You know Amy Learner, right?"

"That's not what I call her, but I suppose you could say that I do."

"Can you get a message to her for me?"

"Well, I can do my best, but I'm not sure she'd get it."

"Because you're crazy?"

"What? No! Because I'm not sure where she is, but I'm pretty sure she's not who her body is. You know?"

"Uh—not ... really."

"I think she's a shade in disguise. Like, I can tell her anything you want me to, but that doesn't mean it'll get to the right persona, you know?"

"Are you trying to say she's possessed?"

"No! She's not there. She never was there. She's a shade in disguise. I wouldn't trust anything I wanted to tell her to her. I certainly don't."

"You don't talk to her?"

"Try not to. I mean, still pray to her, of course, but speaking to her body? I wouldn't."

"You... pray to her?"

"Better than God."

"Touché. Well, anyway, thanks anyway."

"You're welcome. Oh! And by the way!

"Yeah?"

"Someone's telling me to tell you that you shouldn't. You could get into a lot of trouble."

"Sure. Whatever."

"I'm serious. You're playing with fire. Hey. I turned this thing on. Cool."

***

You know what I'm done with? I'm done with answering people when they ask, "Why are you doing X?" when there's perfectly no harm. And it's because of you, Mistress In Absentia. You taught me not to treat everyone like they're my shrink. Because, not everyone is a shrink. So, why do they expect to be treated like it? If I'm not doing something rational, everyone assumes I should be. They shriek "What are you doing!" like acid and ice, as though once you explain what you're doing and the most excellent reason why, they won't call you names. Out of the frying pan, into the... other frying pan, apparently. At least they can't force you to take drugs or eat what you don't want to and when. They don't search your room for the worshipful drawings, the sacred art of your secret heart, and tear it up in front of your face with maniacal anger, then give you the red sneer – eyes, face, nose – and tell you how very disappointed they are in you, Charlene, then tie you to the electric chair till you convince them – tears and snot and sometimes piss, but always begging – you will never worship again, even though you will. Because how can you cease to worship? If a Sufi forget Allah for even one moment, he will perform a full ablution. Someone told me that once and it seems reasonable. If someone submits to a god, then all their thoughts must be governed by that god and once you have seen, how can you not submit? Are you a God, Miss Lerner? I do not know, but I have seen. Whatever you are, I will worship. And I've always known that. So, no matter how they hurt me, I'd always lie. The first while, I tried really hard to stop. I'd try, but I'd feel empty and without purpose – a lump of matter holding anti-matter at bay, and for what? Would I worship and find reason or let the alchemy take me? When I was alone at night I'd take out the one picture they'd never find, thanks to St.

Brittany. I'd stare at it. It was dark so I couldn't see anything, but just knowing was good enough. I could sleep then. So it became a game. And when I lost, I lost hard. But until I lost, I always won. When I lied, I won. And when I told the truth, I lost. But I'm so tired of lies. I've had enough of them. They make this bizarre prison out of freedom. So, do you know what I'm done with? I'm done with answering people when they ask me "Why are you doing X?" when there's perfectly no harm.

***

It's late, and I'm oh, so tired. (Is that a song? It's oh, so tired. Sh, sh. That doesn't make any sense. But lots of songs don't make sense. I mean, why a yellow submarine, and what's up with the band? And they call me heartless? I mean, crazy?)

Anyway, I have a confession. I'm heartless. I hate you. You're all I've got but I hate you. You left me. We were going to go off and get married but you woke up and I was in this darkness, a darkness I became. (Is that a song?) No stars! No moon! They have all been blown out: you left me in the dark. The voices keep telling me you'll do it again. Please don't. I try hard, but you've cast me from you again. That's not a good thing. I don't like hating you. Not to be mean, but I guess I kind of have to.

The sigil itches in the worst way. I'm probably calling on your shade within and not you, what with all the hate. I'd cut the sigil out, but demons like that sort of behaviour. That would only make things worse. Oh! Kill me! Kill me! I hate you so much! Hate me! Have you no heart? Have you no soul? What if you've always been a slave – a shade – that seems likely. I've been wasting my time, haven't I? Praying and hoping and wishing it's been pointless. Because you don't even exist. I don't know. Do I talk to a real person at school? Or am I just talking to myself? Am I deluded to think someone might understand who I am? I think I am. But what do I know? I'm just a crazy person.

***

I woke up this prayer stick under my pillow. It's palm-sized so the nurses will just think I'm talking to myself, not praying to you, oh Shining Host. Praying directly to you.

I've been having these dreams where I'm at school and you're there and I'm allowed to be in love with you. Isn't that a funny dream? Free and in love?

Oh, Shining Lady, I know you're a creature who dwells in the shadow of my soul. (Is that a song?) But I don't care. There is love, I know, even in the darkness. I know the Bible is wrong. Love is light and it illuminates the shadows, but it doesn't have to banish the darkness. That would be merciless.

But that's just heretical. You mustn't trust a word I say. No one does. Oh, but you would, you would! I've dreamed it. No one does and that's why Doctor Krebbs gets to keep raping me. Even Mumma likes him better than me.

I wish I didn't have to go to group today. I only want to talk to you. So, all I do at group is talk about you. They all hate you. They all pretend to be good Christians but telling someone they'll burn in hell – jeering it at them, sneering, and scowling – that's not good nor Christian. Hell is a place where you get sneered at and jeered at and threatened. Hell is a place where smug demons douse you in waves of hate, and berate you with names calling mockingly they can see what's inside you. When you know what's inside them. You know – you can see – if they just turned that same sneering gaze on themselves, they'd see the writhing worms, and recoil in horror.

But I have to go to group. I wish I could bring this prayer stick. I love you, Shining Host. I love you.

amen.

That was exhausting. But I can't go to sleep because Mickey's on his way over. He just called. I'm not sure what I feel about what happened yesterday, but sitting around and brooding about it isn't going to help. Am I scared he'll rape me? A little. Paranoia's a bitch. So is rape culture.

I mean, yeah, he apologised, and I feel sorry for not being able to forgive him right away, but when a guy expresses such vehemence

(I love that word) at a rejection, it makes it really difficult not to be worried. For a long time.

Mirella just called. She says she's on her way over. I tried to convince her that she should wait until at least the Solstice – okay, well, maybe "tried" is a bit of an overstatement. I just don't think I can handle more confusion and heart ache.

Last night I had another dream I was searching for Mirella. There was this, like, hobbity street walker with a bald head. I'm disgusted by her now, because she was – I don't know – dripping sex or something. Like it was melting her. But in my dream, I was in love with her even while I was longing for Mirella.

I'm exhausted and sick and starving, and I've got company coming over. Just a glutton for punishment, aren't I? What sucks is that my mother has this bizarre habit of locking me in the house, so when Mickey gets here, I'll have to get out of bed – hairy legs and all – and open the door to let him in.

I don't even know what I'm going to say to him beyond "Sorry you're house smells like prophet puke." Well, that was weird to write. "Prophet." Right. "Seer sick?" Because "psychic sick" just sounds like my vomit could read your palm. (I'm so embarrassed! I mean, they cleaned it up as best they could – they wouldn't let me help – but it still smelled horrible when I left. I can barely keep water and crackers down. So weak, and hungry. I couldn't fight him off if I had to.

Supplement:

Here's me at dinner tonight, arguing with my parents:

Hey, guys, I think Mirella and I suffered large because we were apart from each other. I think we were both depressed and confused, and vulnerable to attack. I think she was yelling at that church because she was lost without me, and I know I stopped sleeping for a couple of weeks because I was lost without her. So, I think, "depending on the way my marks turn out this semester, I should be allowed to marry Mirella."

Yeah, that was a mistake, saying "marry". I meant to say "see" but once it was out there, I couldn't take it back. I fully intend to marry the girl. (Holy cow! Maybe I can marry her on her birthday! We'll even invite her dad's family.)

My dad was like: How will you support her?

I was like: I'll go to school and become a teacher.

He was all: You have to respect the law for that.

I told him: No. You just have to look like you do.

Mom snorted. I said what. She said: You don't do that. Plus, you've already been to jail.

One drunk and disorderly and I wasn't even drunk! Come on! You've done worse.

"No, I haven't," said Mom.

"It's true," said Dad," she's very boring."

"Rob?"

"Yes, dear?"

"Don't help."

"Yes, dear."

They're kind of funny together.

"Amy?" said Mum.

"Yes, Mum?"

"You really want to marry this girl?"

"I've been thinking about it for a while, yeah."

"What about my grandchildren?"

"Well, you should have thought of that before you stopped at me."

Oops. They didn't have any more kids after me because Pen died. Idiot girl.

"Sorry. Sorry. But look, would it be so bad if the family line ended with me?" (Well, Pen, really.) "I mean, all good things come to an end, right?"

Silence. Mom and Dad looked down at their plates. I think I kind of forgot that the only way they can see Pen is in pictures, and the only way they can speak to her is at her grave. They still miss her terribly.

"Look," I said. "What if I'm called to do this?"

"Called?" said Dad. "Called by whom?"

I shrugged. "Gods?"

He nodded, lips pursed, then shook his doubting head.

Mom said: "Do you know what *folie à deux* is?"

"No."

"It's when a schizophrenic manages to convince a perfectly healthy person of their psychotic world. They share delusions; they share hallucinations. They're often very important to each other."

"Wait, hold on. You think I caught crazy from Mirella? And that's why I want to marry her?"

"Well," said Dad. "You did just say that the gods are calling you to marry her. It's not unreasonable from where I sit."

"This. Is disgusting. And it is a conversation our ancestors would not be having."

Dad snorted. "You're right. If we were our ancestors, I'd have married you off already to someone who enjoys a challenge."

"Or! Or! You would have sent me to the temple of Apollo at Delphi."

Dad shook his head and rubbed his eyes.

"Look," said Mom. "Whether you've developed this *folie à deux* already, or whether you will, I don't want my daughter living her life with a psychosis she doesn't have!"

"Yeah, well, it's not really your decision, is it? Maybe I'll go and say all this stuff to Mrs. Lantigua. I'm sure she'd be thrilled to have someone volunteer to take care of and love Mirella as an adult. I'm not hungry anymore."

"Get back here, we're not done!" called Mom.

"I   am!"

And I was. Until Dad knocked on my door in about an hour's time. I was practising "Death and the Maiden", getting frustrated with all those modulations in the development. He had enough respect to wait for me to pause. I invited him in. He sat on my bed.

"So," he said, looking at his hands. "You think you're a psychic?"

"I do."

"Can you predict something for me?"

"I'm not really all that good at it yet. But! But! I have seen – because I asked what would happen – that if Mirella and I get married we'll be happy. I mean, we won't be rich or anything, but who wants that? We'll be content and crazy and in love. And maybe you don't want to hear this, but the sex will be great."

"Have you two had sex, yet?"

"Yeah. Right after the Hallowe'en concert."

"I see."

"Yeah," I said.

"And it was worth it?"

"Yeah."

He got up to leave, but at the door he turned around. He was smiling. "You've changed, Amymone. You've changed."

Entry #53: Sunday, April 24

I've been sitting here with a pen in my hand for the past ten minutes wondering where to start. Do I just pick up with a new entry, and pretend nothing happened? There's a big gaping hole here between last winter and this Easter. Can I just ignore that and carry on? Somehow, even though I'm sure I'll remember exactly what happened, every last detail, for the rest of my life. The scene in front of the hospital, that sickening feeling of self betrayal – I'll always remember that, but I think it's important to write it. I think in the back of my mind I've got some idea that someone, somewhere, somewhen might read this diary and – what? Find comfort in it? Not hardly. Forgive me? I guess, maybe. I'll be doing little enough of that for myself over the next little while.

Maybe I'd just like any would-be reader, including forty-year-old Amymone (assuming I live that long), to understand. Just understand. Understand that what I did, for better or for worse, I did from love. More than anything, I did it from love. Everything up until this entry I've done for love. This entry, which will probably be the last, describes how selfish I can be.

YOU INCORRIGIBLE HORRID WRETCHED BITCH!

Oh, Mirella! If you can hear me, if you can feel my remorse: my anger and my sorrow! Oh, Hermes! Transport me now! Apollo, strike me crazy! Zeus, strike me down! Good Gods! It was an accident – that's all – just an accident!

I read this over before I decided to write. One of the last things I said was that I can't handle anymore heartache, and now it seems that's all I'll get for the rest of my life. It's certainly all I deserve.

So. Here's what happened.

I went over to Mirella's a couple days after Dad told me I'd changed. I was going to ask Mrs. Lantigua for permission to marry Mirella. I was prepared for anything – a long wait, an involved argument. A no. I *thought* I was prepared for anything.

When I got there, Mrs. Lantigua was out. How long? Oh, an hour or so. I told Mirella why I was there.

"Aren't you sick?" she asked.

"I'm strong enough," I said. "But I can't sit on this. I'm here to ask your mother if I can marry you."

"What? What, really?" She thought I was putting her on. After all, who would marry a mentally unstable woman? But she's not unstable. She may be a little over-protective; she may be completely non-rational. But SHE'S NOT UNSTABLE!!!

I mean, if she's unstable, then so am I. Which isn't really saying much, is it?

Holy fuck! I don't want to relive this but I don't have a choice. I'm living it every moment of my life, wondering what I could have done.

I told her I wanted to marry her and she told me she didn't dare believe it in my aura. Even after all the time I tried to get her to trust herself – she was coming out of her shell, but I guess marriage was a bit too much to believe. She spun in a circle, and accused me of lying, and then thanked me for lying, then told me I was telling the truth. Which I promised her I was.

"Do you think Mumma will let me get married?" she asked. Then, she embraced me, kissed my mouth and said: "I don't care! Thank you for asking!"

But what about Mickey? Wouldn't he be jealous? Well, who cares? I'm in love with you.

We started making out. Both of us had busy, joyous hands, all over each others' bodies. I was screaming in my mind to get her to stop because an out-of-context snogging scene wouldn't help my case. But, oh Gods! – she just felt, and I'd been so long without her amorous touch. in retrospect it seems so foolish now. We both ignored my warning.

Stupid, stupid girl! Getting her all worked up like that!

"You know," I said, between kisses, "if you're mom comes home, she won't like this."

"I don't care," said Mirella. "I love you. Oh Mistress!" She fell to her knees, fell prostrate once again with her forehead on the floor. Thinking now, if I'd ever asked her to get up – ever! That first time I saw her do it, and was awestruck. It seemed so natural for her, and whatever I felt then – am I just making up the naturalness, the way it felt for her to worship me? the way she'd worshiped me for years, for an eternity, on that old piece of paper, all folded into a little square and ragged at the edges.

I looked at her there on the floor like that, and through the discomfort I felt at her worship, and through the fear of knowing that this would be a part of our lives for the rest of them, maybe even beyond, I felt that eerie calm overcome me like the day I told Mirella she couldn't take Gen Jones's tongue. I was an entirely other person with her bowing low to me that way – ageless and cruel and compassionate.

"How sweet," I said, gazing down on her prone form. "Yes, lovely minion. I will take you. and I will love you, Cassandra, until time stands still. And then shall our love be eternal. no man shall come between us; no injustice shall split us apart. So long as we honour the gods with our love, our union will be unbroken. I will take you in and make you a home with my love for you."

Then I dropped to my knees and said, "we may never defeat the Lord God but as long as we have each other, we can live our lives outside his purview. We'll do the spells to keep us safe."

She looked up at me and that's when the door opened. Mrs. Lantigua walked in the room and stopped short. We were rising from the floor, looking oh-so-guilty. Mrs. Lantigua looked pissed.

"What are you doing here, Amy?"

"I—wanted—"

"Miss Lerner is here to marry me!"

"Miss Lerner, now, is it?" asked Mrs. Lantigua.

"No. Amy. I'm here to *ask permission* to marry Mirella."

She set her grocery bag down and stared, incredulous.

After a moment's stunned silence, Mirella said, "Mumma, it's wonderful news! Somebody loves me and it's the Shining Host! Please, oh please might I marry Her?" She grabbed my hand.

"No!" said Mrs. Lantigua. She came toward us. "Absolutely out of the question." She took our wrists and tried to separate us.

"Wait!" I said. "Hear me out."

But she wouldn't. She just took my wrist and pulled me toward the door, saying, "You are never to come near my daughter again!"

"No!" shrieked Mirella. All this time, I was trying to babble my reasons for wanting to marry her. I turned around when Mrs. Lantigua got me to the door. Mirella had caught her mother's wrist. She's taller and stronger than her mother, so pulling her back was no problem for her. I don't know if she was bolstered by faith or adrenaline or what, but I guess she threw her mom pretty hard. Mrs. Lantigua reeled backward, tripped over her grocery bag and fell with a deplorable squelching thud against the corner of the kitchen wall.

In "Ginger Snaps", when that happens, there's blood everywhere, so I was slightly heartened when no inky pool started to spread beneath her. But she didn't move. I mean, she breathed, obviously, but she was out. So I called the ambulance – because someone was hurt – in a kind of daze, with Mirella dancing about, reciting regrettable lines from Romeo and Juliet.

They sent paramedics first, of course. The ambulance showed up soon after to whisk her away. We went with her. They asked us questions. I told them as best I could what had happened and why.

When we got to the hospital, the cops took us off to one side. They asked us what happened. I didn't say. They got pretty aggressive. I asked them if I were under arrest. They pointed to Mirella and said: "What's she on!" (Cops always speak in exclamation marks.) I haven't really been intimidated in a long time, but that tone of voice ripped down a wall of cocky answers, so instead of saying something like: "Ungodly amounts of dopamine" I said: "She's just psychic."

"Psychic! There's a woman in a coma and you want to play games! Tell me what she's on!"

"Nothing! She's psychic! Her mother was just in a bad accident and she blames herself and she doesn't know what's going on! Leave her alone."

His partner piped up. "Do you mean psychotic!"

And for the first time, with a thousand tonnes of lead, it dawned on me just what was about to happen – inexorably, incorrigibly. Why was I so blind!

"No," I lied or not, the shaking already beginning. "It was an accident."

"Is she psychotic!" he asked again.

I was swaying on my feet, stuck half-way between yes and no, because yes, she is, kind of, but no she's not – not in the way everyone thinks psychotic people are psychotic. I held my head and just kept repeating, "It was an accident. It was an accident."

"Sit her down!" said one of them.

"Yup!" said the other.

He took my arm and Mirella flew into a crying rage. She threw herself between us and tried to push him away. In an instant they had her face down on the concrete, screaming and crying and begging me to help her. I wanted to stand up and order them to leave my minion alone and go home. It had worked on Tilley, after all. But what if it didn't work on them? I wasn't about to make things worse by proving myself psychotic too. So, instead, I just say back and felt the tingling in my cheeks, and wished I was dead.

I suspect this will not be one of those moments I look back on in ten or twenty years and laugh about. I hope I'm still pissed about two large and angry men, trained in physical combat and carrying deadly weapons, kneeling on the back of a crying seventeen-year-old waif and handcuffing her so she's even more helpless. It's the last time I'll ever see Mirella.

They hauled her in like she was a drug-dealing child-slaver instead of a high school senior and my would-be fiancée. They say that God – that dickhead, Yahweh – treats all sins equally. I guess they're right.

I got to go home – but nowhere else. In the middle of the night that night, I realised that this diary is a major liability. So, I bundled up, and took a roll of packing tape and this diary and a plastic bag and

Dad's acetylene torch and I stole up the side of the mountain hoping to see the snow spirit. She wasn't there. I walked out onto the ice and at the centre, I knelt down and put the book in the bag. Then I wrapped it full over seven times. Because – I don't know. I look back through this book and there's such heartache! Why would I want to hang onto it? Because it's the only thing I have left of her. I would hate for all my memories to give way to that final image of her on the ground.

I don't know why I thought it would sink. I mean, I'm not particularly good at physics, but it doesn't take a rocket scientist. It's a book. When I bored into the ice and tossed the (hopefully) water-tight book in, it floated. So I went and dug in the snow at the edge of the pool for a stone. Then, with great care, I unwrapped the tape on the bag. It was freezing up there, and my fingers were beginning to turn white by the time I got enough tape off. I unpackaged the bag and stuck the rock in. Then I went back and re-opened the hole in the ice and dropped the book to the bottom. With a prayer, I stood up and turned back where I'd come from. I'd barely taken a step when the ice began to groan. I panicked. I froze.

I tried hard to remember what I'd been told from elementary, but beyond "don't walk on thin ice [that you've made weak by burning a book-sized hole in it]" I couldn't even remember *if* I'd been told anything about walking on thin ice. And while I was thinking, the ice crinkled and cracked. I remember the laughter I heard so clearly, in the crinkly, crackly slither of warm ice. That ice, when I'd bored through it at the centre, it wasn't four inches thick. I thought it would be fine because I'd had a vision there, like, two weeks prior, but apparently not.

I started walking, and then I heard the crackle behind me getting closer. The land seems a lot farther away in that memory than in all others. I took another step, felt the ice give, lifted my foot as quickly as I could, and as I was realising my boot was heavier and much colder than it had been moments ago, my other foot came down so hard I splashed into the pond, banging my chin off the chunk of ice I'd mangled.

There I stood, soaked from bust to boot in the middle of the forest, in the middle of a Canadian winter. Without hesitation, I started down the hill as fast as I could go. My teeth chattered; my feet grew heavy. The wind whipped my cheeks, and snow clung to my boots. The water in my clothes grew icier and icier the faster I moved.

I'm not fully sure anymore how I made it home. I remember it was snowing and the snow was clinging to my coat. I remember the way my coat crackled when I took it off. And I remember the way my shirt clung to my breasts when I stripped for the bath I was running at four in the morning so I wouldn't fall asleep and die.

And I remember the way the warm water made me feel like I was on fire. Fire under my skin. Like truth. And I can remember fighting with myself to stay in the bathtub, sweating and burning up, and crying, praying without the lights on that my diary – all my solid memories of Mirella – would be safe for the winter.

And here they are. All the smoky ones have evaporated or shifted a hundred times. These solid memories are so secure. So comforting.

I gotta take a break!

Entry 54: Monday, April 25

So, yesterday, I went swimming for my diary. Both Mum and Dad had to work Friday, so I could do it without skipping and without worrying they'd be home when I read through it. 202The ice wasn't fully melted, and I had to spend more time in the water than last time. I figured that would be the case. So, this time I stripped naked on the shore, hoping no one would steal my clothes. And my towel.

While I was in the water I was reminded of those dreams I've been having – swimming in the mountains with that beautiful nymph and that lovely, staggy, god-like – wow! Freezing when I got out, but I had my towel and some mostly warm, dry clothes.

Now, I get to finish telling the story of Mirella's railroading. I kind of feel like it's going to be quick. There's a lot of bureaucracy, quite a bit of legalese, not much dignity.

The cops showed up to investigate. They asked how long I'd known Mirella; did I know she was schizophrenic; did I know she'd been off her meds; did I think that was appropriate; how long had I known; didn't I think I had the responsibility to tell her psychiatrist; was I an expert in mental health or child development. Four months;

no; yes; yes; three months; not really; no and no. Then they placed me under arrest for criminal negligence causing bodily harm.

I languored in a jail cell while my parents made money to avoid talking to each other. They wouldn't give me my cell phone, so I couldn't call either one of them at work. I don't think I'd wanted to, anyway. Why ruin their day sooner? So I called them when they were home. In the interim, I signed a confession.

Yeah. That's right. School I can handle. Good marks trumps bad behaviour – always. Shrinks, I can handle. Psychiatry's not that hard. But when you're put in a room with two men who've been trained to blindly obey the law with no regard for personal safety; who've been told that people are mostly bad; who've been taught to assume that everyone is guilty; and who've been given authorization to use whatever intimidation tactics they deem necessary to keep the "innocent" safe – well, you kind of lose faith in your ability to stand up to them. I mean, these are people who will defend each other no matter what happens; and you want to take your chances that one or both of them won't rape you? Well, maybe that's over-stating it. But maybe it's not. And when they're *nice* to you with their exclamation points, then you really start getting worried. So you think that maybe, just maybe, if you cooperate with them they'll let you go home. But they don't because you're a criminal. I was terrified. And you might say, "Well, two men interrogating a young woman and wringing a confession out of her is misconduct" but that's not much good to me now.

And the fact of the matter is, I know it's misconduct. I know if this case were different – if I hadn't had a psychiatric record myself; and if I hadn't had the kind of "pattern of behaviour" I do; and if I'd been a little more careful with "Ms. Lantigua" – my case would have been dropped. But, as it is, people were concerned that together we were both dangerous, when the evidence is clear that it's when we're apart that we're dangerous. But let's never mind that. Psychiatrists and lawyers and judges and cops: they know evidence.

They had me so twisted around about how bad I'd been to be so nice and permissive to Mirella, I pled out. I got two hundred hours of community service and fifty hours of psychiatric treatment. I'll be working for nothing until the end of the summer, and seeing a shrink for about a year. If he – and they're all hes – deems me stable, then I can live my life. But if I'm even just a little bit disobedient, he'll recommend to the state they give me a year's imprisonment. They've been very lenient because I was so cooperative and because so much of the wrong I did I did when I was a minor. For the purposes of this diary, "lenient" means putting any and all my power, safety, and security in the hands of a man who's obsessed with sex – my sex, when I'm with him – for almost a year. I suppose that's better than ten years in prison, but considering Mrs. Lantigua woke up early in the year, I don't think they could have gotten away with much else.

So, I get to live my life when all this is over. Today, I'm going to be working on a letter to Mount Allison in New Brunswick. I have to take a year off to do the court mandated therapy, but I will have to get on with my life. And, yes, I know that Sackville is a small town in a conservative province; and yes I know that small towns are notoriously judgmental and gossipy. The reason I've decided to go there is because it's so far away from here, and I'm not likely to find anyone there who knows me. We did this entire legal thing so quietly, it's missed most of the papers, but my name's out there. Even *if* someone knows me there, it won't have the same power as living here does, with all the memories I have.

Sometimes I go back to that café I found. If I'm going to miss anything here next year it's going to be that café. Isobel is always so pleased to see me.

I missed the date with Sally I had for the vision quest, and by the time I wound up the courage to show up on her doorstep one night, unexpectedly in tears, I didn't really feel much like a vision quest. She and Mackenzie took me in. I spent the night, having called home (I can at least behave myself that way). I told them what happened, and they shook their heads and wished they could have done something. Mackenzie told me she wasn't very happy about the party on the whole, but that I and Mirella – despite our silly nakedness – were a shining light together. She liked Mirella. Mirella's a likeable girl. And Sally told me that that song that's been stuck inextricably in my head since the party is called "Cosmic Love". She put it on for me, and I cried. In the morning, she gave me her copy of the album, called "Lungs" by Florence and the Machine. My paltry sonnetage can in no way compare. Someday, I'll play and sing it for a small crowd, perhaps at an open mic, perhaps at Mt. Allison. I almost forgot:

And, yes. Mickey and I are having sex. I mean, not right this instant, but we do have sex often. It's kind of forlorn and often angry on my part. He's angry too, and kind of abusive sometimes. But who cares, really? You might call him my boyfriend. I'm pretty sane around him. He loves me, and maybe I love him. But I'll never love anyone like I love Mirella. Not anyone.

And yes, Mrs. Lantigua woke up the day after I confessed and was sentenced. She phoned me and we talked. For my part, I tried to be as apologetic as I could, because I lost her her daughter. She was meeker than I'd expected. I wanted her to be livid at me. If anyone has the right to punish me for my misdeeds, it's Valeria Lantigua. But something happened to her in her sleep. I don't know what it was. She was very sad – she cried on the phone – but she told me she wanted only two things: to have Mirella back (naturally), and to forgive me. She told me she hates me, and I told her that was more than reasonable. But she wants to forgive me. I don't get it.

And Mirella? She was sent back. She attacked her mother, who fell into a coma for about a week. They deemed Mirella mentally unstable and dangerous, and they said that she would benefit from "incarceration in a psychiatric hospital for an indefinite period". She's not-guilty by reason of mental defect; I'm guilty because I confessed. She's been imprisoned for as long as it takes to make her normal – which will be forever – and I just have to provide labour. Where's the justice?

I almost forgot: Tilly. Well, she got fired. I got her fired. She told me to be careful, and I wasn't. And I got her fired. Maybe I do need help. Maybe there comes a point when you're so opposed to authority that it hurts the ones you love. Maybe I can take a a more measured approach to injustice, a more balanced approach. Because, when it comes right down to it, I find comfort in rules and discipline. Meter, rhyme, form. These things are my inspiration. Grammar? Rhetoric? Logic? (Well, maybe not so much logic, but still.) I like studying; I like playing music; I like learning and these things all require a steady, measured discipline. Maybe I can be more balanced. Maybe, going forward, I don't want to hurt anyone.

This all goes to show you how deeply cruel and unusual the entire system is, feeding on dissidents and differences alike, consolidating their power so they can enjoy – what? What do they do besides consolidate their power? How much better than us do they live? How much better *can* you live when you're constantly worried about people coming to take your power from you for "no good reason" because they're jealous because you've set up this paradigm where they have to be jealous of what you've got? What have you got besides power? It's not even your power. It's our power that you stole. Aren't we fortunate to have all that we have? Aren't we?

Amymone Simone Lerner.

www.ingramcontent.com/pod-product-compliance
Lightning Source LLC
Chambersburg PA
CBHW050529260626
47157CB00004B/1532